# THE PUZZLE LEADS TO HOME

Hank found her hunched over the table. Her fingers tapped the oak wood of the antique table, as if hesitating, unsure what to do with the pile of jigsaw pieces heaped before her.

Rosie had never been unsure a day of her life. Now, tears streamed down her face following the grooves of wrinkles that life had etched there.

Rosie's nail flipped over the puzzle piece, nothing more than a bit of blue. She rubbed it and then slid it over the table to an imaginary position. Then she reached for another, and all the while, tears glistened on her cheeks. They were pieces of her story, and she was arranging them as she damn well wanted.

She looked up and stared at a distant point somewhere in the dark depths beyond her circle of light. "Home?" she whispered.

She stood up from the table and straightened to her former height that she used to carry around when Hank was still alive. "Home?" she said a bit louder, firmer, in her song-like voice.

CAMERON KENNEDY

OFFERS OTHER WORLDS TO EXPLORE

WITH THESE SHORT STORY COLLECTIONS

**Journey to the Other Side of Life:** Finding resolution after the greatest personal loss.

**The Next World Is Always Better:** Using adventure as an antidote to despair.

Available as e-books from both Amazon and Barnes & Noble.

# THE JIGSAW WINDOW

# CAMERON KENNEDY

D. M. Kreg Publishing

DMKregPublishing.com

Cover Design:  Renee Barratt, The Cover Counts

*To all the families and victims of Alzheimer's disease.*

# ACKNOWLEDGMENTS

Thanks to the many writers of the Oregon Writers Network who believed in this project. This is a work of fiction, conceived entirely in my imagination, but based loosely on optimistic insights gained from my mother's descent into Alzheimer's. Special thanks to my dad, sisters, brothers, husband and daughters as we supported each other during those difficult times. Thanks also to Donald Kreg, my publisher who brought this novel to life.

# THE JIGSAW WINDOW

# CAMERON KENNEDY

# ONE

I am a prisoner, held inside my own head. It's not the first time I am a prisoner. Really, this is not such a bad place, my head. It's a mansion, in fact, a many-roomed marvel. Each room contains a chapter of my life, and oh, I've lived a long one. Too long, some of them think, but that's another story, not mine. Too many sights I've seen in my day. They'll die with me.

Is that what's wrong with me? Am I dying? They won't tell me, but I think they know. After you died, Hank, I wanted to die, too. Now I'm not so sure. I'm not sure about anything. Uncertainty has become my prison warden.

I wish I could ask someone, but words are not mine anymore. Words float around loose inside the dark inside my head. I can't pluck the words from the dark and roll them off my tongue in a way that they can understand. I can't make my hand work so that I can capture words on paper. Oh well. Words won't help me move about in the rooms of my head.

Words... Words...

I don't need words to tell you what you already know. I love you. First and foremost. Always and forever. That's what families are for, for loving. If you know nothing else, you will always know this one thing.

It's the rest of it that I can't tell. The rest, that I'm burning to tell. Perhaps for now those stories are best left locked in their rooms, with me, inside my head. No one would believe me, even if I could make the words work once again.

#

**Rosamonde Ayers Berryhill** was a natural-born storyteller. That skill had always made her a hit at all the dinner parties. She sparkled more than the champagne in her flute. She knew the right questions to ask, when to tease, when to laugh, when to go on, and most important, when to be quiet. She used her body to help her. She knew when to lean forward, as if confiding a secret, and just how close to go, depending on whom she'd captivated with her story. She knew when to shiver, shaking her delicious curves in all the right places, when to seduce with her extra-long eyelashes, when to touch her listener and when not to. Her skin felt like silk, and she always smelled just right — fresh, with a hint of the wild. Like a sunny meadow of daisies planted by God. To illustrate her stories, her piano-long fingers did a little dance that could hypnotize a snake charmer.

Back when Rosamonde was still just an Ayers, she charmed and seduced Hank Berryhill, and by the end of their first two weeks together, they'd found a justice of the peace to marry them.

Rosamonde never wanted her home to end up here in Hawaii, almost three quarters of a century later. She'd followed Hank around the continental United States, and enough was enough. Besides, she didn't belong to the tropics. If it was such a paradise, why did people seek the cold of their air-conditioned homes? Back in the north, folks sought warmth. The Aloha state would always mean Pearl Harbor to her, the beginning of the end for Hank.

They had a good life together, nothing extravagant on Hank's government salary. They didn't need money to feel rich in those days when they had each other. Not even the kids, Melody and Barry, got in the way of their loving. Death managed to separate them eventually, but in the flesh only.

Hank died the year before Lani, their granddaughter, was born. Rosamonde came out for a brief visit to help with the new baby, and so Hank came along, too, in spirit, of course. Right away, he recognized the Berryhill spunk in the little spitball swaddled in pink. Lani and Melody were bound to mix about as well as nuclear fusion.

Hank's hypothesis was tested and verified over the years. Lani would turn sixteen around the same time her mother was going menopause on her.

That year, Lani usually went to the beach with her boyfriend every day after school, because why wouldn't she? World-class Waikiki was only a few blocks from home. She didn't like the crowds of tourists there, but she figured they were better than the way her mother crowded her at home.

All that was bad enough, but then things got worse two days before Lani's sixteenth birthday. That day, she decided to come straight home from school. And she caught her mother — Melody — in the middle of growing a pile of castoffs in the hall outside *Lani's* room: rumpled clothes (all baggy and black — what's wrong with kids these days?), loose CD's and cracked jewel cases, stuffed animals that'd had their stuffing loved out of them, crushed tampons still in their wrappers, and her collection of dog-eared paperbacks from the dollar bin across town. Lani threw a fit like she'd never thrown before.

"What are you doing, MOTHER?" She always saved the formal word for her greatest disapproval of Melody.

"Home so soon, dear?" Melody said with a smile bright enough to sell toothpaste. "Did you have a nice day at school? Did Kapono bring you home in his father's car? I hope you remembered to wear your seatbelt. You didn't leave him sitting out there in the driveway, did you? When are you going to invite him in, so that we can meet him?"

"MOTHER! Are you going through my STUFF?"

"Lower your voice," Melody said. "Grandmum will hear you. Your Uncle Caleb has just brought her home. He was babysitting her in his antique shop, you know, while I had an appointment I had to keep."

"Gran can't hear anything." Lani scooped up an armload of rejects from the pile in the hall. "Get out of my room."

Now, that just wasn't true. Hank remembered how his Rosie could hear snowflakes fall every winter since that first, magical

February of '43, back when they met.

"It's not your room anymore, dear. We're putting Grandmum in here. You don't mind, do you?"

*One Flew Over the Cuckoo's Nest* slipped from Lani's arms and thunked to the floor. She'd read it five times, and now she didn't even notice it fall. She just left it there in the hall and stalked into her former room where she unloaded her things onto the fake wood floor as if she was staking out a claim.

Melody's legs weren't as long as her daughter's, but she had more years of charm school under her belt. Without missing a beat, she floated over to Lani's stake, knelt, and patiently picked up piece after piece.

"Grandmum can't stay upstairs in my sewing room any longer," Melody said, picking lint from the black pants and shirts as she draped them one by one over her arm. "We can't trust her with stairs. This room is so much more practical for her, since it's on the ground level and the bathroom is just down the hall."

"Yeah, and it's closer to the front door, too. Aren't you worried about her wandering off?" Lani grabbed her clothes from her mother's careful sorting and threw them on the unmade bed.

"Dear, I wish you would be more helpful." Melody stood and rearranged the smile on her face, which she always did when she found herself having to look up at her daughter.

Lani folded her arms across her chest, which she always did to show her mother that she was bigger, even in the boobs. "That's not the issue, Mother. No one ever asked *me*."

"Where else could Grandmum go? She can't stay on her own

anymore, not after that last fiasco. Do you remember? When I had to fly all the way back to Baltimore to get her money back from that scammer who promised to fix her roof and didn't? And I missed my connection in Denver and ended up spending more money than what Grandmum lost?" Melody sighed and breezed over to a wall of posters where she used her French manicure to pry loose the first piece of tape she came to. "Your Uncle Barry's no use. What else could we have done but bring her here?"

"I'm not talking about whether or not Gran should live with us."

"Then what's all your fuss about?"

"Can't you like ever *ask* before you go and do something?" In three strides of her long legs, Lani crossed the room and tore the poster from its anchor of tape and from her mother's fingernails.

Melody did her best not to gasp, but a little puff of surprise slipped past her thick layer of lipstick, the shade of sunset. "Oh, too bad. That was your favorite singer, and now he's ripped. Never mind. I can tape him up from the back side so that you won't even notice."

"Mother, he's like so yesterday." Lani crumpled a piece of the torn poster into a wad, assumed a basketball stance on the balls of her feet, and aimed her paper ball at the hoop over her door. Score.

"All right, dear. Let's be reasonable, shall we? Don't you want your Grandmum here with us?"

"That's not the question, Mother."

"You can sleep on the futon in my sewing room. We'll have such fun! We'll be like sisters. Best friends."

"Why can't you move your sewing into your room with you and Dad?"

"Oh, no, no, that just wouldn't work, not at all. You're not being rational. My sewing is a business, not just a hobby. It puts food on the table and buys these posters for you."

"Jewell gave me that poster for my birthday last year."

"Well, you see? That's exactly what I'm saying. Without Jewell, I wouldn't have a store where I could sell my designs, and you wouldn't have your posters. Help me get the rest of these down, will you, dear? Then you can re-paint the walls, and everything will be all fresh and brand new for Grandmum."

"Me? Why should *I* paint? It's your idea, not mine."

Melody sighed. "Are we going to have to go through this all over again?"

"Fine! I can tell when I'm not wanted." Lani strode over to the child's desk she'd outgrown four years ago, but she tripped over her own feet when she saw her papers stacked neatly and her pencils arranged by color in her pencil box. Her hand jerked back, as if a jellyfish had stung her. "What'd you do?" She screeched, then pounced onto the neat stacks, pawing through them and spewing papers onto the floor as her search grew more frantic.

"If you're looking for your journal," Melody said, "I moved it to a better place, rather than under all that mess, which I organized for you."

Lani straightened and stared, stunned and speechless, at her mother. Tears streaked down her cheeks, plastering strands of hair together into ropes of blue-black, a reminder of her father's diluted

Hawaiian blood. Her face puffed to a ruddy shade of heat. She opened her mouth to spit out the insults that scrambled through her head, but only a sob came out. She tried again. "Where?"

"Finish helping me first, then I'll show you."

Lani whirled around and yanked open the drawers of her desk, one by one.

"Oh, it's not there, so you can stop trying to find it. You can have it as soon as we're done. C'mon and help me. Don't you want your journal back?"

Lani pawed through folded notes and mad lib books and puzzle cubes and baseball cards and sparkle fingernail polish and loose jacks. Then a horn honked outside, and her frenzy deflated. With one last sniff, she ran from the room.

"I didn't read it, if that's what you're worried about," Melody called after her.

As Lani stormed down the hall, her grandmother was coming out of the bathroom. With split-second timing, Lani tacked to one side to avoid knocking Rosamonde over. Her grandmother was a lot more frail these days and seemed to shrink a little more, each time Lani saw her. Rosamonde sucked in her breath. Her eyebrows arched high, and a look of terror flitted across her face. Rosie never used to be afraid of anything.

"I'm sorry, Gran," Lani said, steadying her by the arm.

"Home?" Rosamonde asked.

"Yes, I'm home," Lani said, swooping down to pick up her backpack from the floor, where she'd left it by the front door. "But I can't stay. I'll come back to see you, Gran. I promise." She bent to kiss her grandmother on the cheek, then she sailed out the front door and slammed it extra hard behind her.

Rosamonde watched the door quiver. She could see all the splinters of glass shake inside the door's little window. It wouldn't take much to blow them apart into thousands of shards, like jigsaw pieces, once they started shaking like that. It seemed that she stood there a long, long time, watching. Waiting. Of course, she never was very good at telling time. Suddenly, Melody appeared at her side and smiled for her toothpaste commercial.

"Home?" Rosamonde said.

"Yes, Mom, you're home. Aren't you glad that you're living with us now? We'll take good care of you. This is your home now."

But that's not what Rosie meant, either. Hank knew, because he knew her better than anyone. Rosie wanted to know when *she* was going home.

# TWO

I have made another mistake, and now the door is breaking. It is my fault, as always. Melody looks at me with pity, as if I'm some half-formed twit. I am not a breaker of doors, although from time to time, I would like to be. I do not believe in doors.

I thought I knew that tall girl who kissed me, but I was wrong. She is no one to me, but she seems nice.

I wonder if she's my sister who died?

Not even you can tell me, Hank, for you never knew my sister who died. She came from before your time.

No, I do not think that girl is she, for I do not recognize her dark coloring. Although, I am no longer sure of my sister's coloring. There is no one left who can tell me. My sister who died is hidden away in one of the rooms of my memory.

I shall have to go in search of her myself.

It is as if I am caught between two worlds: yours and theirs.

Mine is yours, but it's not here anymore, and neither is yours. I wonder, as I roam through my memories. Only memories are real. Memories are footprints of one's life. I can't make anyone see my footprints, so I have to ask, do they exist? Without my footprints, do I even exist?

#

**Hank murmured to** Rosamonde that yes, of course she exists. That without her, that tall, kissing bandit would never have become who she is. That his Rosie was not to blame for Melody and Lani's differences. They were two hot-headed chemicals that couldn't co-exist in the same universe. Rosamonde had nothing to do with that — only with their existence.

"I know, Mom," Melody said in her sing-song voice, "we'll have some tea. I grew the herbs myself in my garden and then dried them, so this tea is the best." Melody spoke in a breathless stream of words, as excited as if she'd won the lottery. She thought tea could fix just about anything, but it sure as heck wasn't Old Grandad, which was Rosie's favorite right around sundown, following a long, end-of-the-day walk with Hank.

But then, it wasn't sundown yet, either. Good thing, too. Time was what Lani and Melody both needed before they could cool down. If Lani wasn't home shortly thereafter, Hank didn't want to be anywhere near Melody. Even though she was his daughter, too.

Melody led her mother into the sunny kitchen and brought a chair from the dining room for her to sit on. She couldn't risk one of the tall barstools at the kitchen counter. Her mother couldn't balance on them without falling off and killing herself.

"Don't let Lani upset you," Melody said. Once she had Rosamonde carefully installed on the cushioned chair (she'd sewn the cushions herself from Thai silk) she breezed through the kitchen, setting the kettle to boil.

Hank had to remind Rosamonde that Lani was Melody's daughter.

"She's going through a difficult time right now," Melody continued, oblivious to Hank's presence. "What's so sweet about sixteen? That's what I want to know." She laughed, and her voice trembled ever so slightly. "I should cancel her party. That would show her who's boss. But I won't. The plans are already set, since the party is just day after tomorrow. Besides, she'll thank me for it later. I know she will. Remember when she was brand new, Mom, and you came out to help? Hard to believe sixteen years have gone by already."

Carefully, she pulled out mayonnaise jars of dried herbs and measured out the precise amount into metal tea balls.

"She's been a smart mouth," Melody continued, "ever since she started hanging around that boyfriend of hers. He's too old for her. He doesn't go to the high school, so I can't find out much about him, and Lani isn't talking."

To be more accurate, Melody wasn't listening. Melody didn't want to hear what she didn't want to know, and she didn't want to know about the way Kapono was unsupervised most of the time. That's what happens when a kid enrolls in college. Melody didn't want to think about college, either, but when the time came, she would pick out a nice, small one for Lani. Something that she and Martin couldn't afford. She would find a college that could serve as an extension of her protective umbrella.

Hank ruffled the air, making the light over the sink flicker. He didn't like his role as mediator, but he had to do it for Rosie. Family was everything to his Rosie. Maybe she couldn't always remember Lani's name in her head, but her heart knew better. Her heart kept track of her own flesh and blood. There was nothing more important in life than family. Without family, what was the point of life?

So Hank followed the family all around, watched over them, so to speak, keeping the connections alive for Rosie. He couldn't leave her side very long, or else she got too agitated. Hank didn't want to see her suffer, but truth was, he could hardly wait until all this was over and the two of them could slip away together forever, fading away into oblivion, unburdening themselves from all the world's problems.

Problems he'd helped put out there.

Melody peered up at the flickering light as if her glare could fix it. "I wish I knew what was wrong with that light," she said. "The bulb must not be any good. I should buy the expensive kind of light bulbs, but my budget can't afford it. We have over a hundred light bulbs in this house, can you believe it? And to replace them all at once would be too much." Then she turned and studied her mother. The way her eyes narrowed in thought, Hank knew what she was thinking. Having Rosamonde here was a burden to the budget, too.

"I think it's about time for Martin to get a raise, don't you, Mom?" Melody searched the top rack of the dishwasher for the cup she always used for her mother. It was plastic with a wide bottom and a big handle for easy grasping. Hank expected that before too long she'd end up getting one of those toddler training cups like the ones she'd made Lani use all the way until she went to kindergarten.

"Do you remember what you said about Martin when I brought him home for you to meet that first time?" Melody laughed. She found the cup and filled it with her tea, even though the faded gold letters indicated another intent: "Flynn's Coffee, Hawaii's finest."

"You said not to give up my dreams for a man." Melody laughed some more, but Hank didn't see what was so funny about it. Had Rosie really said that?

Melody finally controlled her laughter and brought the plastic cup to Rosamonde. She turned the cup, offering the handle to her mother for easy grasping. Rosamonde stared first at the handle, then at Melody, then at the barstool where Hank perched.

"It's not too hot, Mom. I made it just right for you. Just the way you like it, with a little dollop of honey."

Rosamonde's gaze returned to the cup's handle. Finally, she spoke in her startling, clear voice, the voice they hardly ever heard anymore. "What am I supposed to do with it?"

"Why, you drink it, of course," Melody said. "Just like this." Melody showed her how, using her own porcelain mug covered with purple orchids. They matched the flowers on her flowing dress. Melody always liked to match.

Rosamonde grasped the handle and lifted the cup to her lips, imitating their daughter. A dribble of tea ran down her chin.

"See? I told you you'd like it." The ladies sipped in silence, then Melody continued. "What you didn't understand back then, Mom, when I first brought Martin home for you to meet, was that Martin was my dream. *Is*, I mean. I'm living my dream here. Isn't it just wonderful here? Life couldn't be more perfect. Especially now that you're here with us. A girl needs her mother. Having you here with us makes everything complete now. Thank you for coming, Mom."

That wasn't how Hank remembered it. Melody had practically kidnapped Rosamonde. Melody had arrived at the little house overlooking the Chesapeake, the house where Hank had died almost two decades earlier, and she wouldn't leave until the house was sold, its contents carted away, and Rosamonde's possessions were reduced to what would fit inside two suitcases. Melody had made all the decisions, and in a way, Hank felt relieved that someone had taken charge. Hank couldn't do it anymore for Rosie.

"Oh, I know, Martin may have his faults," Melody said, "but one of these days he'll have his family's business all for himself, and then things will be easier. I think we deserve a little more of the share, and I'm sure that will happen soon. Maybe I should have a little talk with Dad Flynn and speed things up. It's time he retired."

Melody set her flowered mug on the counter, then took Rosamonde's cup away from her, then dabbed her mother's chin with a napkin. "Oh, there goes that darned light bulb again."

Hank couldn't take it anymore. He decided that since Melody

had everything under control here, he'd better go check on Lani. He rather liked her young man.

#

**I don't know why** Melody shouts at me. She is saying something about changing sheets, whatever that means. She is asking me if I am okay, but of course I'm not. She knows that. Why does she ask what she already knows?

I look to Hank for help, but Hank is not here. Hank? Hank? Where are you?

I look back to Melody and open my mouth, but the words are not working anymore. That's what happens when Hank leaves me.

Alone.

Alone.

I do not know this place.

I must go look for Hank. He must've gone home.

# HONOLULU, 1990

**The day Rosamonde** became a grandmother was the first day she got through all twenty-four hours in a row without thinking of Hank, not even once. Not that she was proud of this achievement, for the pain in her heart was still raw. She'd lost him just twenty-three months earlier. However, on the day little Lani entered the world, it was as if Rosamonde took a vacation from her grief. She was a grandmother!

She'd waited for this day from the moment Melody first brought Martin Flynn home for her to meet. Rosamonde had looked him over thinking, *is this the one who'll make me a grandmother?* He had a golfer's clean-cut physique, good manners, and job security in the form of his family's coffee business. At first she thought, *what couldn't a mother like about him?*

Well, for one thing, he lived in Hawaii, a place so far away from Maryland that it might as well be another country. In fact, she wasn't altogether convinced of the correctness of Hawaii's status as one of her nation's states, although she'd never admit that aloud, not to anyone, and particularly not to the Flynns. She'd been raised with better manners than that.

And for another thing... Rosamonde couldn't quite put her finger on it — Hank would've been able to, if he'd been there with her, since he was always so logical and precise. He'd always been good at analyzing a situation, which was why he'd turned into a successful scientist against the odds, meaning his origins. Yes, he *had* been successful, regardless of the harsh words leveled against him later on. Even so, no one could deny that his team at Los Alamos had accomplished what they'd set out to do, even if it was Pandora's Box that he'd helped to open.

Rosamonde couldn't quite identify that nebulous other thing that was wrong with her son-in-law, besides the unfortunate geographical blunder of his birth, which unlike Hank, Martin had not overcome. Even though she couldn't identify the problem, she could almost sniff its foul presence, like a dirty pan that had been left to soak in the sink a day too long. No doubt about it, Martin was at fault about something, she could tell, on account of Melody. While Rosamonde may not be good at Hank's scientific process, at identifying and classifying what was there, she was good at identifying what was *not* there. The pieces that were deliberately left out spoke volumes to her. She was a reader of clues, of faces, of hidden meanings that lived between-the-lines.

The clues regarding Martin's shortcomings appeared in Melody's face. A mother could always spot trouble in her daughter's face. Melody had been blessed with a dazzling smile, one that warmed the coldest of hearts, but nowadays, Rosamonde noticed that even though her daughter still flashed her brilliant smile, there was a slight sag to her eyes — no, not a wrinkle exactly, which would've been expected for a career girl in her mid thirties. The sparkle behind her daughter's eyes had fizzled, an eternal flame gone out.

Rosamonde noticed the sag and lack of sparkle over the last four or five years. No, it was five and a half years ago, at Barry's graduation, when Rosamonde first noticed. Whatever troubled Melody, Rosamonde bet that it had been going on longer than that. It was a boil festering, and oh, how she ached to lance it for her daughter. Trouble had been festering maybe as long as ten years, since Melody's marriage and subsequent move to Hawaii.

Yes, it was definitely Martin's fault. Martin was lacking in Melody's life. The baby would bring him back, so little Lani was a blessing in more ways than one.

Rosamonde booked the very next flight she and her son Barry could get to Honolulu. Lucky for them that Lani came when she did, far enough ahead of Thanksgiving that there were still seats available. Taking the time off from work was no problem for Barry since he'd planned to quit his job at the bar anyway. Bartending was only temporary work until his screenplay sold.

By the time they arrived with leis round their necks at Melody's cute little house near Kapiolani Park, the baby Lani was already four days old. Melody had hired a nurse to watch the baby upstairs so that Melody could sleep undisturbed in the tiny den downstairs. Considering the cracker-box size of Melody and Martin's house, it surprised Rosamonde that they could afford a private nurse at all. Why didn't they just ask one of Martin's sisters to help out? Not the younger one, of course, but the older one seemed sensible enough.

Rosamonde didn't wish to probe into her married daughter's financial matters, but she wished they would let her help them out. A loan, perhaps. Martin could scarcely afford a house. Then again, houses in Hawaii were no cheap matter. They were lucky to have something, anything at all, even though small. Their neighborhood was nice enough. Lush. Green, ferny-looking trees that were nothing more than over-grown houseplants made one think of summer when in fact, they were heading into winter. Perhaps Martin's family business was more lucrative than Rosamonde had realized.

Well, Rosamonde decided, it was none of her concern. Her daughter was getting along, with or without her sparkle. Rosamonde was glad to take over when Melody let the nurse go. She was glad to take the baby while Melody healed.

And, oh, such a precious bundle was she! Reflexes were one of nature's miracles of survival, and Rosamonde loved checking them off: the flutter and flicker of the tiny face behind closed eyelids during sleep; the miniature fingers wrapping around one of Rosamonde's, a giant by comparison; the eager muscles rhythmically sucking from her bottle. All the baby's parts worked fine, including the gurgles and burps and grunts and sighs as formula passed through her system.

Rosamonde loved reading aloud the book she'd brought with her on the plane, *Clan of the Cave Bear* (such a marvelous view of another world), while the baby rested peacefully against her heart. Lani was a good baby, one who hardly ever cried. Occasionally, the baby would rear up from Rosamonde's shoulder, resisting the burp that rose from the churning turmoil within her brand-new insides. Rosamonde helped to ease it out, and when it finally was released in an explosion of bubbles, Lani settled back against her grandmother's shoulder with a sigh and those tiny fingers grasping, winding, kneading against Rosamonde's shirt.

"Mom!"

When Rosamonde heard the urgency in Melody's voice, her heart skipped a beat. Her book slipped from her one-handed grip and fanned shut, losing her place. She straightened against the cool leather of the sofa, where she'd been slouching in utter contentment with the baby dozing against her breast. On the opposite side of the room, Melody stood, leaning against the doorway to the hall as if she was about to faint. Her face was as white as the orchid sitting in the filtered light of the atrium entry behind her.

"What's wrong?" Rosamonde felt the baby stir beneath the tension stiffening the fingers of her hand that secured Lani to her shoulder. "Do you feel okay? Couldn't you nap?"

"Mom! You don't have a burp cloth on your shoulder. The baby's going to spit up all over your nice blouse."

Rosamonde laughed, feeling the alarm drain from her. "It'll wash, honey."

Melody crossed the room with that ghostly, floating step of hers. Her pale face and the pastel blue of the robe she'd made for herself out of flowing silk didn't diminish the image in Rosamonde's mind. It was the same mental image she'd held of other famous ghosts whose stories she'd devoured over the years.

She shook herself. Her daughter wasn't a ghost. She took the burp cloth that Melody dangled before her, because doing so would make Melody happy, and it was just easier to keep everyone happy than it was to have to mend the hurt later on.

A better question was what had happened to the men? Why weren't they back from the store yet? How hard could it be to buy a turkey? She needed to start it defrosting.

Melody burst into tears.

Her daughter's cry of anguish sent a knife piercing through Rosamonde's soul. Carefully, she laid the sleeping baby down on the sofa. At less than a week old, Lani wasn't going to go anywhere. Then Rosamonde stood to scoop her daughter in her arms, the way she used to do, whenever Melody let her.

"There, there, dear," she murmured while Melody sobbed against her shoulder. "Everything's all right. Mama's here."

"Oh, Mom." Melody pushed away from Rosamonde and wiped her eyes with the back of one hand. "I'm sorry."

"You have nothing to be sorry for. It's best to get it off your chest. Want to talk about it?"

"Oh, no. It's nothing like that. It's just that..." Melody sniffled and cocked her head sideways, gazing at the sleeping baby. A look of endearment softened her sagging eyes. "Is it fair to bring her into this world? Sometimes I've wondered, but now looking at her, I can't bear the thought of not having her. Oh, Mom, what if something happens to her? What if I can't...take care of her right?"

34

"Honey, it's perfectly normal to have your doubts and fears." Although Rosamonde suspected that Melody's doubts and fears went far deeper than a question of hormones. Was this the Martin problem, finally coming out? "Trust yourself," she said, steeling her voice, "and just love your baby the best that you can. You'll do fine as a mother. If you have enough love, everything turns out all right in the end."

Melody's head jerked to one side, but not before Rosamonde could see a fresh flow of tears. *Oh lord*, Rosamonde thought. Her heart skipped a beat. *What's Martin done? Or not done?*

Melody dashed to the kitchen on the other side of the open counter that separated the combination dining and living room from the kitchen. Rosamonde followed as far as she dared go without losing sight of the baby on the couch.

"What if I can't do it?" Melody said. She opened the refrigerator and poked around inside.

"Of course you can. You're not the first mother to experience doubts."

"But I don't know how to take care of a baby, and I don't want to make a mistake. I need someone to help me. I need you, Mom. Without Dad around anymore, you ought to think of moving permanently to Honolulu."

A shudder rippled through Rosamonde. She'd been uprooted enough. She'd struggled all her life to put down roots for her family, and now that she finally had, she couldn't just yank them up and toss them aside. No, it was too late for her to move again, and even if it weren't, who would take flowers to Hank's grave?

It was time for someone else to accommodate *her* for a change.

She ached at the thought of missing watching little Lani grow, but life had to go on, and Lani was Melody's responsibility, not Rosamonde's. When the time came for Rosamonde to move again — for the last time before she joined Hank — she'd never willingly choose a place like the tropics. She could hardly breathe here, where the very air was green. Air was not meant to be liquid and its scent full of decay. Hawaii had its own type of beauty, she couldn't deny that, but it was one of parasites. She wasn't accustomed to beauty feeding off of other life, beauty that depended on decay. Besides, there was no change of season here, and she was too old and set in her ways to learn anew again.

Rosamonde cleared her throat, a signal that indicated a compromise. "I'm sure your sister-in-law will help you. Silvia has five children, doesn't she? She must know a thing or two about raising kids."

"Mom, *no.*" Melody straightened and pulled a plastic container from the fridge. She opened the lid and released the sweet scent of pineapple into the room. "Silvia's the last person I'd ever ask for advice. She doesn't supervise her children, and they've gone completely wild. Thank goodness they're older. I believe the youngest one is seven now. I should be able to keep them from corrupting Lani." She carefully arranged the pineapple on a plate, then offered it to Rosamonde. "Want some?"

Rosamonde helped herself. She couldn't resist the sweets of nature. *You had to go to their source to get the best samples*, she thought. Melody was deliberately tempting her, but tasting the fresh fruit, she didn't care.

"Lani won't need cousins," Melody said, "but she *will* need a grandmother."

"I'll come every year to visit."

"Once a year isn't enough."

"True, but you could come home from time to time."

"Maryland is not my home and never has been, not even when I lived there. I always missed New Mexico after we moved."

"Well, there's no going back, is there, honey?"

"That's right, Mom. That's why you should move here."

Rosamonde sighed. She should've seen that one coming.

"Now that I have a baby," Melody continued, "it's going to be too hard for me to go there to take care of you."

"You need to take care of Lani, not me."

"Why won't you come, Mom? You have nothing keeping you in Maryland anymore."

"Well, that's just not true. I have my job at the library, reading to the children."

"It's a volunteer job."

"They need me, all the same."

"More than your own family?"

Rosamonde hesitated. She couldn't answer that because nothing mattered more than family.

"Oh, honey," Rosamonde finally said. "I can't leave your dad."

"He's dead, Mom."

"Who would plant flowers on his grave?"

"We'll go back every year and do that, I promise. Just think about moving out here, that's all I ask. I have to take care of my business, and I need your help more than Dad needs you now. Otherwise, Lani has to go to a sitter. She starts next week."

"Dear, is that necessary? Can't you sew at home? At least take off more time?" Money, she thought, it all boiled down to money. Maybe it was Martin who was too proud to ask for help.

"Of course, Mom, but I have to go out and sell my designs. What's the point of creating fashions I can't sell? Mine is the perfect job for raising a child. Most of my work will be done from home, but I still have to count on someone who can take Lani when I have to meet with clients. It'd be so much better for you to be that person, instead of a sitter."

"I wish I could."

"Thankfully, you're in good health now, but we can't predict how much longer that'll last. It's best to get you settled into a new place before you actually need to be there. It'll only become harder to move the longer you wait. There's a nice complex not too far from here that we can go look at."

Rosamonde was being selfish. Was Rosamonde being selfish? The thought of moving again — anywhere — terrified her. Flying out here once a year was frightening enough. This time she'd had Barry for company, but she couldn't depend on her son to accompany her every time. More than anything, she refused to become a burden for either of her kids. Why, she'd move into an old folks' home before she did that! It couldn't be time already for her to make that kind of move. She was only sixty-seven. She had plenty of years ahead of her, and she wanted to take them one year at a time.

"Honey, I didn't come all the way out here to talk about growing old. Why, you're only old when you give in to it in your mind. I came out here to meet my grandchild, and that's what I'm going to do. I only wish your dad could've met her, too."

"Okay, Mom, but I warn you. I won't be satisfied until you're here with us full time. If you insist on staying in Maryland, then Barry will have to move in with you. I'll have a little chat with him."

"That's not necessary."

"Oh, yes it is. It's time for him to finally grow up and face reality."

Melody was right about one thing. Once she decided on a course of action, there was no letting go of it. All Rosamonde could do was change the subject and hope to re-direct Melody's fervor. "Lani's name is Hawaiian, isn't it?"

"Uh-huh. It's so much more evocative than 'Melody'. What on earth were you thinking when you gave me such a silly name?"

"I was thinking that it's a beautiful name to match my beautiful daughter. Just like Lani. Is Lani a family name on Martin's side?"

"It was Grandad Flynn's mother's name. She was part Polynesian."

"Really? You'd never know it to look at the Flynns today. Martin and his sisters with their blonde hair don't look as if they have a drop of Polynesian blood in them."

"You'd better not let them hear you say that. They're very proud of that one little drop." Melody's face switched to listening mode. "Speaking of the Flynns, I believe they're back from the store. I hear a car in the drive."

Melody wiped her fingers on a towel, then breezed past Rosamonde. Martin's baritone voice rumbled from the atrium entryway. Despite the low register of his voice, Martin was not a man whose presence filled a room. Not that she meant that in a derogatory manner, no. He just wasn't very effective. Rosamonde supposed he had other things on his mind, like work. Even though he was lucky to have a flexible schedule, thanks to being the boss, Rosamonde was sure he'd bring the worries of the office home with him. As Hank had done.

Grocery bags rustled as her son-in-law entered the room and greeted Rosamonde with a nod of his sandy blonde head. He was well tanned from his lifestyle on the golf course, two days a week, rain or shine. Work might worry him, but he wouldn't let it get in the way of his golf game. Maybe he'd stopped off to play a few holes on his way home from the store.

"Where's Barry?" Rosamonde asked. "Didn't he come back with you?" *Men,* she thought. *You can't trust them with a household task so simple as a quick trip to the grocery store.*

"We ran into Caleb," Martin said, as if that explained everything.

"Caleb?" Melody said.

"Silvia's husband."

"I know who Caleb is. What was he doing in the grocery store?"

"I never said he was in the grocery store. You said that." Martin winked at Rosamonde, crossed the living room, set down the bags of groceries, then beamed at little Lani. "She looks just like me, don't you think?"

Rosamonde nodded and grinned. Newborns mostly looked alike, a breed of their own, more similar to wet rats than bearing a resemblance to any parent, but she wasn't going to argue. Let him think so, if that made him happy. Fatherhood seemed to agree with Martin. She'd never seen him happier than now, including at his own wedding. There was a virile air of cockiness about him. Most important, she hoped his joy would infect Melody.

It was working already. Melody laughed. She actually laughed. "Okay, so you picked up Caleb. What happened to my *brother*? Did you forget him at the store?"

"Don't I wish."

"I beg your pardon," said Rosamonde. No one appreciated how hard her son tried to succeed.

"Sorry, Roz. What I meant to say was that, uh, he got distracted. With a *wish*. Yeah, that's it."

Melody groaned. "Don't tell me. Let me guess. Caleb told him about the green flash."

"More or less, but anyway, you can blame Caleb. We'd no sooner gotten into the car, Barry and I, on our way to the store, when Caleb pulled up, looking for me. He's got some hair-ball scheme to buy a business, and he wanted me to take a look. I think he just wants a loan."

"Why didn't he go to your dad, then?"

"He knew the old man would throw him out in the street. He figured I could make a case for him, to make up for Silvia getting screwed out of Flynn's — "

"Martin!"

"It's true, isn't it? Dad's not going to leave any part of the company to a woman, not when he has a male heir. The least Dad can do, in my opinion, is help Silvia and Caleb get a start in something of their own. It's only a loan, for god's sake — "

"Martin!"

"Anyway, we had to see the place right away because Caleb thinks it's a hot property and it won't last long on the market. He's got that all wrong. It's an antique shop of all things."

Rosamonde gasped. "Antiques? You have antiques here in Hawaii?"

"Caleb is kind of an antique himself," Melody said.

"I told him he's crazy. Dad won't go for it. Caleb should find something else to do than warehouse other people's junk. No one wants that old crap."

"I think it's a charming idea," said Rosamonde, raising her voice to be heard. It worked, too, because they both fell silent, as if she'd dropped a bomb.

Melody shook her head. "It's no use to give it another thought. By tomorrow, he will have forgotten about the whole thing. What's more important now is what's happened to Barry? How did you lose him?"

"He got distracted by the ocean while we were checking out the property, and he wandered off. I had to go on to the grocery by myself, damn him."

"Martin!"

"Don't worry about *him*. He'll find his way back. He always turns up."

"Maybe *I* could give Caleb a loan," Rosamonde said.

"Oh, Mom. No!"

"Honey, collecting antique pieces of glass was your dad's hobby. He loved to visit antique shops. Using some of his nest egg would help out your brother-in-law *and* be a way to honor your dad at the same time."

Hank was gone, and now Rosamonde would have to find something to do with the rest of her life. Doing something useful with Hank's money would help everyone involved. What better way than an antique shop?

# THREE

Hank, where are you? He does not sit on that thing anymore, whatever it is called, here in this place that I do not know. My words are gone, along with Hank.

I look to Melody for help, but she is not here, either. I believe this place must be her house. If it is my house, they have changed it. It is so dark and so empty here. I do not recognize this place. No, I have never been here before. I am sure of that. I think.

I am tired of strange things and new places around me. I am tired of telling them how unhappy I am, and I am tired of not being heard. I wish Melody would let me go home. She is a good girl, but she has always had a mind of her own.

Perhaps I shall just go. Hank is waiting for me outside. I will find him outside, and he will show me the way. I stand up and test my legs. There is nothing wrong with my legs. I think they are wrong about me. I want to be sure, but I cannot be sure. There is something they know that they aren't telling me. They think I wouldn't understand, but there is nothing wrong with me. Why do they take me away from my home, only to leave me all alone?

So alone.

I walk through the valley of the shadow of death, but you are with me. Is that what this dark room is? Cold. I am so cold. This dark place is green, but it's not the right green.

I cross the room and bump against that thing. Another thing for sitting. A couch, yes, that's what they call it. It is my couch, I believe, since I remember the slick feel of it against my skin. What is it doing here? They have moved it. Why are they confusing me?

Hank, wait for me.

I reach the door that I thought I broke. It is not broken anymore. I do not have to break the door to open it. I know how to turn the knob, because there's nothing wrong with me. That's what I do. Hank, I'm coming for you.

#

**Hank found Lani** in one of her favorite places, the beach closest to home. It spread out as a sinuous ribbon of sand beneath its famous backdrop of Diamond Head, which was nothing more than a lopped-off volcano, truth told. It was actually kind of puny compared to some of the calderas he'd worked around back in New Mexico.

Lani didn't come here for a dead volcano but for the beach. It wasn't Waikiki, which she loved for its vitality, a place where she could lose herself in the anonymity of crowds, but this beach had the advantage of being within walking distance both of home *and* Waikiki. This beach was a good enough place for times like this when she needed to decompress.

Hank knew such things because as a ghost he could hear people think. Not really (he would've scoffed if he could), but that was as close as he could come to describing the process. Drifting in and out of other people's heads could've been a handy skill at one time, but now there wasn't much he could do about anything he learned. He couldn't always interface with any of them except for Rosie, and that was only when he caught her just right in that in-between state of hers they wrote off as dementia. Mostly, no one else knew he was there or paid any attention to him. He didn't think of himself as a ghost in the traditional sense, not the way kids used to throw sheets over their heads for Halloween and shout "boo!" nor the way B movies made ghosts frightening, hell-bent, and full of revenge. Hank wasn't like that.

At least, not in this post-corporeal stage he wasn't. That's how he preferred thinking of it because he didn't like the D word. Before, life had been a whole different ballgame. He'd been scarier then than he was now. He wished he could've re-done his life before its corporeal end.

This transition phase he was in, otherwise known as being a ghost, was temporary. Thank goodness. It'd last only until he finished his business of protecting Rosie. Transition was always an awkward time for anyone, but soon, they'd be together again, he and his Rosie, and he could stop this ghostly business.

In the meanwhile, he knew that Rosie would worry about Lani, who'd taken off from home in such a huff, leaving Rosie in that state of terror. So once again, Hank was doing what he had to do. He'd watch out for Lani and bring her back to Rosie.

Lani sat with her back leaning against a palm tree, staring out beyond the ancient fishponds, beyond the reef where the surf crashed, as if she could see the ends of the earth. "I can't believe what a bitch!" Lani told the young Japanese man who squatted next to her.

Hank understood that Kapono wasn't really Japanese, but the kid had enough of his ancestors in him to make him appear like one of them. What Hank had trouble understanding was how Hawaiians could've interbred with Japanese after the disaster of Pearl Harbor. That was his own prejudice, Hank realized, which only supported the stereotype of his being a crotchety old fart. Kids today didn't appreciate the choices Hank's generation had had to weigh. Hank couldn't help himself anymore than Kapono could help his part-Japanese, part-Hawaiian blood.

Kapono listened patiently to Lani's tirade. He wore a worried frown that creased his smooth, hair-free face. His eyes disappeared into slits. Hank didn't trust a man whose eyes he couldn't read, but he realized his mistrust went deeper than the question of slitted eyes. It was the blood.

Despite all that, he actually liked the young man, which was different from trusting him. Hank liked anyone who cared about his granddaughter, even if it wouldn't last. The poor kid needed someone to care about her. Right now.

Sure, Melody cared too, and he supposed Martin cared in his

own way, but Lani couldn't recognize her parents' concern at this time in her life. She needed someone to tell her in a way that she could understand. Like the way Kapono rubbed her back while she sobbed and spit out all her hurt feelings.

"I can't take it anymore," she said. "I have to get out."

"You can come stay with me," Kapono said.

"Really? You mean it?"

"Sure."

"But what would your mother say?"

"She doesn't have to know."

"How can she not know? You still live at home. What would you do? Hide me under your bed?"

He chuckled softly. "Not *under*." Maybe Hank didn't like the kid so much after all.

Lani squealed, her tears forgotten. She was still a virgin, thank the good Lord, but that was her deepest, darkest secret.

"I don't get how come you still live at home," she said. "Didn't you ever want to go away?"

"Sure, but not all of us are privileged like you."

"You're just lazy, that's all. If you weren't so lazy, you'd get a job and get a place of your own."

"I got to study if I want to stay in school."

Attaboy, Hank thought.

"So what? That's boring."

"Yeah, but the pay-off for the boring stuff is that you get to study the fun stuff."

"What's fun about school?"

"High school doesn't count. You'll find out."

"Don't talk to me like that. That sounds like my stupid mom. The bitch."

"Yeah. So anyway, where're you going to go if you don't come home with me? You got to go someplace. You want to sleep on the beach?"

"Maybe that's not so bad."

"Sure, if you like trouble."

"What else is there?"

"Trust me, you don't want that kind of trouble."

"Anyway, your mom would just send me home. Then what would I do?"

Kapono sighed, and by God, his eyes opened. "You got aunts. What about them?"

"Silvia would rat, and Vanessa never has anything to eat. I dunno. I need someone who'll let me stay and not rat on me. Someplace nearby, 'cause I'm gonna have to sneak back home and find my journal... I know! Jewell. She's way cool."

"Yeah, but she's your mom's best friend and business partner besides."

"She's still cool anyway."

Hank drifted over to Lani and hovered above her. Then he stepped into her mind and flashed an image of Rosie. *Don't forget your Gran.*

He didn't really understand how this worked. He still felt new at this, even though he was long overdue for transitioning to the other side. Time was relative. He'd been a scientist most of his life, for chrissakes, and this transition period just went beyond all the physical laws he'd thought he understood. What mattered now, though, was that his ghostly essence was no longer ruled by those physical laws. He could somehow insert himself into the physical space that the dearly pre-departed occupied, and then through that intersection he could implant his thoughts or wishes into the living. Sometimes it took, but not always. Not even usually. He had no idea of the physical laws of this place, or why it worked with some and not others. It shouldn't work. It depended, he supposed, on the receptor.

Anyway, it was worth a try, so he fluttered there, shimmering in Lani's physical space, sending warm thoughts of Rosie.

Rosie, living with the Flynns now, waiting for her time with Hank.

Rosie, comfortable in Lani's old room. It wouldn't be much longer. God, he hoped not.

Kapono tried his best to derail Hank's efforts. "You'd put Jewell in a tough situation," he said, "staying with her. She may be cool, but her first loyalty will be to your mom. You should stay with me, instead."

Lani sighed. "I guess I'll have to take that risk. Jewell's condo is nearby, and you live way the hell away. I don't want to stay that far away from Gran. Gran needs me."

Good girl, Hank thought. She got the message. Now he could go back to Rosie.

#

**Rosie was gone.**

When Hank returned to the Flynns' house, he found Melody on the phone to Martin.

"You need to stop what you're doing and go look for Mom right now," Melody said, enunciating each word slowly, carefully, as if speaking to an idiot.

"Yes, I know Mom couldn't have gone far," she continued, nodding. "I know I'm closer to wherever she is than you are. I have to stay here, in case the police bring her home."

After a pause, she said, "Of course I phoned the police first. What did you think?"

Hank heard the catch to her voice. He wondered if she would've smiled her brilliant smile had she known anyone was here with her.

"Yes, they wanted me to stay on the line," she said, "but of course I couldn't do that, so I hung up. I had to call you."

Then she shook her head. "No, Lani's gone. She's out with that boyfriend of hers." Pause. "I know." Another pause. "I know. Maybe we could talk about that later. Right now, you need to..."

Hank didn't stick around to hear the rest of it. He had to find Rosie.

#

**I can't see a thing** out here. White light blinds me. I don't know if the white light is better or worse than the dark I left behind me. They tried to tell me that house is mine. It's not my house. I would know my own house. Yes, I would.

I am not stupid. Just because the words have gone away. They think they can fool me. But they cannot.

Hank, wait for me. Why are you hiding from me? You can't hide, because I know where to find you.

I feel the ground with my feet. It is hard and flat and warm through my shoes. What is wrong? Has the whole world gone mad but me? Winter is not a warm time, and I know it should be winter now. I am a winter baby, that's how come I know. The white light around me does not feel like my winter. I am hot, I think. Maybe I am cold. I am something that's not right.

I cannot hear. No, that is not true. I hear everything. And nothing. The air roars around my head, wanting to get in, while I want to get out.

Hank, you always called me clever. If I cannot see you or hear you, then I will find you by smelling you. Is that clever? You are always Old Spice and engine grease to me.

What I smell now is...ocean air and exhaust fumes. You are not here in this white light, but wait for me. I am coming for you, Hank.

#

**Rosamonde pushed the** baby buggy into the glare of afternoon sun and felt blinded for a minute, until her eyes adjusted. Lani fussed, even under her cute, pink sunbonnet and under the pram's sun shade. It didn't feel right, walking without Hank. He'd always enjoyed walking. It was nothing to him to walk a couple of miles first thing each morning, before going off to work. He called it his thinking time. Hank was good at thinking, and Rosamonde was good at telling. When she walked, she wanted to tell stories. Most evenings, Hank would walk again, just to unwind from his day and get his mind off his work. She always walked with him in the evening, and she prattled on and on about her day, turning insignificant daily drudgery into glorified stories, adding hooks and cliffhangers and quirky details, distracting him from his anxiety with the details of her day.

She missed Hank dreadfully, especially when she walked. But now she had a granddaughter to walk with and tell stories to. She steered the buggy along the cement sidewalks that radiated heat and tension even here in the suburbs, and she told Lani about the first Polynesians. She'd read about them (Michener, wasn't it?), sailing the seas in their dugout canoes, chasing the stories of the stars above. They were a storytelling people, too, just like Rosamonde. They could spin the ordinary details of their day into amazing tales about gods and goddesses and little people with magical powers.

She knew that little Lani heard her tales, in spite of the noise of traffic speeding past. She knew the baby could hear, because she'd checked off all the reflexes, as outlined by Dr. Spock. The rhythmic motion from the buggy's springs was putting the baby to sleep, but still, the stories Rosamonde told her had to go into that little head somewhere. She'd done the same to her own children when they were babies. Storytelling was like making bread. *You stir in all the ingredients and wait to see if the dough will rise.* Her efforts took with Barry but not with Melody — *you just never know.* Barry would one day become a famous screenwriter, and she supposed that one out of two wasn't a bad score so far. Who knew what the future held for little Lani?

Considering all the noxious fumes Lani would have to grow up with, Rosamonde wondered if her granddaughter would have any kind of a future at all. Fresh air was good for babies, had been good for her babies on the high mesa, and because of that, Rosamonde wanted to take little Lani with her on her walk over to the antique shop Caleb hoped to buy with her money. Caleb wanted to show her the place. Melody had happily agreed — to the walk, not to the loan — and besides, the buggy was Rosamonde's gift to the baby. She wanted to give it a trial run. But now Rosamonde realized her mistake. Perhaps she was doing more harm than good. Exhaust fumes hung thickly in the sea breeze, covering up the salt she should taste in the air instead. She supposed her granddaughter would adapt in time. Life had a way of going on, despite human errors. She wished Hank could be here with her, to advise her. He would know.

#

**Hank? I cannot see** in all the white light. I will find you. In white light, not dark. My feet know the way. I have gone this way many times, and now I do not have to tell my feet where we are going. We are going home. I am coming. Wait for me, Hank.

I cannot hear your voice. I cannot smell Old Spice and engine grease. But I do smell engines.

That is the noise I hear! Engines are all around me, engines with their honking horns and squealing tires, and now that I know, I am afraid. Knowledge is a terrible thing. Terrible, when it should be good. My feet stop. My feet know.

They know that they will fail me, have already failed me. I am dying. Perhaps I am already dead. I wait for the pain. I wonder where I will feel it first and how it will spread through my body, but all I feel is...nothing. Nothingness fills me.

Angry voices, strange voices, shout. They shout at me. I do not know why. I do not know their words. Their words are not my words. I try to understand, but I cannot. My feet will not move. I feel my eyes open wide, but all I see is the white light. I sweat from the cold.

Then something clamps onto my arm. It is someone's hand. I do not know whose hand it is. I think it is my sister who died.

"Gran, what are you DOING here?" my sister-who-died says to me. She pulls on me and makes my feet work again.

She is nice, and the pitty-pat of my heart settles. My eyes relax, and now I see that the light is not so white. I am not cold, but hot instead. I am both.

"God, this is so weird," the nice one says. "I just had a feeling you needed me, like you were calling to me, or something, I don't know. And I wasn't so far away, and then I heard the traffic, and horns honking, and people shouting, and it was YOU they're shouting at. God! Come on, I'll get you home."

"Home?"

"Yes, Gran, home. Come on with me, now. I'll take you."

My sister who died does not know the way home. They think I'm stupid, but I am not. I know home is not back there, the way she tries to take me. She is nice, but she can't fool me. My feet stop.

"What's wrong, Gran? Don't you want to go with me? Oh, I get it. You're running away, too, aren't you? It's okay. I'm with you."

It is not okay, and my feet will not move, not in the direction the nice one wants to go. There is nothing wrong with me. I can see shapes now in the light that is not so white. The nice one, I think, is not my sister who died. She is family, but I cannot for the life of me remember her name. Hank, what is this one's name? Why did you leave me, Hank?

Hank?

Hank?

"Okay, Gran, calm down. I won't make you go home if you don't want to. I know, I have an idea! Uncle Caleb's store is just another block away. Was that where you were going? Let's go there now, and you can sit and rest and have a glass of Unca's lemonade. How about?"

I do not know, but my feet are moving again. It is the way they wanted to go all along, so it must be right. It must be where Hank is.

#

**The antique shop** was little more than a showcase window sandwiched between two high-rises. The window with its streaked pane of glass, painted list of merchandise, and a formerly green awning now bleached and dusted with a fine layer of sand was a bridge between the modern towers to either side. It was a refuge that offered watches, furniture, toys, books, glassware, and china, or so the window informed. A refuge from the world of today.

Rosamonde breathed a sigh of relief and pushed against the door with her backside. She wasn't about to relinquish her grip on the buggy.

The door opened behind her and a bell tinkled above her head. "I wasn't sure if you'd come or not," said a man with a voice so soft he seemed to caress his words. "Let me help you with that."

"*That* just happens to be your niece," said Rosamonde, "and I said I'd come, didn't I?"

Caleb made appropriate adoring sounds as the pram wheeled past him, into the store. "I never expected Melody and Martin to have a baby," he said.

"It's high time they did." Rosamonde nodded. The dim interior of the store took the strain off her head, and the musty smell made her feel at home.

"I didn't think Melody would find time to be a mother, not with her career."

"Kids today have too many irons in the fire, if you ask me."

They stood there in the gloom, silently appraising each other. Caleb reminded her of a disheveled teddy bear — a little plump and in need of a haircut. She could almost see the heart stitched onto his thread-bare shirt that made her want to squeeze him. Then something about his furious blinking caught her attention. His eyelashes were too long for a man's and curled up like a kewpie doll's. His eyes, though, were a clear, topaz brown, like the glass eyes you'd see on a teddy bear. His left eye ticked.

He was nervous apparently, and Rosamonde suddenly felt sorry for him. Melody berated her brother-in-law for going nowhere in his life, but Rosamonde thought that having five kids and a wife, and providing for them to boot, made him pretty darned successful. Yes, he was a man in his forties who'd drifted from one job to another, but that told Rosamonde that he hadn't found his passion yet. Maybe this place was it. The possibility of losing out on his chance-of-a-lifetime would be a frightening thing, indeed.

"Show me around," she said. "Tell me why you think this is a good deal for us."

#

**"This way, Gran,"** says the nice one. I follow her into the cool dark, filled with the calm of the past. A clock ticks. The floor squeaks. This place could be home. It smells old. There is engine grease in the dusty air, but there is no Old Spice. So I know this calm, clock-ticking, shadowy place is not home either.

#

59

**"They keep the big** pieces up front and cut glass in the back," Caleb said, striding through the store as if he already owned the place. "I'd switch that around. Let the crystal sparkle in the window and draw window shoppers inside. In the back of the store, that's where I'd put the furniture. Maybe arrange some pieces into a cozy lounge. A place for conversation. Camaraderie, y'know? Maybe offer some lemonade to weary shoppers."

"Sounds like you already know what you want to do."

"I've been thinking about this for a long time. Silvia says I'm a packrat, that I could open a store with all the junk I like to collect."

Just like Hank, Rosamonde thought.

Caleb stopped by a display of toys and stared deep into the eyes of a walking doll. "I bet if this doll could talk, she'd have some stories to tell about the little girl who once walked her. I want to keep the past alive. That's why I want this place."

Hank always said that memories were stored in people's things, that's why they're valuable. You have to preserve their things to preserve the past.

Rosamonde rocked the buggy. The baby was trying to wake up. "You think the past deserves to be preserved?"

"You betcha."

"Including all the mistakes we've made over time?"

"Especially. How else are we going to learn anything? Would you go back and change anything, even if you could?"

"Change? Never!" A wave of horror engulfed her mind. If she'd made other choices in her past, better choices or not, she wouldn't have Lani today. Or perhaps she'd have a whole slew of different Lanis. She ached for the lost ones, the children and grandchildren that might've been. Such thoughts made her head hurt. "Maybe it's better to forget some things," she finally said.

"I hope you don't mean you want to forget about your kind offer to help me acquire this place."

"Not at all. I meant what I said. I always mean what I say." Boxes of games stacked on the shelf next to the doll caught her attention. She'd always loved games more than dolls. She picked up the box on top — a jigsaw puzzle — and saw a picture of a rural landscape at the peak of summer fertility. Its picture could've been painted of the farm where she'd grown up in eastern Ohio. She hadn't been back there since she buried her mother in '46.

Distant memories drew her to a time when she'd sat round the kitchen table with the family long after supper was cleared and the chores were done for the day. It was the dead of winter, but they were warm inside with their laughter and stories they shared over a game of homemade dominoes or cards or the jigsaw puzzle they worked again and again. It was family that turned a place into a home.

Caleb peered over her shoulder. "If I was in charge here, I'd set out a puzzle for customers to work in the cozy room setting along with lemonade. Make this into a homey place where people want to come back to. Work a little puzzle, buy another trinket."

#

**"Hey, Unca Caleb,"** the nice one with no name says. "How's business?"

I look at her, and I look for the buggy, but the buggy is gone. The baby is standing. The baby is *talking*! Oh, my! What is wrong with this world? Oh oh oh! Whatever have we done?

"Same old same old," says a teddy bear. "Hi there, Mrs. Berryhill. Come on back and sit a spell. I've got a fresh pitcher of lemonade."

#

**The picture on the** box-top showed the farm as much more idyllic than the way she remembered life on the farm had actually been. The picture didn't show the hours of chores and the dog-tired muscles and all the work that summer fertility created. There was no end to putting up vegetables, and just when you thought it was over, the apples would be ready. Rosamonde had always been eager to escape to school at the end of summer vacation, even though she had to get up when it was still dark to do her chores before the long walk to the schoolhouse. It was a time of innocence before her world got yanked into adulthood with the atomic era. There was no going back.

#

**The standing-talking** baby pulls me through the dark to a rocker just like the one my granny had. It feels good to take a load off my feet in Granny's rocker. Granny is not here anymore, but she has left her things in Mama's world. There are no worries here, and I feel almost happy for the first time in a long time.

Mama took care of me then, just like Hank did later.

Hank is here, somewhere. I feel him.

We wait for Hank, my sister-who-died and I.

As we wait, she bends over a table. It is covered with tiny pieces. Broken pieces. A picture is broken.

"Hey, Unca Caleb!" she says. "You've got a new puzzle. I've never seen this one before."

"It's special," the teddy bear says back. I do not like teddy bears who act as if they know me.

"How come?"

The teddy bear winks. "It's magic."

I may not know the standing-talking baby's name, but I know that she is my blood. I have just forgotten her name, that's all. My mind works tricks on me like that. She sees me watching her, and she hands a box to me. What am I supposed to do with it? Eat it? I feel the question on my face.

"Hey, Gran, remember how I always used to give you a puzzle each year when you visited us for Christmas and I was little?"

I do not understand. Is this box mine? I do not know what is inside. I do not know what she wants of me.

"This is like old times, huh?" she says. "I'd give you a new puzzle, and you'd let me help you work it. Do you remember?"

I wander through the rooms of memory inside my head. What she means must be here somewhere. Somewhere.

"Let's work this one together, how about?"

Hank, what does she mean?

"This is way cool. Look, the picture shows some sort of Grandma Moses snow scene, and all the people are busy doing their own thing, even though there's clearly a storm coming. Look at those dark clouds — oooooh! Dude! Look at that horse and sleigh. Look how old it all is. This must be from back when you were a little girl, huh? What are those men doing to the trees? With buckets? Oh, I bet I can guess. They're making maple syrup, aren't they?"

The sweet memory of maple flows through my head. That is what Hank tastes like. I remember now. I know...this place... Hank and I have been here... And...now I know what to do. I open the box to look for him inside.

# ARNIE

**Arnie Trimble was the** sort of man who'd never had to ask for help before. He wasn't asking this time, either. Nossir, he was paying Lyman. That is, he *would* pay him a share once this season's maple syrup sold. Assuming there'd be any sales at all this year, thanks to the war.

Arnie stepped into his snow pants and slid them up his stocky frame, covering denim overalls. Stepping into the rubber galoshes was less easy, more like stretching a second layer of skin over his work boots. He wrapped Grandma's woolen muffler round his throat, snapped up his jacket, and tugged the earflaps down from his cap. Peggy always told him he never could hide his ears from nobody.

All the better for hearing the sap flow, come sugar season.

*Oh Daddy, stop teasin'*, Peggy would say. *No one can hear sap flow.*

Arnie snickered at the memory and stepped outside into the bite of morning air. Lyman was already there, waiting in the yard

65

with a pair of horses, all three of them blowing steam.

"How long you been standing out here?" Arnie asked.

Lyman shrugged.

"How come you didn't say you was here already? You could've come on inside. Had yourself a cup o' coffee. It can't be above freezing yet."

"Twenty-seven degrees," Lyman said. He was bundled up for the weather in roly-poly gear that mirrored Arnie's. Except for the red tip on the end of his sapsickle-shaped nose, he probably couldn't even feel the cold.

"I ain't paying you to freeze to death on me. Let me grab my snowshoes from the woodshed, and then we'll be off. We got us a trail to break out."

They fell into a rhythm. Nellie and Jasper plodded flank to flank, sinking deep, up to their joints, as they worked their way through the drifts left over from winter snow. On either side of the gray workhorses, the men scrunched across the snow's crust, skimming its surface with the paddles that attached to their boots. Come summer, this would be a dirt road again, the road that headed up to the lake where Arnie liked to fish for bass, but every spring it was the sled route through the sugarbush.

"Hardly feels like spring can be around the corner," Arnie said.

Lyman grunted.

"Last week of February we always break out the trail."

"Storm's coming," Lyman said.

"Maybe so, but we got to get ready for tapping all the same. Pops always said you got to time it just right. You could set your calendar by him. First Tuesday of every March, that's when he'd start drilling, and that's the way I learned to do it, too. Trimbles have been here in Dillon Falls for six generations, so we oughta' know. Legend has it that the Indians taught the first Trimbles the secrets to sugaring."

Arnie waited for a response, or a comment, or a complaint, but Lyman said nothing. He kept trudging along, blowing more steam. By now, both men were breathing deeply, filling their lungs with aching air.

"You don't talk much, do you?" said Arnie. "Well, I ain't paying you to talk, neither. Anyhow, storm or no storm, we got to be ready for next week." Arnie glanced up at the sky. Gray clouds piled on top of each other, each roll of gray darker, more ominous, more stuffed with fresh snow than the next. He frowned. He didn't need another set-back. That's why he'd hired Lyman.

"Where'd you say your people come from again?" Arnie asked. "I didn't."

A man who had his secrets too, Arnie thought. He could respect that. "Well, I figured if we was going to work together, we might oughta' get to know each other a bit more. Folks are like that around here. Ain't got nobody else but theirselves to depend on. Know what I mean?"

Lyman grunted.

"We're a closed-mouth folk up here, so you come to the right place if you're shy. I know you like to come up here fishing every summer, but something made you come early this year." Arnie paused, giving Lyman the opportunity to expand on that.

He didn't, so Arnie went on. "You come way early, didn't you? Lucky for me, what with my little girl all grown up and gone away. Said she had to work in one of them factories that make bombs or something. 'What about me?' I told her. She'd rather help make bombs than help her own daddy. What's the world coming to? I tell you, them wily, yellow Japs sneaking into Pearl Harbor like that — "

"They're people, too, just like me and you."

"Well, son, they may be like you, but they ain't nothing like me." Arnie wasn't really old enough to be Lyman's father. He was 42 to what he guessed Lyman to be: scarcely thirty. But using that term made him feel older and wiser.

They plodded on. Arnie's legs felt numb, and he didn't think it was entirely due to the cold. One more week of this cold. It'd been a hell of a winter. Next week, come Tuesday, it wasn't going to freeze no more at night. That's when the sap would start to flow. It'd always been that way. The war may change his private world, but not even world war could change sugar season.

"They're the enemy, son," Arnie said.

Lyman fixed his attention straight ahead, deeper into the sugarbush, a field of towering maple trunks.

Arnie felt a buzzing in his head, and he wondered if it was the sap awakening, and he was, in fact, hearing it flow. "What else you gonna call them?"

But Lyman still didn't answer.

"If you're running from something, son, maybe I can help you."

Lyman snorted and plunged ahead. "How much farther you want to go?"

"It's a couple more miles to the other side of my sugarbush. Then we got to go back and do it again. Only the next time it'll be easier, 'cause we can hitch the horses to the sled."

"When that storm comes, it's going to dump at least a foot of new snow all over our work."

"Maybe so, but this is when we always go breaking out."

"Things don't always stay the same."

"No, they don't," Arnie said. At least he had Lyman talking now, even if what he had to say, Arnie suspected, was only meant to divert him from probing into the mystery of what Lyman was running from. "But around here, we don't like to change."

Arnie wasn't going to box Lyman into a corner. He'd been there himself. He was willing to bet his last nickel that whatever it was Lyman was running from, it had to do with the war.

Try as he might, Arnie couldn't escape war. The first one was coming back to haunt him again. He'd managed to avoid his duty with that first one, the great one they used to call it, by running off to Mexico, putting Pops to shame, and because of that shame, Pops had kept quiet about the truth of Arnie's absence. Let folks think he'd gone east instead of south.

Even though he hadn't seen action himself, the war had touched Arnie all the same. He'd lost all of his best buddies to the fighting and even one sister in a field hospital. To think that Arnie was a bigger coward than his sister had stuck in his craw all these years, especially since Arnie was certain that such an unfair turn of events had caused Pops' death sooner than he should've died.

Now Arnie figured that Lyman just might be doing the same thing he'd done, hiding out from duty. Arnie could relate to that, so he'd hired the summer man on, no questions asked.

With Peggy gone off to the bomb factory, Arnie'd had no choice but to find someone to take her place with the sugaring. He couldn't tap all the trees by himself and get the sap to the sugarshack at the same time. Nossir, it took a family to keep things running smoothly, and now the war was disrupting families everywhere. He and Pops used to do it together, then it had been Arnie and Peggy. Now he figured it'd be Arnie and Lyman. Most of the young men round here had already signed up and moved on out.

Everyone was on the move these days, now that the nation was finally at war once again. Arnie was too old for action, but not too old to regret the mistakes of his youth, so when the Japs, those wily yellow bastards, yes that's what they were, snuck into Pearl Harbor ten — no, eleven — weeks ago, Arnie saw his chance. He was the first one from Dillon Falls to sign on with the Office of Civilian Defense.

It was utterly important to cover up his cowardice and keep up the right image, and the right image right now was to serve his country. No one paid him much attention, though, when he insisted his neighbors hang blackout curtains. At least they obliged him enough to shut off their lights and head to bed. This was an early-to-bed, early-to-rise place anyhow. It was no small task to keep one's business to oneself in a small town like theirs, but Arnie had done a pretty good job of it. The OCD was useful in helping keep the truth of his cowardice secret from his neighbors, secret at least for now.

Then he realized that it must be his role with Civilian Defense that kept Lyman quiet. Good Lord, could Lyman be a spy? What on earth would a spy want from these parts? Scoping out the place for a Nazi invasion he suspected, that's what. Never mind that Dillon Falls was a couple hundred miles inland from the coast of Maine. Maybe them Nazis would sneak down from the north instead. Use their submarines to slip down the St. Lawrence, on to Champlain, then hit all the major targets in the east from inside.

And it was up to Arnie to stop it. This was Arnie's chance to redeem himself. He would, too, but first he had to collect sap. Sugar season was a narrow window, and he wasn't going to miss it.

"Hey, what's that?" Lyman said, pointing into the thick of the sugarbush.

"That's our gathering tank, son." Arnie was preoccupied wondering how he would handle the spy in their midst. Would he miss his chance if he waited till after the sap was collected and boiled? No, he thought not. Lyman would stick around long enough to get paid, and he couldn't get paid until they sold the bottled syrup. That was the agreement.

"No, I mean *that*."

Now Arnie's gaze followed Lyman's pointing arm some fifty feet or so down the hill from them. A patch of blue interrupted the white expanse of snowy ground carpeting the sugarbush. The blue bundle was large enough that it hadn't blown there on its own. Someone had to have dumped it, probably from a sled. Except, no team of horses could pass through the deep snow yet, since the trail hadn't been broke out yet.

"I think," Lyman said, his voice quivering, "I think it's...a body."

## FOUR

"**M**other! I've been looking everywhere for you! How'd you get here by yourself?" Melody sounded both irritated and relieved as she stormed through Caleb's dimly-lit store. Her gauzy island prints billowed behind her, and Hank couldn't help but be reminded of a bird of prey swooping down on its target. The target in this case was Rosamonde, rocking gently back and forth back and forth in the platform rocker in the back corner of the antique store.

Rosie clutched a piece of the jigsaw puzzle to her breast, and her eyes were closed as she listened to Hank whisper soothing endearments. Thank God he'd found her. Rosie'd been in Lani's capable care until Hank got here, but still... He couldn't keep this up forever.

At the sound of their daughter's voice, Rosie's eyes flew open and her body tensed. Hank knew Melody's was a silly question. His Rosie couldn't answer something like that, and Melody knew it, too. He'd finally managed to calm Rosie, and now, with Melody's sudden appearance and outburst, all his work was undone. Tension was her answer for their daughter.

Following in Melody's wake, Caleb clomped across the wooden floor. Each of his steps rattled china in cabinets along his way. "Lani brought her in. Said she found her over on Kalakaua, stopping traffic. Lucky thing Lani got to her before the cops did."

"Lani?" Melody said. Her voice lifted. "Where's Lani?"

"Not here anymore. Only stayed long enough to get her grandma settled down and have me call you. Then she took off again."

Melody sagged and sank into a chair opposite Rosie. She studied her own mother as if their roles had reversed, and Melody the Mother had just spotted dirt behind her kid's ear. "What's that you have in your hand, Mom?"

Rosie arched her eyebrows, looking like a deer caught in someone's headlights.

Caleb answered for her. "Mrs. Berryhill has been back here working that jigsaw puzzle."

Melody leaned forward to inspect the partially assembled puzzle on the dining room table in Caleb's Corner, the cozy lounge for which he'd named his store. "That's not possible. She can't work puzzles anymore, Caleb."

Caleb shrugged. "Okay. Maybe Lani worked it for her. I had a customer I was helping at the time, so I wasn't paying close attention."

"Lani's good for her," Melody said, staring wistfully at the developing picture. The rectangular outline was done, along with one corner that was filled in. Two men in snow gear bent over buckets that hung from the sides of two sugar maples, bare of their foliage in a wintry landscape.

"Mrs. Berryhill was pretty agitated when Lani brought her in," Caleb said, nodding. "Now look how happy she is. Must be my store that she likes."

"I'm sure she likes your store, Caleb, but it's Lani who brings that look of contentment to Mom's face."

Melody always knew she was right, even when she wasn't. Hank remembered that she'd been that way from day one, and when she went through the terrible two's, that was the most certain of her times. Now it was true that Rosie felt comfortable in Caleb's store, but it was Hank, of course, who'd actually satisfied Rosie, once Lani had done the footwork for him. It was Hank who'd managed to get Lani off that beach and go find her grandmother and bring her here to a place where she felt safe.

"Mrs. Berryhill can come and sit here anytime she likes," Caleb said.

Melody laughed. Hank recognized the high-pitched sound. It was her aren't-you-an-idiot laugh. "No, no, no, that won't work at all. I can't let her walk anywhere on her own. We were lucky this time, but Lani won't always be available to rescue her."

"I could swing by and pick her up anytime you want."

"That's very nice of you, Caleb, really, but no. That would impose on you, and we can't have that. No, I have another plan in mind."

"It's not an imposition. Anything I can do, you just let me know." Caleb reached over and fit a piece into the puzzle — a solitary woman in a yellow coat waited in front of a grocery store — then he headed back to his cash register.

Melody sprang up from her chair and ran after Caleb. "Did she have that boy with her when she came?"

"Who?"

"Lani, of course. She was with a boy, wasn't she?"

Caleb scratched his forehead where a stray lock of hair tickled him. He'd always looked like he needed a haircut, and now that he sported more gray than sandy color, his hair was shaggier than ever. "Nope," he said. "No boy. Just the two of them, Lani and Mrs. Berryhill."

"So. That's why Lani ran off again in such a hurry. She had to get back to *him*." The way Melody pronounced "him" could curdle blood. Luckily, Hank didn't have any left to curdle anymore.

Let her go, Hank thought. Lani's young, and she'll have her flings, and there ain't a dang thing you can do about it, Mel-poo.

Melody wasn't receptive to ghosts, though, and even if she were, she wouldn't have paid Hank any attention.

"Keep an eye on my mother, Caleb, while I make a phone call." Melody pulled her cell phone from a pocket and wandered up to the front of the store. She stood before a shelf of cut glass vases, sparkling in the sunlight, and used her thumb to find the tiny buttons that punched in her instructions.

She put the little bugger up to her ear, then smiled. "Martin? Yes, it's me. We found her. You can stop worrying now."

76

She listened a while and ran her fingers across a nick in one of the vases. "Yes, I know. But everything's all right. We'll have to keep a better eye on her from now on. And I have an idea. We can't depend on Lani, so I'm going to have to hire someone to sit with her. You know, like I used to do for Lani when she was little...

"I know it's expensive, Martin, but listen to me. It's worth every penny for the peace of mind...

"I know, Martin, but maybe you should talk to your dad. You deserve a raise. Maybe it's time you took over the business. Dad Flynn can't keep going forever...

"Anyway, Martin, Jewell knows someone." Melody lowered her voice, as if it mattered. No one could ever change her mind about anything anyway, once she'd set her mind to a course of action. "Jewell told me about this therapist who'll come to the house. It would be the perfect arrangement, don't you think?"

Melody pretended to listen, and then went on. "Well, Martin, you just wait. You'll see. I've already made an appointment. He's coming to the house tomorrow. Nolan Penrose is his name. What's that? Oh, I had to phone Jewell and tell her I can't come in tonight after all, on account of Mom's disappearance. I'll have to make it up next week. No, *next* week. I can't go in the rest of this entire week, not with Lani's party day after tomorrow."

Melody shook her head at the vase before her. "You didn't forget, did you? No, I didn't think so. Still, I can't go in tonight. Mom's had too much trauma today for me to leave her, like I'd planned...

"Jewell understands. She doesn't mind. That's why we get

along so well. We think alike. Yes, I know, Martin, but nobody knows Jewell as well I do."

Melody moved on to another vase and rubbed at a spot. "When will you be home for dinner? Oh? You think you'll have a chance to talk to Dad Flynn instead? Of course I don't mind. You have to catch him when you can, since he's such a busy man. We won't wait for you, then. I'll keep a plate warm for you. Just bring good news home with you, all right? I'd better get back to her now. Love you." She thumbed off her phone and tucked the gizmo back into her pocket.

She stood for a long while, gazing across the store at her mother. Something was forming in her mind, but Hank was too afraid to get any closer to find out. Her plan would activate soon enough, he figured, and meanwhile, he and Rosie could enjoy the calm before the storm.

#

**My mind is like one** of those glass balls that you shake. Snow swirls and swirls. And I am trapped inside. Inside a snowy world. Where nothing changes. It snows, or it does not snow.

I am looking out through the glass wall of my bubble mind at the other world. *Their* world. They are close, but I cannot touch them anymore. Did I ever? I see them looking at me with pity. Their faces press against the glass wall. They see me seeing them, but they do not hear me. They do not hear my heart. Why can they not let me be? Mine would not be a bad place if they would just let me be.

I do not feel alone, Hank, when you are here with me. Shall we go home now?

Home?

Will it be time soon? You want to hear one more time about home? I know the place. They say that home is in the heart, but that's not true. Home is where the rooms of our minds intersect.

Come with me, and I will take you.

#

**Melody planned to** take Rosamonde home in her car, even though the distance was only a few blocks and Rosie had already managed it by foot, most of the way by herself. Hank thought for sure that Caleb's store was where Rosie had intended to go all along. She'd always had a soft spot for Caleb. Hank wasn't sure why, except maybe because Rosie always had a way of mothering everyone. Something about Caleb made him particularly motherable.

Caleb watched Rosie while Melody went to fetch the car. She had to double park in the alley that fronted the store while she went back inside to coax her mother out. It ticked off more than a few drivers, meanwhile, who usually chose the alley over gridlock on the busier streets of this district.

"Mom, whatever did you think you were doing?" Melody scolded Rosie once she thought they were alone in her sedan. A Toyota, but still, it was the latest model and top of their line.

Rosie rubbed her thumbnails with her index fingers. Her

eyebrows arched as she stared at the cars and pedestrians fighting for space outside her window.

"I could've brought you here if you'd only told me you wanted to come."

Rosie gaped at the clamor of traffic.

"See how dangerous it is out there? Yet, you managed to walk through all that without killing yourself. How'd you do that? You must've had an angel on your shoulder looking out for you. Was it Lani? Lani probably walked with you the whole way, since you couldn't have done so yourself."

Round and round, Rosie's fingers polished her thumbnails.

"Oh, I know you used to do it all the time. You probably didn't even have to think about where you were going. Your brain already knew the way so well. But really, Mom, you can't do it anymore, you know."

Rosamonde stared at the people on the other side of the window. She wondered if it was snowing yet inside her glass bubble. Perhaps that's why they watched her back. They waited for snow.

"Say, Mom, we're so close to Jewell's boutique, do you mind if we stop off for a minute? I need to collect my new orders, and besides, she'll want to know that we found you safe and sound."

Maybe Rosie didn't mind, but Hank sure as heck did. There was nothing worse than a bunch of women gabbing about clothes. But no one asked his opinion, and even if they did, they wouldn't listen.

At least Melody had her own parking slot off the alley behind

Jewell's boutique. This place was only a few blocks from Caleb's, but it might've been another planet. It was on a classier piece of real estate, closer to the hotel strip and closer to the beach.

Melody had jumped at the opportunity to display her fashions here when she befriended Jewell Mattingly about a year before Lani was born. Over the years, their partnership had boosted each half of the business. Jewell's location brought tourists in, and Melody's fashions kept them coming back, digging deeper into their pocketbooks.

Whoever said that best friends couldn't be business partners?

Melody took Rosamonde by the elbow and steered her from the car to the back entrance. Rosie hung back, fixated on a cat sitting atop a garbage can and licking one paw.

"Don't touch it, Mom. Remember the feral cats that took over our neighborhood one year when we lived in New Jersey? You told me not to try to catch them because you couldn't be sure what diseases they carried."

Rosie cocked her head to one side, trying to make sense of Melody's words, but it was true. Hank remembered. Nobody kept a cleaner, tidier house than Rosie. Cleanliness was next to godliness, she always said. Not that God ever mattered all that much to her besides being a convenient explanation for questions she didn't have handy answers to.

"Come inside, Mom, and we'll find you some fresh papaya."

Papaya had never been one of Rosie's favorites, and Melody never could remember that. Rosie liked both sweet and natural things, and papaya just didn't have enough of the sweet stuff for her. So Melody's bribe didn't work. Rosie was far more interested in the feral cat than the prospect of papaya. The cat reminded her of wild things. She had a streak of the wild in her.

What Rosie wanted didn't matter, though, because Melody wouldn't turn loose of her mother's elbow. They clattered up the three metal steps. Rosie tried to pull free, but Melody hung on tight.

"I want to go home," Rosie said.

"In a minute, Mom." While Melody struggled with the door, she almost lost her grip on Rosie. "It's cool inside. You'll like that."

It was dark, too. Rosie had never liked the dark. A long hall led from the back door off the alley, past a bathroom, past the ladies' office, which doubled as a fitting room, past three curtained-off changing rooms, and then into the cluttered store itself. A ceiling fan clacked overhead, stirring the air that was already cooled by air conditioning. Soft ukulele music floated along the rows of clothing racks that formed a maze between two display counters on either side of the store.

A pair of customers inspected the swimsuits while Jewell busied herself over one of the glass counters. Her long and straight hair made a dark brown curtain across her face as she bent over an array of coral necklaces. When Melody swept into the store, dragging Rosie behind her, Jewell stood up, pushed the hair off her suntan, and smiled. Her complexion was flawless, at that in-between stage past acne and before wrinkles, a stage Melody had exited around the time of Hank's death.

"Hey, there," Jewell said. "What's up?" Jewell's voice always lilted like a song, as sensuous as Peggy Lee's.

"We found her," Melody said, beaming.

"Thank God. You are so lucky."

"No. Mom's the lucky one, aren't you, Mom?"

Rosie scowled. She wanted to go home, and she knew this place wasn't it. What exactly it was, she couldn't be sure, but home it was not.

"Hey, it's a good thing you showed up, because that agent for your movie star client — "

"Shhh." Melody glanced over her shoulder, but the customers were too busy sliding garments along the rack to pay them any attention. She lowered her voice. "That's top secret. No one's supposed to know that Lacey Glade is in town. She's managed to dodge her fan club, and she wants to keep it that way while she's here on vacation. Keeping her whereabouts a secret is part of her deal, coming here for fittings."

Jewell laughed. "You really believe that? Honey, take it from me, that type thrives on attention."

Melody flashed her toothpaste commercial smile. "I believe whatever my clients tell me to believe. Now, what did her agent have to say?"

"Lacey's coming in tomorrow for her fitting."

"But she's scheduled for next week."

Jewell shrugged. "Too bad. I guess you'll have to cancel."

"And lose her account? No way. I'll manage. What else?"

"One of your clients phoned this morning — a Mrs. Tate? She wanted to know how her order is coming along, and she said she plans to come in tonight. That was before I knew of your change of plans for tonight."

"Okay, I'll call her. That woman always thinks she can come in for a fitting without an appointment, and she's a nobody. Anything else I need to know about?"

"You'd better check your inventory. Two families on holiday together came in this morning and purchased quite a few of your coordinates off the rack."

"That's great!"

"They wanted to know what else you have, so I showed them your catalogue. They might come back tonight, too. They didn't leave a number, though."

"Then Natalie will have to take care of them. I don't like her being alone in the store at night. Don't you think you could stay late with her?"

"Nope. I already have plans. I have a life too, y'know, and besides, Natalie's really good chatting up the tourists. Most of them aren't serious shoppers after they've had their dinner and piña coladas."

"I hope you're right. Sorry I have to bail on you, but I can't leave Mom alone, not after what we went through today. And now Martin says he won't be home, either."

"Working late again?"

"Talking to his dad."

"Oh. He works late a lot, though, doesn't he?"

"Are you suggesting something?"

"Heck no. Not me. You must be awfully sure of him."

"Why wouldn't I be?" Melody laughed, her all-knowing laugh.

"I mean, y'know...?"

"Surely, you're not implying... I mean, just because I choose to believe my clients, you can't really think... Oh, no. Not Martin. He's just too... Well, I don't know what he is, but I know he'd never dream of doing anything he's not supposed to do." Melody's jaw tightened, and she turned away, searching for a distraction with which to hide the way her heart was careening into a bottomless abyss.

Her gaze locked onto the customers, who wandered toward the back of the store with an armload of bathing suits. "I'll take care of them," Melody said to Jewell, "and I'll bring some papaya back from the office. Watch my mom, will you?" Then she sprang after the customers. "You're going to love those bikinis," she told them. "Let me show you the changing rooms."

Jewell studied Rosamonde when it was just the two of them plus Hank. "So, Mrs. Berryhill, tell me about your little adventure today." Clearly, she was trying to distract Rosie from worry about Melody's sudden absence.

Rosie's eyebrows arched. She ignored all of them and stared instead at the front door, a glass door between two windows. In the show windows, mannequins wore Melody's breezy sundresses and matching cover-ups and hats.

"Hot," Rosie said.

"That's right. Things don't change much around here. But it beats the winters in Maryland, don't you think?"

Rosie moved toward the front door. A patch of glaring light

shone through the glass. Beyond that was a fringe of palm fronds that framed the line where ocean met sky.

"Hey, Mel," Jewell called. "I think your mom wants to go for another walk."

Melody scurried back, carrying a plastic bowl. Her brown eyes widened with alarm, and her usually brilliant smile drained from her face, leaving her flesh pale and her lips thick. Bloated.

"Oh, no, Mom! We can't leave yet. Look what I brought you. Some wonderful papaya. See?"

Rosie glanced at Melody, then turned back to the rectangle of bright light coming through the door. "Snow," she said.

"No, Mom, we don't have snow in Hawaii, remember? You come right over here and sit down and have your snack. It's fresh papaya. We get it fresh every day." Melody chased after Rosie, then steered her to a chair behind the counter and thrust the plastic bowl before her. Rosie stared first at the salmon-colored cubes then at Melody. She didn't understand.

By the time Melody returned to Jewell, she'd restored both color and smile to her face. "See what I'm dealing with?" Melody whispered to Jewell. "I think that friend you recommended is going to be just what we need."

"Nolan, you mean? He's not exactly a friend of mine. He has an apartment across the hall from me. We only chat coming and going. Usually going."

"Naturally, I checked his references," said Melody. "Everyone sings his praises. Best of all, he's coming to the house tomorrow. That's fortunate, now that Lani's become so unreliable after school.

That's the thanks I get for all the years of taking care of her. All I ask is a little bit of help now."

"Hey, she's a kid. She wants to have fun."

"Too much fun. She needs to learn that life is more than just having fun. She has to learn responsibility, too."

"She thinks you're too hard on her."

"Thank you for your concern, but it's really none of your business, is it?"

"No, I guess not." Jewell sighed. "I never meant to intrude in your family. Sometimes things just happen. Things that you never plan to have happen, and then they happen, and you can't stop it, because it's meant to be."

"That's because we're tied together in more ways than one," Melody said. "We sure have been through a lot together, haven't we? Look, I'm sorry I snapped at you. I know you only mean to help. Things aren't easy right now." Melody rolled her eyes in the direction of Rosamonde. "And to make matters worse, Lani and I got in a big fight today. She ran off, and to be honest, I don't know when she'll be back. You haven't seen her, have you?"

Jewell shifted her weight instead of answering. A flush crept across her tan, and she turned back to arranging her collection of coral necklaces.

"Have you?" Melody asked again. "Has she been by here?"

Jewell studied Melody through the glass of her display case. She chewed on her lower lip, then finally she said, "Okay, yeah. She's been by here. But don't worry. She's all right. She just needs a little space for a while, y'know?"

"Space? *She* needs space? She doesn't know how lucky she is. She gets to go off to school every day and be with her friends and learn interesting things and play the sports she loves, while I..."

Jewell closed and locked the display case, then stood up straight. "Yes? While you what?"

"Oh, never mind."

Tears formed in Jewell's eyes. She took small running steps to Melody and hugged her. "I'm sorry, Mel. I'm so, so sorry. I didn't know it'd turn out this way."

"Don't worry," Melody said, patting Jewell. "Everything's all right. I don't blame you. Actually, I'm glad that Lani came to you. That's one less thing for me to worry about. It's such a relief to have you as my best friend. Thank you for being my friend!"

Jewell sobbed, then sniffed away her tears. "I told her we'd have a slumber party tonight. She needs someone to talk to. Someone who'll listen to her. I didn't mean to hurt anyone. I'm always, like, the big sister."

Melody smiled. "You said you had other plans tonight."

"Um, yeah. Those *are* my plans. She doesn't want you to know, that's all. But, um, I don't want you to worry."

"I'm soooo glad."

If she only knew the rest of it, Hank thought, she wouldn't be so glad. Some things he tried to stay out of. Soon enough, she'd find out on her own. Tonight, maybe.

# FIVE

Sometimes I wander into one of the rooms of my mind and I think I know the place. I cannot be sure. I hear you, but you are not here. Is this place real? Was it ever real? It would not be in my head if it is not real.

Where are you? Where am I?

The longer my life, the more rooms I grow in my head. Already, my mind is a larger world than the one I remember as real. So I have to ask, "Is this me?"

I have grown too many rooms, and soon they will all be gone with me. But I cannot go yet! I have too much to tell you before I go. I have to make you understand. I have not yet cast my footprint in their world. My footprints I leave in the snow, and with the spring thaw, they will melt away.

Too many rooms to choose from. Too many places to search. I follow your footprints, Hank, wandering from this room to the next. But they will never find mine, not until I make them understand me. My sister who died is my only hope. Perhaps she hides from me in the next of my rooms.

#

**The air of Melody's** living room that night after dinner felt thick and sour to Hank. Melody sat Rosamonde down on the leather sofa, then she put some music on, some soft Hawaiian love songs, and she lit a ginger candle on the coffee table. Sound and scent didn't cover up the heaviness radiating from her heart, though, so Hank drifted away from her, over to the foyer, a shadowy place beyond the smoggy cloud of Melody's influence. From the foyer, he could track Rosie and at the same time watch for Martin, who wouldn't be returning from any meeting with Dad Flynn, not as Melody thought. What Hank would do to head off the inevitable disaster, he had no idea.

Luckily, Melody was too focused on Lacey Glade to worry about Martin. Melody spread out her sewing on the dining room table, then pulled a scrapbook from the shelf and opened it up on the coffee table before Rosie.

"Remember when you came out for a visit right after Lani was born?" Melody asked, returning to her shimmery piles of silk on the dining room table.

Rosie rubbed her thumbnails and studied the photos of herself in various positions holding baby Lani, burping the baby, strolling with the baby. Rosie cocked her head to one side, then to the other side. Her eyebrows arched, and she frowned.

"My baby," Rosie finally said. Her lips twitched, trying to remember how to smile.

"No, Mom, Lani is *my* baby. That's you in the photo with *my* baby. Lani."

"Baby."

"Yes, that's right. My baby."

"No. My baby. I have two babies." Rosie held up two fingers to show Melody. "Where is the other one?"

"That's good, Mom!" Melody flashed her brilliant smile, and her sewing scissors clattered to the table. "That's so good! You had two, and I have one." She held up two fingers on one hand and one on the other. "How many does this make?"

Rosie had no idea what Melody wanted from her, and her two fingers wilted into the ball of her fist. Her attention wandered to the next page of the photo album.

"It makes three, Mom," Melody said. She sprang up from the table and marched over to the phone. She punched in some numbers, listened for a while, then ran her fingers through her hair, messing it up, making her look newly electrified, the way she'd looked as a toddling baby after sticking her fingers into an outlet. Rosie had gone hysterical then, calling Hank at work.

Melody let out her breath in a whistle and dropped the phone into the cradle with a little more force than necessary. "They're not answering, but I know they're there. Jewell told me so." She stormed over to the sofa and plopped down next to Rosie, bouncing her mother as if she'd caught a wave. She fixed her attention on turning the pages, regaining her composure. Even the ends of her electrified hair smoothed into place.

"Oh, look," Melody said, pointing at a photo. "This is the time when we came to visit you, and we rented that cottage on the ocean. Remember? We've always had such good times at the beach. That's why it's just perfect that we're all here together now, forever. Well, except for Barry. But he's close enough in L.A. that he can hop over for visits easily. He'll be here soon, for the holidays."

"Soon?"

"That's right, Mom. I hope Lani shapes up in time, or else there'll be coal in her stocking this year."

Rosie tilted her head again and blinked several times in rapid succession, indicating her confusion. Hank knew. Holidays weren't an easy time for his Rosie. She remembered, even though she didn't want to remember. If Hank had been able to control his own death, he'd have never died during the holiday season. The memory of his death would always taint this time of year for Rosie.

"She'll come out of it," Melody said. "It's only natural for sixteen-year-olds to rebel, right Mom? Well, she's not sixteen yet, but she will be, all too soon. You were lucky that Barry and I didn't give you so much trouble. Not like Lani. She must get her rebellious streak from Martin's side of the family. Not from Martin, of course, he's too kind and gentle. It had to be from his sisters, Silvia and Vanessa. Maybe I can get them to tell me some stories about when they were sixteen, so I'll have more ammunition dealing with Lani."

"Stories."

"You always liked stories, didn't you, Mom? You won't want to hear their stories, though. Vanessa still hasn't gotten over her problems, but at least she's not Mom and Dad Flynn's problem anymore. I'm sure they weren't firm enough when Vanessa was still living at home. You have to be firm with your children, don't you agree?"

Melody flipped through more pages of the scrapbook, and Rosie stared at the faces flashing past. She was captivated but quizzical. She knew they were familiar faces, but she didn't know the faces anymore as her extended family. She couldn't put them in context.

Thirty minutes later, Melody flounced back to the phone, as if an internal clock ticked within her, making her redial at that moment. She listened again to nothing and slammed the phone down again.

"I know they're there. Jewell's too busy taking *my* place, having a 'slumber party' of all things, to answer her own phone." Melody stared at the front door, and for a minute, Hank startled, thinking that Melody had actually seen him. Sometimes people saw ghosts, but he didn't think anyone other than Rosie had ever spotted him. Being discovered made him uncomfortable. He shouldn't be here, and he wouldn't be, if not for Rosie. He would vacate this dimension of unreality just as soon as he could.

Then he realized that it was the door Melody was staring at, not at Hank's spectral essence. She threw out her vibes, and he couldn't help but wade through them, escaping them as if he were a drowning man. Melody wanted to go to Jewell's apartment herself and drag Lani away. She would, too, if not for having to leave her mother behind unattended. Damn that Martin! Melody never swore, so Hank understood the level of her frustration. She blamed Martin for her situation, being stuck between opposite ends of the spectrum of problems: her daughter's teenage rebellion and her mother's aging dementia.

And it was all Martin's fault. If he were here, she wouldn't be stuck. She could become unstuck. Where in hell was he, anyway? Dad Flynn should've heard him out by now. Unless they were drawing up papers or something. Yes, that must be it.

Melody settled back down on the couch beside Rosie and pulled out another scrapbook. "Oh, look, Mom, this is your album. It's one we found in the house when we were cleaning it out for you. Maybe you'll remember some of these people, and you can tell me who they are? I recognize some of these pictures — they were taken in Los Alamos, weren't they? But I don't recognize the people. Are they some of your friends from that time? I'll bet they're all famous scientists. I wish you could tell me about that time. I'll bet it was exciting to be there, while history was being made. You never liked to be in the limelight, though, did you? I wonder what your part in all that was?"

"Socks," Rosie said.

"Socks? What do you mean?"

"Socks."

"Ah. You mean when are we going to hang the stockings for Christmas? Good question. We should've done that by now, but we got distracted."

Thirty minutes later, Melody raced to the phone, as if it called to her. She hit the redial button and listened, rolling her eyes around to inspect the shadowy corners of the ceiling. Her smile contorted into a look of wild desperation that would frighten any kid at Halloween, and she threw the phone at the cradle.

"She's there," Melody said in a quiet voice, as she floated back across the room. She'd perfected a sort of sliding step that enabled her to move soundlessly. "She knows I'm calling her, too. I know she knows, because I'm her mother, and I know everything she's thinking, even though she thinks I don't know. Just like you know what I'm thinking. You know, too, don't you, Mom? Mothers know."

Melody gave out a loud sigh and sank back onto the sofa. "And to think, I almost didn't get to become a mother." She took Rosie's photo album away from her, snapped it shut, and slid it back on its shelf beneath the coffee table. Then her fingers skimmed across the bindings until they found the certain book she was looking for. She pulled it out.

"Do you remember our wedding, Mom? Thank you for giving us such a nice wedding. Even though it's been almost thirty years. Can you believe it? It's never too late to say thank you again." Melody studied the photos of the wedding party. "Look how skinny and gawky Barry is! Well, he was only eighteen then. He'd just graduated from high school. What a whirlwind of events that weekend was. There you are, Mom, all dressed up in that pretty pink suit and matching hat. It's too bad hats aren't popular anymore as part of an outfit. I think it's so important to add finishing touches to dress up an outfit, to make it special. For special occasions." Her voice faded to a dreamy tone as she flipped through the pages.

"Oh, look, here are my first views of Honolulu after Martin brought me here. That was a difficult time for me too, back then. Everything was so different for me, coming from the east coast to a tropical paradise. I found out it wasn't such a paradise after all. But that's only because I didn't know my way around then. Now I do, and so it really has become a paradise. That's why I can make it a paradise for you, Mom."

Rosie's eyebrows arched, and she rubbed her fingers together.

"You're getting tired. Let's put you to bed. You don't have to wait up with me. You'll be sleeping in Lani's room tonight. From now on it's your room. Tomorrow we have a big day planned for you, so you should get some rest now."

She stood up and helped Rosie to her feet just as the front door opened and Martin staggered in. She froze in silence and inspected him. The air chilled several degrees, and Hank drifted up, seeking the warmer air currents trapped by the ceiling. Martin's necktie draped around his collar, but Melody's gaze fixed on the buttons of his shirt that had been buttoned, off by one, pulling the fabric of his shirt into uneven creases. Even from the ceiling Hank could smell Martin's breath, reeking of alcohol.

Melody's eyelids fluttered as she took it all in — the rumpled jacket, the cowlick standing up the way it did each morning. She lowered her voice to a chilling level and told him, "You're late. Which has been no help to me. After all this, I certainly hope you got him to agree."

"W-who?"

"Your dad, Martin. Your dad. Remember him?"

He shrugged and walked past Melody and Rosie, aiming himself more or less in the direction of the kitchen. "I believe I'll have a nightcap before turning in," he said, louder than necessary.

Rosie's eyes opened wide as she watched him, and her lips parted, forming an "o."

Melody pasted on her brilliant smile, looking more forced than it usually did, and she grabbed Rosie by the elbow. "Come on, Mom. I'll have to deal with him later." The two of them leaned into each other as they moved down the hall to Lani's room, Rosie's now.

#

**Cuddling close to** Rosie under Lani's quilt, Hank yearned for the warmth of her flesh. He had to hear out the uneven voices the rest of the night that fired like bullets down the stairs. Martin's voice bullets were elevated, bellicose, and slurred, while Melody's return fire hovered barely above a whisper, blizzard cold.

"No, I'm not gonna lower my voice," Martin shouted. "Who're you afraid's gonna hear? Lani? You chased her off, r'member?"

A gust of air off the glacier of Melody's heart howled through the canyons of the house. Hank whispered soothing endearments in Rosie's mind.

"What're you afraid of? Your mother? You're too late, Mel'dy. You can't fix her. You can dope her up till you're blue in the face, and it's not gonna change one thing. Might as well let it go."

Another blast of icy air whistled down the stairs.

"Just leave her the fuck alone, Mel'dy. Let her die in peace, 'cause that's what's gonna happen no matter what you do. You're more worried about what you can't control, like your mother and Lani, than you care about me. Always have been. You don't even know when I'm here, so how come you care that I was gone? I told you already. My, er, meeting with Dad ran late. So we had a couple of drinks, what's the big deal?"

Something crashed upstairs, followed by a moment of silence. Then the floorboards creaked with the weight of movement. A door slammed.

Rosie lay stock still on her back. She never slept on her back, only on her right side. Now her body was as stiff as a corpse and her eyes wide open and fixed on the ceiling fixture. Hank's endearments couldn't penetrate the steel trap surrounding her mind.

# EFFIE

**If the Nazis didn't** kill Effie Boatman's husband first, she'd do the job herself when he returned from the war. Harold could've gotten a deferral if he'd only tried, but no. He hadn't even waited to be drafted. The day after Pearl Harbor he'd simply gone to Burlington and enlisted. Simple as that. He hadn't talked it over with Effie first. Hadn't even told her he was doing it. He'd just gone and done it. Told her he was going into Burlington for supplies. Couldn't even tell her the truth, that he'd made the decision without her. The coward. Now she was the one left in sole charge of Boatman's Grocery here in Dillon Falls.

The bell jingled over the door and Effie looked up from the columns she couldn't get to balance in her ledger. Rolph Ingersoll, a jack-of-all-trade who called himself a wood cutter, strode inside, grinning like the cat that got the mouse. There was a fine-looking man if she'd ever seen one, broad shouldered and well muscled from all that chopping and hauling. *He* hadn't gone off to war.

'Course, he was older than Effie's husband, even though he didn't look it.

"Morning, Effie," he called. "You got any of Widow Wallis' eggs left?"

"Sure do, Rolph." Effie laid down her pencil and reached under the counter for the basket of eggs. "Wallis brought them in herself earlier this morning. How many you need?"

"Gimme four. What else you got under there?" Rolph leaned across the counter, pushing past the rack of cigarettes.

"Never you mind. Four? You sure that's all you want?" Effie whisked a page of newsprint from last week's paper and wrapped the eggs, one by one.

"Four is all Opal and me need for breakfast without the boy. He hardly ever eats at home anymore, now that he's got himself a girl. Oh, what the heck. Make that a half dozen, if you got 'em to spare."

"You bet, Rolph. For you, I do." She reached into the basket for a couple more and blushed. Something about his powerful presence made her forward.

"Mind if I look around?" He waved a scrap of paper. "Opal give me a list."

"Help yourself. That's why we're open for business."

He wandered off down the rows of shelves that grew more and more sparse these days. When the weather turned bad and the delivery trucks couldn't get through all the snow, her supplies always slimmed down, but now with the war on, it was worse than ever. Bad enough that maybe she should think of closing. If she didn't get these columns to balance, the bank would close the store for her.

She sighed and turned back to the ledger. If Harold had only asked her opinion about enlisting, she would've agreed. It was about time America joined the fight against evil. Dillon Falls would do their part to show the rest of the world that the little tyrant with the moustache couldn't run all over them. But Harold hadn't asked because he apparently thought her opinion didn't matter, and that's what really irked her. As if she couldn't be trusted. Truth was, she didn't care if he was here or not. Keeping the inside of the grocery neat and pretty and ringing up customers had always been her part of the business, anyway. His was the gas pump out front. He sold tractor tires and kept all the books, too. His absence didn't really affect her job, since she could get by without selling gas and tires at all. Tires weren't to be had, anyway, and word was, gas would be rationed soon. Come spring, probably. Although she wasn't convinced spring ever would thaw out this place again. As for the books, she figured she'd learn how to do them. No reason why she couldn't. Maybe the bank could give her an extension.

Rolph whistled one of those new tunes that'd been filling the airwaves, the one about making changes, while he plucked items off the shelf. Changes. Wasn't that the truth?

"What've you got to feel so chipper about today?" she asked when he returned to her station by the cash register with an armload of goods.

"Cheer up, Effie, this war will be over before you know it."

"I sure hope you're right. My supplies are already running low, even though the neighbors are doing their darnedest not to horde. They even pitch in and bring me their extras."

"Ya. We depend on you, that's why. No other store around here for ten miles. No one wants you to close with Harold off to war."

Effie shrugged and added up his items. "What would I do if I didn't have the store to run?"

"Other women are going off to factories to help build planes and bombs. I figured you might, too."

"I'm not like that."

"No, I reckon not. You like to doll yourself up too much. Sure is a shame Harold's not here to appreciate that."

Effie's heart flipped over in her chest, she swore to god. They were alone in the store. Not a single other soul here, not even in the conversation pit. No boys around no more to play poker back there. Not even Old Man Dent come in to sit a spell.

She swallowed long and slow until her heart stopped its flutter. "What are you saying, Rolph? You saying I shouldn't try to make myself look good just because Harold's gone?"

"Not at all, Effie. Not at all." He handed her two crisp ones in exchange for his groceries.

"Well, you just mind your own business, Rolph. You got Opal to take care of."

He laughed. "Listen to you. Opal can take care of her own self better'n any woman I ever seen. You know what that woman's planning on doing next? She swears she's going to start tapping next week and make her own sugar."

"But you don't have a sugarbush. Where's she going to tap?"

"She's not going to start a business. She's just going to make enough for us to use. We got a few sugar maples around our place. We never tapped them before, because why bother with just a few? Besides, they weren't old enough until now. Her daddy planted them to ring in the new century. She figures there's enough sap in them to tide us over till next year."

Effie shook her head. It seemed like a lot of bother for a little sweetness in return when you could just as easily get by without the sweets. It's not as if sugar was a basic necessity in one's diet. Why not do without? Like Rolph said, this war wasn't going to last much longer, not now that America was finally in it.

But folks around here went crazy over their maple syrup. They put syrup in everything. She'd like to see them try to do without. She bet they couldn't get through the cold of winter without their syrup. It was more than a signal of spring coming — syrup was a way to keep warm through the cold of winter. She wondered if they liked the syrup that much, or if it was the tapping that they really liked. Tapping was a rite of spring.

"You tell her that if she ends up with more than she needs, she can always bring the rest of it over here to sell. I sure could use something extra to stock my shelves."

"We all could, Effie." He rattled the few coins of change in his pocket and stood there, holding his cloth bag as if he didn't want to leave. Finally, he cleared his throat and spoke, slowly, in a low voice. "You ever get any customers asking for...things besides what you got on the shelves?"

"What things, Rolph?" Effie's heart had flipped, and now it was running away from her, like a motor gone wild.

"Like the way you hold back those eggs behind the counter."

"You want more eggs, Rolph? I can't let you have any more than half a dozen, otherwise there won't be enough for my other customers."

"I'm not talking about eggs. That was just an example."

"What *are* you talking about, then?"

"Oh, let's just say, for instance, tires."

"Where would I get tires from, Rolph? They're not selling cars while the war's on, and that goes for tires, too. Rubber's scarce. It comes from those countries we're fighting."

"Not all of it, it doesn't."

"What we got has to go to the war effort."

"That doesn't stop farmers from needing tires for their tractors, and now that spring is on its way, there's bound to be a farmer or two round here who can't patch up their old tires one more time."

She rubbed her upper lip in thought. "I see your point. I bet they'd pay for 'em, too, but back to my first question: Where am I going to get tires from? Harold donated the ones he had leftover from his supplies. There won't be any more, not for a good while."

"What if I could get you some?"

"Rolph? You in some kind of trouble I should know about?"

"Not at all, Effie, I'm just saying 'what if?' What if I could lay my hands on a supply of tires? You got any customers who'd be interested in buying them?"

"That would be breaking the law, Rolph."

"Effie, Effie. Now don't get yourself all hot and bothered. I'm just theorizing, that's all. Forget it. Forget I said anything."

"No, I'm not going to forget it, and I'm not hot and bothered. I'm just pointing out a fact. You're talking about breaking the law. Now, I respect the law, but I also understand that in times of need, folks have got to look out for themselves, even if it means looking past some details of the law. So, if you want my help on anything, Rolph Ingersoll, you'd better tell me the truth about what you been up to."

"So you can what? Snitch on me to Arnie? Have him turn me in? You get some reward for snitching on your neighbors? Before you know it, we're going to have our own Gestapo right here in Dillon Falls."

Effie snorted. "I wouldn't give Arnie Trimble the time of day, not after the way he stole my pop's sugarbush."

"Opal says he bought it fair and square."

"Don't you believe everything you hear."

"Okay, I won't, and you neither, you hear? Turns out, I don't have tires. That was just another example. To see how you'd react."

"React to what?"

Rolph leaned closer and lowered his voice, despite their being alone in the store. "What if I knew about a few extra guns for sale?"

Effie sucked in her breath. "Is this another of your 'what ifs'?"

"I might need a favor, come Tuesday. You still got that empty barn up at Dead Man's Curve?"

Effie nodded. She didn't trust her voice to use words.

"What're you using that barn for, now that Harold ain't here and he got rid of his supply of tires?"

"N-nothing."

"Good. I got me some cargo running across the border, and I need a place to store it for a day or two. You interested?"

"What sort of cargo?"

"Don't worry none, Effie, it's for the cause."

She slapped the side of her face. "The cause?"

"What if we ordinary citizens got to fight the Gestapo in our own backyard?"

"You think it's going to come to that?"

"You just never know, Effie. That's why we got to be prepared."

"Be prepared about what?" said a new voice. Effie looked away from Rolph and bit her tongue. Kipp Lehnert! Somehow, he'd slipped into the store without being heard. Somehow, he'd made the warning bell above the door not jingle.

Of all people to sneak in on them! Kipp was their postmaster. Called himself American, but he was still German. He was fifth-column, sure as heck. How long had he been standing there?

Effie drew herself up tall and stiff. She knew what she had to do if she was going to survive.

# SIX

When Nolan Penrose showed up the next morning, he had the rumpled appearance, Hank thought, as if he'd slept on a couch. Same as either Melody or Martin had. Hank couldn't be sure which one of them had gone to the futon in Melody's sewing room the night before, but he was willing to bet it wasn't Melody. Martin came out of the shower, looking as if he'd nearly drowned there, all slicked down and dressed in the fresh clothes Melody had chosen for him. He passed through the house like the wind, gulped down a cup of coffee, glanced at the *Wall Street*, then left. Not a handful of words were exchanged.

Nolan's arrival was less dramatic than Martin's passage, except that Nolan wore a satisfied grin of relief, as if he'd come to stay, which was more than Martin ever did. Nolan reminded Hank of a lost puppy dog, a yellow lab, he thought, friendly and willing to follow anyone home who tossed him a morsel of kindness. His mission in life was to serve others, to make others happy, to just be there, available at a moment's notice to do their bidding.

"Speak, boy!"

And Nolan would tell whoever wanted to listen whatever said person wanted to hear.

"For the first visit, Mrs. Flynn, I really don't advise you to leave. I mean, not right away. We should give your mother time to become comfortable in my presence — "

"That's impossible." Melody flashed her all-knowing grin that suggested she actually knew more about his practice of social work than, quite possibly, he himself knew. Social work was a sort of hobby with her. Her work dealing with difficult clients over the years couldn't be very different from Nolan's, after all.

Melody elaborated, ticking off points on her fingers, the nails trimmed neatly and close and painted with a clear lacquer of hardness. "First, my mother is never comfortable. She hasn't been comfortable, not really, since Dad died eighteen years ago. There is not a person alive who makes her feel comfortable, not even me. Secondly, my most important client so far — an academy award winning actress here on holiday, and no I can't tell you who, because I have to protect my client confidentiality, I'm sure you understand — insisted on meeting with me this morning. If I don't show up, I'll lose her account. That means I won't have the funds to pay *you*. And finally, what difference does it make, since I ultimately plan to leave her in your hands, anyway? If it's your first visit, or the second, it's all the same in the long run. Are *you* sure you know how to handle her? No, we don't have a diagnosis yet, but we all know what's wrong with her. I'm expecting an official diagnosis within the week, when I take her in for testing. I would've had it done by now if only Martin had... Oh, never mind."

Nolan listened patiently, watching her intently with his puppy-dog eyes of devotion. He loosened his collar, even though it was already loose. In fact, the top button was missing, probably tugged right off with all that squirming of his. Then he told Melody what she wanted to hear.

He told her about his confidence that he knew exactly how to handle Rosie, and that Melody could rest assured that Rosie was in his good hands. Rosie would respond well to him, he promised. He'd worked with plenty of patients before, just like her. Melody could go to work without a worry in the world.

Melody bought it, even though Rosie wouldn't come out of Lani's bedroom, not even to meet Nolan. He was a stranger, and strangers frightened her.

"You're sure you can handle her?" Melody asked again as she collected her purse and car keys.

"Believe me, it's better this way. No offense, but your presence during my treatment would only interfere with your mother's establishment of boundaries for our relationship." Nolan gestured with his hands in what looked to Hank like he meant "back-off buster."

Maybe he was exactly who *Melody* needed, not necessarily Rosie.

"My role at first," Nolan continued in psycho-speak, "is simply to observe her patterns — "

"Yesterday, she decided to go for a stroll through traffic." Melody gave him a pitying smile.

"Don't worry, Mrs. Flynn, that won't happen on my watch."

"Just see that it doesn't. You have my number? And Martin's, too?"

"Yes, Mrs. Flynn. Relax, Mrs. Flynn."

"I'm not upset. There's nothing wrong with me. Just so we understand each other." Melody jangled her keys and flounced out the front door.

Nolan stood in the hall, staring at the closed door for what seemed an eternity. Finally, he tiptoed down the hall to Lani's room and lifted his knuckles to rap twice on the door. "Mrs. Berryhill?" he asked. "Are you in there? Do you need anything? Will you talk to me?"

He waited. His fists dug into his pockets. He leaned against the wall. He stared at the ceiling. He examined Melody's orchids. Then he started to whistle. The melody carried a vague resemblance to one of Rosie's favorites from the good old days.

Lani's door flung open, and Rosie stood there. "Barry?" she said in her clear voice, staring straight at Nolan.

Nolan swiped his fingers through his hair. "Um, Barry?"

"Barry!"

"Okay, you can call me Barry if you like."

"Barry!" Rosie opened her mouth, imitating a smile. If she could've jumped up and down, she would've.

"So...tell me about Barry. What does that name mean to you?"

"My baby."

# BOULDER, 1985

**Rosamonde and Hank's** baby was graduating from college, and they couldn't be more proud. They'd driven all the way out here to Colorado from their house on the Chesapeake, because they expected to load up the car with Barry's things. They expected him to come back home with them, at least while he job hunted. The east coast would have more opportunities for an English literature major than a provincial place like Boulder. Rosamonde and Hank knew about the provinces, having been assigned to such places for several years. New Mexico, not Boulder, but the west was all alike. Both their children had been born in New Mexico. Probably it was on account of Barry's birth in the west that he'd chosen to head west to school. He was drawn to his origins.

Either that, or the proximity to skiing.

Anyway, provincial or no, the university here was a nice enough place, and god knew, expensive enough, especially for the out-of-staters. That's why Barry took off a year from school when he first moved out here. He worked as a bartender in Colorado and established his residency. Barry was on the five-year plan, but then, he had an extraordinary amount of reading to do, being a literature major. Rosamonde read all the time, but she couldn't keep up with Barry's reading lists. And there was his writing. He'd taken as many creative writing classes as possible, to which Hank always protested.

"They think they can *teach* you how to write?" Hank would huff each time Barry asked for a bit more money. Hank inhaled air, puffing out his chest until Rosamonde pictured a geyser, building up pressure, about to erupt. "Why are we paying them to tell you to go away and write on your own?"

But whether it was the writing classes, or the bartending, or the skiing, or the extra time needed for reading, it didn't matter anymore. Because now Barry was graduating.

Now it was all over. It was the end of an era with no more school expenses for their children, and while Hank would probably lift a glass of bourbon in celebration tonight and tomorrow night and the following night, Rosamonde would quietly mourn. She could see her connections to her children being severed, one by one, with each of their accomplishments. Accomplishments were like ribbons that had to be cut in order to celebrate a groundbreaking. Instead of thinking ahead to the new beginning beyond the cut ribbon, Rosamonde always thought backwards at the past she was losing with each step of her children's progress.

For her, her babies had never stopped being babies.

She wasn't ready to release them to the world. To let them

go. It was hard enough, losing Melody to a husband and Hawaii. Hawaii was a place where you went on vacation, not to live. Her daughter might as well have gone to the moon, it was just about that hard to get to Hawaii from Maryland. And expensive, oh my.

No wonder Melody showed up for Barry's graduation with dark circles under her eyes. The poor girl was working too hard, trying to make ends meet. It was a wonder she could take off time from her struggling alterations shop to come here. Time was the issue, not money. Hank had sent her a check to cover the airfare along with a handwritten scrawl, "Be there." He wanted Barry to have his moment to shine before his own private audience.

"Where's Martin?" Hank asked Melody when they picked her up at Stapleton the night before the ceremony.

"He couldn't get away. Dad Flynn needed his help because Vanessa's in the hospital."

"Oh dear, is she all right?" Rosamonde asked.

"She's fine, Mom."

"But if she's okay, why is she in the hospital?"

"It's not exactly a hospital," Barry said. "It's de-tox."

Hank grunted. "Just as well Martin didn't come."

"It's not his fault, Dad," Melody said. "You shouldn't blame him. He can't help it if his family is...difficult."

"Dysfunctional, you mean."

"Barry! You should be ashamed of yourself. That's just not true at all. The Flynns are a very respectable family who've been in Hawaii for generations. Grandma has native blood."

"I stand corrected," Barry said. "I see you haven't changed,

Mel.  Marriage must agree with you."

"It's something you should think about trying.  Got any girls in your life?"

"None that you'd want to call your sis."

"Don't be so sure.  I can do wonders with raw material."

"How raw do you want them?"

Melody ignored that.  "I'll bet one of them is more special than the rest.  Will we get to meet her this weekend?"

"She's arranged to be out of town while you're here."

"What a shame."

"Not at all.  It's better for everyone this way."

"If she doesn't want to celebrate your graduation with you, then she can't be the right girl for you, Barry."

"Okay, Mel.  If you say so."

"Don't worry.  We'll find the right one for you."

"With you around, I'm never worried."

"I love you, too, little brother."

Rosamonde's heart warmed.  Her children had always played well together.

# IMOGENE

**Imogene Teasdale thought** that Dillon Falls ("Dillon Fell" she and her friends called it) had to be the most boring place on earth in February of 1942. Not that it had been all that exciting before the war. At least before the war she'd had dreams of fun, as any normal sixteen-year-old would have. She hadn't settled exactly on how that fun would play itself out. She couldn't decide between a modeling career in Paris or an acting career maybe on Broadway or maybe in Hollywood. Well, those were just her dreams. More than likely, she would end up going to the city (and there was only one real city in the entire universe, and it happened to be only a day's drive away) and becoming a waitress. That was okay, too, because the city never slept. The city, her mother always warned, was a den of corruption, where girls didn't have their mothers breathing down their necks every minute of the day. Even though Imogene had never been to the city, she knew how the city was. She'd seen the matinees, most every Saturday.

The war had changed all that. The war had robbed her of her dreams. Now there was no place to dream of going, leaving her stuck here in Dillon Fell. All the interesting people had already left, and those who stayed behind could talk of nothing but war. War, war, war. She'd had it with the war.

Their teacher had gone off to war, and his replacement was Grandma Moses' twin, the pastor's mother. Even the pastor himself had gone off to war. Imogene didn't consider herself religious, and god forbid that she was a brain, but the church and school were the only places in Dillon Fell that even thought of providing fun activities for the teenagers. Now she had to find her own amusement.

Paul Ingersoll and Troy Dent.

She took turns on the sled with them and couldn't decide which one of them felt better riding beneath her, through all the thick layers of their woolen coats. They'd tried piling all three of them atop the sled at once, but the boys had squished her till she couldn't breathe. Besides, the runners sank into the snow with their combined weight and they'd tumbled off, laughing, into a snow bank.

"My turn next," Paul shouted, chasing the sled, half running half sliding and tripping down the snowy hill overlooking Dillon Pond.

Imogene lay in the snow at the bottom of the hill, where she'd tumbled off the sled with Troy, who lay next to her, deliciously close to her own heat. She stared up at the gray sky, and clouds frowned back at her in her mother's absence. She'd come out here to the pond with the boys to get away from her mother's disapproval, but she never could quite escape. It wasn't fair. She was doing nothing wrong. She couldn't help it if she made boys trip over themselves, vying for her attention.

And then Paul stood over her, blowing steam with each excited gasp. "Come on, Imo, let's go. You and me this time." He held out a gloved hand, brushing across her right breast. Her nipples instantly hardened.

"Give a girl a chance to breathe," she said. She took his hand and yanked, pulling him off balance so that he fell on top of both her and Troy. The three of them wrestled, the boys trying to push each other away while Imogene wriggled out of the pile. She laughed, watching the boys fight over her.

It wasn't a real fight, she knew. Paul and Troy were best friends, different as night and day but equally eager to show Imogene a good time. She would have to decide between them one of these days, but she kept putting that off. Once made, her choice would break up the boys' friendship. She didn't want to be responsible for that.

"What are you laughing at?" Paul said, once he'd pinned the smaller Troy beneath him. He sat astride Troy's chest like a conqueror riding an untamed steed.

"Get off, you big oaf." Troy gasped, squirmed, and with one mighty buck, rolled Paul off him into a snow bank. Troy sprang to his feet, thumped his chest, and bellowed like Tarzan.

Imogene felt a flame worm its way through her body. What she liked about Troy was the way he could imagine they were in some far-off place, like Tarzan's jungles. He told her about all the stories he read about those different places, and just hearing them set her on fire and took her away from boring Dillon Fell.

She wondered if there'd be any jungles after the war was over. She wondered if the war would ever be over. She wondered if life would ever be the same again. She hoped not. Life was boring. War was even more boring. How could this be?

Paul, on the other hand, didn't have much need for books and stories. He was always tinkering with his hands. She liked the way his hands worked her body. His hands were expert hands, and her body juices flowed, singing in response to his touch. So far that's all it had been — touching. Troy wanted to touch her too, she could tell, but he didn't know how or where. He also didn't know that Paul had already beat him to it.

More than anything, she liked the boys as a pair because that's how they were fun. They encouraged each other's craziness, fed off each other. And they made her crazy, too. She scampered away, bounding through the snow, to the edge of the pond.

"Let's go ice skating!" she called, stepping onto the ice.

The boys shouted in unison. "No, Imo! Stop!"

"Who's gonna stop me?" She took baby bird steps, testing, testing, listening for tiny cracks and pops that would splinter the ice.

"The ice is too thin!"

"Uh-uh," she sang. She couldn't slide anyway, not in her galoshes, so she pranced around, close to the edge.

"It's starting to thaw!"

"You boys are just ninnies. I'm going home. Home is more fun than you boys, and that's not saying a lot, 'cause home is the most boring place on earth."

"Don't go home." Paul followed her out onto the ice.

She thought he'd be the one to rescue her, not that she really needed rescuing. What she hadn't counted on was how loud the crack ended up sounding, almost like a gunshot, a crack that ripped not only ice but also the air. Paul grabbed her by the elbow and yanked her back.

She fell smack on her butt on the ice, and the impact was so sharp and so bruising that it knocked the wind from her. She gasped for air. "Oh!" Maybe this hadn't been one of her smarter moves. Being dumb always called for a distracting tactic.

She clawed her way up onto the snow bank at the ice's edge. "You boys ever think about what it'd be like to live somewhere else besides this boring place?" With her mitten, she massaged her sore rear end.

"I don't have to," Paul said. "Uncle Sam's thinking for me. I turn eighteen the week before graduation."

"Wait for me, bud," Troy said, "and we'll enlist together. I'm not eighteen till the end of summer."

"They'll think I'm yellow if I wait."

"I mean besides the war," Imogene said, pouting. She knew the boys wouldn't be around much longer, but meanwhile, she was determined to have her own good time. "Let's just pretend there's no war. Where would you go after graduating if there's no war? What would you do? Would you stay here or go someplace else?"

"You're just jealous 'cause you're not going to get to shoot any Nazis." Paul climbed up onto the bank after her. He assumed a stance with a pretend rifle and went "bla-a-a-a" towards the woods.

"Says who? There's talk of a women's force, and I could join them if I wanted."

"You're better off staying here, waiting for us to come back," Troy said while Paul defended them from gathering shadows.

"Who says you'd come back? Besides, I'm not going to end up stuck here. Not me. I'll go to that factory where Peggy went, if I have to. She'll get me a job there. It's not my first choice, but at least it's away from here."

"Let's me and you run away together, babe. Time's a'wasting." Paul slid one arm around Imogene's waist, then dipped her as he grabbed the sled's rope with his free hand.

Imogene squealed with pleasure, and they ran up the hill, dragging the sled behind them. Troy trudged along behind. At the top of the hill, Paul positioned the runners of the sled the way he wanted them on the hill's crest. "After you, madam," he said, gesturing with a gallant sweep of one arm toward the wooden seat.

"You'll squash me," she said, then giggled. "Oh, you want to do it sitting up this time? With your arms and legs wrapped tightly around me?"

"Right. Let's do it."

"Oh, Paul." She approached the sled as if it were a wedding bed and seated herself, bending her knees to place each boot on the steering bar. Her position summoned up an image of giving birth, and she giggled again at the thought.

"Nope, I'm going to steer." Paul sat behind her, embracing her with his entire body. His legs encased her, and his boots nudged hers inward. She leaned back, against his chest, and he scooted forward enough so that his hardness pressed into her lower back. A thrill of pleasure tickled through her.

Troy caught up to them. The spring was gone from his step. The way he bobbed from side to side gave him a dejected air as he approached the rear of the sled. The non-rider's job was to give the sled a running start and push it off the crest of the hill. "Ready?" he said, bending low and grasping the back side of both runners.

Paul's breath tickled Imogene's neck as he nodded. She held her own breath as his arms crept around her, teasing her breasts. Her heart raced, her pulse hammered, fever coursed through her veins, and she thought she would explode.

"Wait," Troy said. His voice dropped to a whisper. "Did you hear that?"

"Hear what?"

"I dunno. Something in the woods. Listen."

It was hard for Imogene to hear anything over the pounding of her heart, but then she heard a distant sound, a hollow sound. A wail.

"Someone's crying," Paul said. "So what? Let's go."

"No, you dope," Troy said. "It's wolves."

Whatever it was that they'd heard, the sound that came next chilled the air with its crisp, clear report. This time it wasn't the ice cracking. It was a real gunshot.

# BOULDER, 1985

**The morning of Barry's** graduation dawned bright and clear for everyone except Rosamonde. Not that she wasn't proud. Her heart was filled with enough pride that she feared she might float away as easily as the helium balloon Melody had bought for the occasion. She just hated to see it end, that's all. She hated giving up her children to the world.

Still, it was a special occasion, and she'd dressed for it in her best rayon suit. She wished she could've worn her cameo too, but she couldn't find it among her things, and Hank had been in such a hurry. He hadn't slowed down one whit in retired life, not one whit.

The bumping bouncing of the balloon against low-hanging branches served as a background beat while they walked the few blocks, mostly uphill, from their hotel to the stadium where the ceremony would be held. Goodness, Rosamonde, thought, puffing. She'd forgotten about the altitude and the difficulty breathing. Each gasp for air punctuated the suffocation of her heart. She'd been used to the altitude at one time, back when they lived in New

Mexico, but after that she'd adapted well to sea level, as comfy as a clam in mud. Certainly, she couldn't talk and walk at the same time. And if they didn't hurry, they might not find a suitable seat.

Hank set the pace, then Melody followed, flip flopping her balloon with each step. Rosamonde brought up the rear, and she fell farther behind the closer they got to the stadium atop the endless hill.

"Hank!" she called, gasping. *Slow down, Hank! Your heart!*

Then they were caught up in a sea of people, separating Rosamonde from her family. "Hank!" she called again, but her voice couldn't rise above the merry din that engulfed her. She lost sight of them, but there was the balloon, thank goodness, and she followed its bobbing, weaving pattern above the heads of the crowd.

She hated crowds. She'd always hated crowds. Crowds were the worst thing about living on the east coast. You couldn't get far enough away from people without walling yourself up inside the cell of your home. Rosamonde was an outdoorsy sort of person, always had been. She liked her home, but she liked being able to escape home to the outdoors and enjoy God's landscape in solitude. Well, as long as that solitude included Hank.

"Hank, wait for me!" she called, but it was no use. She couldn't expect him to hear her in all this noise.

It was a happy crowd, a celebrating crowd, full of proud parents like herself. Aunts and uncles and grandparents. Would Melody ever make her a grandparent? Rosamonde wasn't sure she'd live to see that day, since Melody seemed more interested in her career than starting a family.

There were quite a few children in the crowd, too, siblings with starry eyes who wanted to model themselves after their big brothers and sisters. For the big sister, like Melody, it was an obligation to be here. Hank had made that clear. Being here gave Melody the chance to relive her own moment of glory. Hank had been right about that, about wanting to give Barry his moment to shine, with the family spotlight directed entirely on him, rather than on the successes of Melody.

Truth told, they'd never expected Barry to make it this far. Barry was a dreamer; Melody, a doer.

The balloon led Rosamonde into a dark portal, a tunnel filled with pressing bodies. Their rush reminded her of lemmings, funneling along in the same direction, toward an arch of light ahead. The crowd kept pushing her along, and she wondered where the folks in front of her went to make way for those behind. Not over a cliff, she hoped.

Why hadn't they stopped to wait for her? Surely they must've realized by now that they'd forged ahead. Anger flared within her at their lack of consideration, their downright rudeness. Hank had never been like that, and she'd raised Melody better than that. It must've been the anticipation of the big event that made them forget all else. To forget her.

Finally, the portal's tunnel opened onto the light of the outdoors and a narrow walkway that circumvented the stands surrounding the oval field below. The balloon bobbed directly ahead, but Hank and Melody were not here. She glanced around, confused, back and forth between the balloon overhead and the small child who held it by a string.

This child was not Melody, and Rosamonde realized her mistake. She'd followed the wrong balloon. She stood there, paralyzed. People bumped against her as they swept past her to find seats. Some of them mumbled apologies, but most didn't even notice that she stood there. She felt like an invisible person.

She glanced back at the portal and wondered if she should try retracing her steps to the point where she'd actually lost sight of Hank and Melody outside the stadium. They could've ducked into any of these portals that riddled the outer wall of sandstone. Surely they'd come into *this* one, though, since it was the nearest entrance via their path up the hill. If she just stood here and waited, letting people flow around her, one of them would find her.

So she stood and waited to be found. That was it. They'd chosen seats, and Hank was saving them while Melody went back for her mother. It shouldn't be much longer, Rosamonde thought, before Melody would find her.

People continued to pour into the stadium from all directions. Their paths criss-crossed, creating a melee of disordered movement. The tinny sound of a band echoed off of somewhere. Hoots and hollers punctuated the noise of the crowd, which grew steadily to a roar. She scanned the sea of celebrants, but it was impossible to pick out Hank and Melody, or even which of the balloons was Melody's.

Traffic on the walkway thinned, but still Rosamonde didn't see Melody rushing to her. Rosamonde's feet hurt, and the sun, already intense this early in the morning, fried her skin. Sweat poured down her sides as if a fountain had been turned on.

"Oh dear," she said when long lines of black-gowned graduates filed onto the field to the familiar tune that made her pride bubble up in her throat. She choked and dabbed a finger to the corner of her eye. Oh my, she thought. *How has it come to this?*

"Ma'am, can I help you?"

She followed the sound of the voice to a young man, no older than Barry, an usher, no doubt, judging from the stack of programs he held.

"I wish you could, young man, but I seem to have lost my way, and now it's too late. The ceremony has started, so I'll just have to watch it by myself." Rosamonde hated being by herself almost as much as she hated crowds. Being alone wasn't the natural state of things. Coming from a rural community, there'd always been someone, even though the spaces were wide open and mostly empty, unlike here, where people crowded together. How could so many people co-exist and yet still be alone in the world?

"Don't worry, Ma'am," said her young usher friend. "I'll help you find your party." He thrust one arm into the air above their heads and waggled programs until he got the attention of the next usher at the next aisle.

And the next thing Rosamonde knew — it was a miracle, really — here came Hank pushing his way through the sea of strangers. It was as if her own private usher had somehow scared him up for her.

"Rosie Rosie christ Rosie here you are thank god Rosie," Hank said, his words rushing together in the mumble that Rosamonde recognized indicated her husband's extreme anxiety. His arms encircled her, and he leaned into her, his entire body shaking just a bit. He nuzzled her ear, where recalcitrant strands of hair that had come loose from her bun wisped in the breeze.

"Hank, how on earth did you ever find me in such a crowd?"

"Nothing can keep me away from you, and christ, I thought I'd gone and lost you. No way will that stupid blunder happen again. You can't get rid of me. It's you and me forever, babe."

She squeezed his hand. "Look, the ceremony has already started. Where's our boy? Do you see him?"

"I only see you, old girl."

# SEVEN

Hank knew that Barry was the apple of his mother's eye. And puppy dog Nolan-the-therapist somehow reminded her of their wayward son. Was it his lack of fire? Rosie, back in her day, wouldn't have put it that way. She'd have called it his gentleness, or some other such tom foolery.

Whatever, in hiring Nolan, Melody had stumbled across a good thing, for Rosie was content under Nolan's pretend care. She followed him, lamb-like, one lamb following another lamb, to the dining room table where he'd spread out cards showing numbers and shapes in some sort of game doubling as a mind test. Nolan aka Barry was determined to find Rosie's elusive mind. Where had it gone? And with Barry on his side, he just might find it.

Hank watched for a while until he realized that his Rosie had almost but not quite forgotten his own presence. Not that she'd actually forgotten him but was distracted instead.

He could take advantage of her distraction to take a well-deserved break. After all, there was no rest when he had to guard his Rosie round the clock and keep Melody and Lani from going at each other's throats. Melody could take care of herself, but Lani... Well, his granddaughter was another matter. He didn't know her, couldn't know what or who she needed. She was young enough to accept her grandmother as she was, and for that, Hank was her advocate, as much as a dead person could advocate anything.

He found her in Jewell's condo. Her long form twisted the sheets, wrapping them around her legs. Her painted toenails hung over the end of Jewell's pull-out sofa. Some electronic gizmo plugged into her ear, and she wagged her foot to whatever beat filled her head through the insert.

The closed door to Jewell's bedroom squeaked open, and Jewell staggered out into blinding light reflected off the ocean and through the slats of louvered blinds. Eyes still closed, she paused in the doorway, yawned, and rubbed her head. She looked like shit, Hank thought, with her hair bushed out and tangled as if she was going for dreadlocks. Bags under her eyes were heavy and deep enough to sink an aircraft carrier.

"Coffee," she mumbled, holding her arms in front of her zombie-like and groping her way through the living room. She stubbed her toe against the open frame of the sofa bed and cursed. Her eyelids flew open and she stared uncomprehending at Lani, sprawled on the mattress. Her hand jerked up to her brow. She frowned. Cursed again. And closed her eyes again.

"Shouldn't you..." Jewell's fingers slid down to her mouth, covering it, stifling a yawn, or else something bigger bubbling from within.

Hank floated up, out of the way.

Jewell burped. "Shouldn't you, like, be in school or something?"

Lani didn't respond, and Jewell reached down to tweak the painted toes. Lani yelped and pulled the thing out of her ear. "What?" she said.

"School, kiddo. You're late."

"I'm not going."

"Yes you are."

"But Jewell — "

"No need to shout. School, or home."

Lani glared at her. "You *said* you understood." Her lower lip stuck out, the same way Hank had seen Rosie pout. The difference was that Rosie's pouts were in jest, while he suspected Lani's lip meant serious business.

"No argument. Get moving." Jewell massaged her forehead.

Lani bounced on the mattress, shaking the entire frame. "Don't treat me like a baby, same as everyone else treats me. I'm not a baby!"

"No," Jewell said, her voice barely above a whisper, "you're not." Her fingers trembled, and she dropped her hand from her forehead, down to clasp her own arms that she wrapped around her own waist. She looked as if she needed to cling to something. "Being responsible doesn't give a person the right to...to ab... abdicate my responsibilities."

"Huh?"

"I mean...you have to earn the right to slough off every now and then."

"Like you?"

"Yeah, like me. At least I finished school. Got my own place now, my own business. Wouldn't've happened without school."

Lani plugged her gizmo back into her ear. "They don't teach you how to surf in school."

Jewell bent down low, fanning out her bushy hair over Lani's head as she plucked the thing from Lani's ear. "Fine, then, if that's your choice. You don't need school. You don't need me, either, if all you want to be is a surf bum. You don't need anyone. Unless, of course, you happen to want some breakfast."

"Hey, are you mad at me, or something? I can go to Aunt Vanessa's. She doesn't think school's such a big deal, either."

"If that's where you want to go, sweetie, then by all means. Go. I'm sure she'll give you breakfast."

"Oh, all right. Have it your way. I guess I can go to school, if it means so much to you."

"Your Aunt Vanessa doesn't cook, does she?"

"How'd you know?"

"A lucky guess. Want some coffee?"

Lani nodded. "Mom never lets me have it at home. Says coffee's not for children." She screwed up her face in distaste and wiggled out of bed.

"She's right," Jewell said with a laugh. "It's for women like you and me. C'mon." She led the way into the kitchen, a galley, no bigger than what they inserted on planes, a compact version of a real kitchen. Rosie, back in her day, never could've operated in anything less than a country-sized kitchen, filled with the sweet aromas of her fresh-baked breads.

Lani settled onto a barstool and watched Jewell bang open cupboards and drawers. She pawed through the refrigerator and unscrewed lids and rattled through mugs. She mumbled and grumbled to herself.

"So where were you last night?" Lani said.

Jewell dropped the bag of coffee, spilling a fine trail of grounds onto the counter. She looked up from that mess to stare at Lani, as if seeing her for the first time. Her face went as white as the Formica. "Don't tell me you were afraid, being by yourself last night. I thought you said you're not a baby."

Lani's face mottled, and her brows twisted. "I'm *not*. *You* said we were going to have a slumber party."

"I'm sorry. Something came up. I'm so, so sorry."

Lani went still on the barstool. "S'okay."

They stared at each other in silence, then finally Jewell said, "Um, your dad's sister sings at the Koa Mo'ole, doesn't she?"

"Aunt Vanessa? Yeah. Is *that* where you went last night?"

"No. I was just wondering."

"Okay, I get it. You don't want to tell me. Must've been some hot date, huh? You going to see him again soon?"

The mug Jewell was retrieving from the cupboard slipped from her fingers and crashed to the floor. Ceramic chinked against tile, and the broken handle skittered away. "Oh, damn!" Jewell cried, sinking into a heap on the floor.

Lani sprang from her stool. "At least it wasn't full of coffee yet." She scooped up the trash bin and brought it to Jewell, whose cheeks glistened with tears. "You okay?"

Jewell looked up, pondering the question. She rose slowly and pulled a tissue from the pocket of her robe, blew her nose and then studied Lani through reddened eyes. "Sure, I'm okay," she finally said. "It was my favorite cup. That's all. No harm done." She dropped the broken pieces in the trash along with her tissue.

"So are you?"

"Am I what?"

"Going to see him again?"

Jewell sniffed. "It's not like that. You make assumptions, just because. I dunno. But you're wrong, kiddo. Totally." She clamped her jaw shut.

Lani's face flushed with splotches of heat. "Oh, I get it. You like girls instead."

"Sure, but not like that. Look, don't worry about me. Maybe there *is* a guy. But it wasn't a date. God, no!"

"Maybe? Tell me about him."

"Um, no, kiddo. We're talking about you, remember?"

"Okay." Lani yanked a bagel from a bag and munched in silence while Jewell flitted about the kitchen. "Hey, you don't have to do the dishes too. I can do them for you. After school, okay?"

"What about Kapono?"

Lani shrugged. "Like, I don't have to see him *every* day. Y'know?"

Jewell smiled. "A woman needs her independence."

"Tell Mom that. The bitch."

"You may not believe this, but your mother loves you very much."

"Sure, stand up for her. Kapono was right. I shouldn't've come here after all."

"Why *did* you?"

"I thought I could..." Lani scrunched up her eyes, deep in thought. "I dunno. Something...about Gran. Gran *needs* me. I can't go too far away from Gran. Poor Gran, she doesn't have anyone else, no one to fight for her against Mom."

Good girl, Hank thought.

"*Against* your mom?"

"They hate each other."

"Oh, I doubt that."

"Hey, believe me, I know. You haven't been there to see for yourself. Gran always loved Uncle Barry more, and Mom couldn't stand that. It's gonna be hell next week when he arrives. That's why I'm staying away. Maybe I'll go stay at Kapono's then."

"Are you sure that's a wise choice?"

"Why not?"

"You don't want to make a choice that you'll regret later."

"Yeah. He wants to...you know."

"Jesus, I hope someone's told you about the birds and the bees. What about *you*? What do *you* want?"

"I've never — But don't tell Mom that!"

"Don't worry. You can trust me."

"Yeah. I can, can't I? Y'know what? I wish I could stay with you forever."

"Really? You wish that?"

"Yeah."

"Well, sweetie, I'm honored. Especially because I know you must have lots of other possibilities. Like your aunts and cousins. Does your aunt sing anywhere else, besides the Koa Mo'ole?"

"Aunt Vanessa? How come you're so interested in her?"

"I'm not, I was just wondering. Don't you think it's fun to have a celebrity in your family?"

Lani shrugged. "None of my friends know who she is."

"Maybe not, but I'll bet the tourists know her. Sometimes they ask in the shop if I know where so-and-so does shows."

"Grandpa Flynn doesn't think she's good enough, and she's his own daughter."

"He's too hard on her. He's just disappointed that she chose not to work for the family business."

"How do you know *that*?"

"I don't, I'm just guessing."

"Well, you guessed right. Sometimes I think I'm an outcast, too, just like my aunt Vanessa."

"Why, honey? You think your family is disappointed in you?"

"I don't think — I *know* it."

"I'm sure you're wrong."

"There you go again. You're treating me like a baby."

"Maybe there are some things that are better for you not to know."

"See? That's what *they* say."

"They?"

"The fam."

"What else do they say?"

"It's like... Oh, I don't know. They're keeping something from me. Something big."

"Maybe they don't want you to feel hurt."

"I have rights, too, don't I? Besides, they don't care if they hurt me with other things. Like that thing with my journal. Can you believe my mother the snoop?"

Jewell blinked, and her eyes widened, then teared over. "Shit," she said.

"What?"

"Oh. My. God." Jewell threw her arms around Lani. Her forehead sagged against Lani's shoulder. Her back heaved, and gurgling, coughing sounds hiccupped from her. "What...have I... done?"

"Hey, it's no big deal. That's cool. You're cool." Lani patted Jewell then gently untwined herself from Jewell's grip. "Hey, look, I'm late. I gotta get dressed for school, y'know?"

Hank drifted into Lani's head and hovered there with an image of his Rosie, comfortable in their farmhouse kitchen. Even though they'd never lived together on a farm (both of them had come *from* the countryside) she'd always insisted that the homes they bought each time they moved had to have a kitchen reminiscent of down home.

"After school I gotta go visit Gran," Lani said.

*Good girl.*

"But I'll be back after that, that is, if it's still okay. You won't send me to live with Aunt Vanessa, will you?"

Jewell wiped her eyes and shook her head. "Not if you don't

want to go there. I'm here for you, kiddo, in spite of everything else. I don't want to interfere. I only want what's best for *you*. Remember that."

Yeah, right, Hank thought.

# EIGHT

He is here with me, Hank! Our baby! I found him! All along I knew that I would find him if only they let me search long enough through the rooms of my mind. I know that what I think is right. All that is real is inside my head, not in theirs. They try to tell me I am wrong, but no, *they* are wrong, and I am right. I have known it all along, and they cannot fool me.

They try to fool me. I do not know why.

Hank, our baby sits before me, and he shows me some of his work. Oh, his words are mysteries to me, the words he's caught in his work. I have never heard his words before. I am sure of that. I think. I cannot understand my own boy, but I'll bet you could.

Hank? Have you gone away again?

There was a time once when I knew more than our boy knows, a time when I owned the words he owns now. I gave them to him. I lost the words, but they are not gone. Words only hide from me. The words I used to teach our boy are the words of what I used to know. He took my knowledge from me and turned it into his. Not that he meant me any harm. Oh no. I didn't really lose the knowledge I gave him. It's here somewhere. In all that I have seen of life, I have grown more rooms than I need, and that's where my memories go, to one of the rooms of the mansion of my mind. It is a rich mansion because of the rich life we have led, starting with... I do not remember, but I know they're here somewhere. I have to search harder. I have to...

Hank? Where are you? Is it time to go now?

Our boy shows me words and tells me words, and his words used to be mine, but they are no more. Words are hiding in the rooms of my mind. Are they hiding with you, Hank?

Hank, don't hide from me!

#

**"All right, Mrs.** Berryhill, it's okay. We don't have to do this anymore if you don't want to." Nolan the puppy dog swept up his cards into a loose pile and shoved them to the far end of Melody's dining room table. His eyes darted back and forth, and he swiped pudgy fingers through a shaggy lock of his hair. "We're going to do something else now, okay?"

Hank returned from Jewell's condo just in time, apparently. He had to spend some time soothing Rosie while Nolan's fingers drummed against his brow, summoning an idea. Nolan glanced at his watch. Four hours still remained before Melody's promised return.

"You want some lunch?" Nolan said, jumping to his feet. As if food solved all the world's problems. Hank *wished*. How differently would the world have turned out if the Enola Gay had dropped ten thousand pounds of food instead of a ten-thousand pound bomb?

Nolan looked at his watch again. "Naw, I guess it's too early for lunch." Then he looked back at Rosie's beautiful, calmer face. "Oh, you liked that idea, did you? All right, tell you what, how about a cup of tea to tide you over till lunchtime? You like tea, don't you?"

Good lord, now he was doing a Melody, Hank thought.

"Let's move you over here to the sofa where you'll be comfortable while I fix some tea," Nolan said.

One lamb followed the other lamb, allowing him to seat her on the leather, then plump up a pillow behind her back. From the sofa, Rosie could see Nolan aka Barry move about the kitchen.

"So, your daughter says you recently moved here from Maryland," he said. "How do you like it here so far?"

"Home," Rosie said.

"Yes, it's your new home. You've been here before, haven't you?"

She frowned and rubbed her thumbnails. "I want to go home!"

"You *are* home, Mrs. Berryhill." Nolan whistled as he moved about the kitchen, filling the teakettle, searching for teabags, pulling cups from the cabinet.

"Barry?"

"Barry's your son. You'll see Barry soon when he comes for the holidays. Maybe you'll introduce him to me."

"No! Damn you!"

Nolan stepped out of the kitchen, and his eyes widened as he stood in the doorway staring at the gray-haired granny with the sailor's mouth. Hank moved close to Rosie. He murmured soothing endearments, reminding her of his presence. Nolan wasn't Barry, not who Rosie thought he was, but that shouldn't matter, because she had Hank in reality.

But Rosie wasn't going to settle this time, no matter how much Hank tried. Christ, he was getting tired of this. If he could've died all over again, he would've, just so he could've picked another time of year to die. The holidays always set her off, reminding Rosie of Hank's death. He knew. Soon, not soon enough, she'd be with him, and they would drift away together to oblivion and be done with all this tom foolery.

"Damn, goddamn hell! Damn! Damnit to hell! Go to hell! You go to hell!"

*Rosie, that's enough.*

"Now, Mrs. Berryhill, I know you don't mean — "

"Fuck you! To hell! Damn goddamn fuck you to hell — "

*Rosie, that's* enough *already.*

She tasted the forbidden words, rolling loose in the flood that was drowning her mind. Words could never flow freely again for her, regulated under the control of her mind, like a dam that released so much and no more. She liked the sense of power that came along with capturing any words at all, sampling them on her tongue, and hurling them for the reactions they caused on the faces of others. He understood. But really. You had to conform to the reality of others around you.

As quickly as her tirade had exploded, it finished now. Her head leaned back against Melody's hand-sewn Thai silk pillow and her eyelids closed, long lashes resting against the flush of her cheeks. Nolan tiptoed to her side and stood over her, examining her first from one direction then from another. Her chest heaved with a sigh. She was asleep. Nolan backed away slowly to a dining room chair, where he eased himself down, propped his elbows onto his knees, and leaned his forehead into the cups of his palms.

# NINE

Hank found Melody sitting on the floor of the fitting room of Jewell's boutique. A tape measure draped around her neck, and pins poked out of her mouth like porcupine quills. A woman, looking not a day older than Lani except that she wore too much make-up and too few clothes, spoke into a cell phone as she played the part of human mannequin before Melody.

Hank drifted through his daughter's mind with an image of her distraught mother and a nervous Nolan, clearly in over his head. The image didn't take, for Melody continued to frown at the hem before her.

"What do you mean that bitch Paulette got the part instead of me?" said the near-naked model. Hank tried not to look. "It was practically promised to me! Look, I have to have that part. You understand me? It's not just any part. It was written for me... No, I didn't know Chad before his last hit, but I know him now, and he agrees. It's so me. Totally... What? Well you just make a few phone calls and see that it happens. You can do that, can't you? What kind of agent are you, anyway? Yeah, I'm stuck here through Thanksgiving, damnit. Don't call back until you have something I want to hear."

The model stabbed her phone and hurled it across the room. Papers skidded to the floor from Jewell's desk, where the phone hit.

"We'll never get this done if you don't hold still," Melody said through the pins in her mouth.

"Oh, what does it matter? I'm finished."

"You're young and beautiful, and your entire career is ahead of you. With your Academy award now, you can have any part you want."

"Apparently not."

"You'll find a better part."

"You don't know what it's like. You're just a seamstress."

"Actually, I'm a designer," Melody said, pulling the pins from her mouth and stabbing them one by one into her tomato cushion. Then she dazzled the kid with her smile. "*You* get to show the world on the screen what beauty is all about, but I'm one of the people who helps create that beauty, so I think that qualifies me to know a thing or two about it. See?"

"Yeah, so what?"

"So I get to meet a lot of celebrities in my business, and they come in all types. People like you who are recognized everywhere you go, and some famous people nobody knows, at least not by face."

"Like who?"

"Like a few screenwriters. And I happen to know that there are lots and lots of really good screenplays out there that'll probably never be made into movies. It's so sad. I bet if someone like you found the right movie, it'd become a big hit."

"Yeah, that's the key, isn't it? Finding the right movie isn't so easy. Then some bitch comes along and snatches right out of my hands the one I want."

"Then all you have to do is find a better movie."

"Not so easy."

"It is if you know the right people."

"I suppose you do?" The girl's voice iced over with sarcasm so thick that Hank shivered.

"Now that you mention it," Melody said, "I do happen to know a brilliant screenwriter who just happens to have a screenplay available and just happens to be coming *here* in three more days."

"Oh, yeah? What's his name?"

"Bartholomew Berryhill."

"Never heard of him. What's he done so far?"

"Oh, you probably haven't heard of his credits. He's only recently moved to Hollywood. All the stuff he's done was back east."

"Are you shitting me? You want me to talk to an unknown writer? Like, who cares?"

"Well, for starters, it's got a great love story. And I couldn't help but overhear you talking about a Chad. Is that Chad Diamond by any chance? It is? Well, I happen to know that Mr. Berryhill's script is on Chad Diamond's desk right now. He asked for it. If you're interested, I might be able to ask Mr. Berryhill to send you a copy of the script, too."

"It's a love story?"

"Oh, it's a *beautiful* love story."

"Yeah, but what's the female lead like?"

"She's young and beautiful, just like you, and she's a strong woman, besides. She's supporting her entire family by working in a war factory — "

"So you're talking a *war* movie? Are you serious?"

"Then, when U-boats attack New York City — "

"Wait, I never knew that happened."

"It's a movie."

"Oh, so it didn't really? Well, I don't know. Maybe that could turn out sexy. If Chad's doing it, then there must be *some*thing to it. And that bitch Paulette is sure to want the female lead as soon as she hears about it. Okay, maybe you'd better get this guy to send it to me. Fast. Wait. He's coming *here*? Maybe he could bring me a copy?"

"Whatever you say." Melody grinned. "Now hold still and let me finish this hem. You're going to look gorgeous in this."

# TEN

When Melody returned home, Rosie was in the middle of obliging Nolan (the Barry look-alike) with one of his tom fool games. Not that she participated in the way he'd instructed her to. Mostly, she watched him with wide-eyed wonder while he moved his cards of pictures and numbers around the table. She was willing to do this much because she'd awakened from her nap in a better mood and had even eaten a bit of lunch.

"Hi there, Mom," Melody said-sang, sailing into the house. Certainly a different entrance, Hank thought, than everyone's sour exit that morning. "Have you had a good day? If it's been half as good a day as mine, then yours has been wonderful too." Smile smile smile.

Nolan answered for Rosie. "Today's been okay."

"Just 'okay'? That's all?" Melody turned to Rosie. "Mom, do you agree? Was your day just 'okay' and nothing better than that?"

"I'd say today's gone smoothly enough," Nolan said. "Nothing to worry about."

"That's very nice, but I want to hear it from Mom."

His face turned beet red, and his glance darted from Melody to Rosie. "Mrs. Berryhill? Can you tell your daughter about the bird we watched today? The one that came to the lanai? Remember?"

Rosie looked down at her thumbnails. Round and round and round her fingers rubbed and polished her nails. Her lips moved, but she made no sound.

"She doesn't talk much," Nolan said, turning back to Melody, "at least not to me, she doesn't. Maybe you can get her to talk."

"Oh, no. She can't talk anymore."

"Maybe she doesn't have anything to say." He chuckled, and so did Hank. Melody had always had a selective memory. She ignored them both and turned to Rosie.

"Mom, I have some great news." She faced Rosie, but her eyes rolled in the direction of Nolan. "I'll have to tell you later."

Nolan must've gotten the hint, for he gathered up the cards he'd laid out. "Anyhoo... I guess our time is up for today, Mrs. Berryhill, but I'll be back... Tomorrow?"

"Yes, tomorrow, that's right," said Melody. She swept over to the table and straightened the edges of his piles of cards. "Tomorrow at ten, okay? Remind me then, and I'll show you a better way to organize your materials." For now, she let him put his sloppy stacks of cards away in his briefcase in his haphazard fashion. Apparently she was in a hurry to escort him to the door.

"Goodbye, Mrs. Berryhill." Nolan tripped along behind

Melody while fumbling with the latch to his briefcase.

Suspicious, Hank followed the pair to the atrium entry while Rosie stayed busy with her thumbnails. Melody blocked the door and let out a long sigh before letting Nolan go. She crossed her arms and frowned. "Just because Mom can't talk anymore doesn't mean that we've given up trying to get her to talk. I wouldn't expect you, of all people, to give up on her."

"Mrs. Flynn, I assure you that's not exactly — "

"I had *so* hoped that you would make a break-through with her."

"There's always tomorrow."

"You may as well give me your evaluation of her. I can handle the truth. How did it *really* go today?"

"Fine. Just fine. I promise. No problems." Nolan shifted his weight, looking like a sprinter readying himself for the dash past Melody to the door. A muscle twitched in his jaw. Apparently, he could be as stubborn as Melody. He had no intentions of revealing the sailor language episode. Good boy!

"It's okay," Melody said. "I still want you to work for us. I *know* you had problems today. There are always problems."

"No, really, it was fine. We did a few activities to exercise a wide range of cognitive skills and a few fine motor and gross motor activities.

"Really? You did all that? And nothing went wrong?"

Nolan nodded.

"I don't believe you."

"I assure you, everything was well under control." Nolan

switched his briefcase from one hand to the other, then smoothed his tousled hair with his free hand. Sweat rings showed under his armpits.

"Because I know what's wrong with her," Melody said. "We all know. It's Alzheimer's. Anyone can tell that."

Nolan cocked his head to one side. "Maybe, maybe not. There are many forms dementia can take, and her case is a bit unique."

"It's okay, you don't have to spare me. I already know. I just need to have an official diagnosis, that's all."

"I'm afraid I'm not qualified to — "

"I know you're not, and that's okay, too. That's not why I hired you. I have an appointment for next week at Golden Crater, even though there's a super long waiting list, just to be seen. You know why, don't you? Because it's the very best Alzheimer's care center in the entire nation, maybe even the world."

Oh, Christ, Hank thought. What's Melody up to now? He whirled about, a silent tornado of consternation. The weeping fig in the atrium rustled its leaves.

Melody glanced over her shoulder. "Did you leave a door open somewhere?"

"No, ma'am."

Just then the front door rattled behind Melody with enough force to shake her out of her stance. She sidestepped past the door as it pushed inward, and she turned to aim a frosty glare at the new arrival. Martin.

"Oh. It's you," Melody said. "You're the breeze we felt."

Martin chuckled. "That's me. Nothing more than a passing wind."

Melody laughed too, but neither of the Flynns sounded very happy. "What are you doing home this early? The golf course too crowded for your tastes?"

"And what is my charming wife doing here at the door, waiting to greet her weary bread-winner?"

"*Martin*! Yours is not the only income in this house."

"Oh? Did Lani get that job flipping burgers after school?"

Nolan cleared his throat and ducked past Melody. "I'll just be going now."

"Martin! Now see what you've done? Do you realize how lucky we are to find Dr. Penrose, who's willing to come here to the house to care for Mom?"

"Actually, I'm ABD. It's not doctor, not yet."

"Details," Melody said, flicking her wrist. "Dr. Penrose was just telling me about Golden Crater when you interrupted."

"You can call me Nolan," Nolan said, extending his hand to Martin. They shook, and they went on shaking.

"So sorry," Martin said. It was as if the two of them formed a secret club with their handshake. "What's this about Golden Crater?" Martin finally broke the handshake and patted Nolan on the back.

"It's one of our full-care centers for geriatric care," Nolan said.

Martin frowned. "Sounds expensive."

"Believe me, I wasn't going to bring it up. Competition for my services? Are you kidding?" Nolan laughed, but it sounded more like trembling lungs.

Melody leveled her gaze back at Nolan and evaluated him

with a look of pity. "You *should* be working *with* them. Don't you understand the wonderful resource we have with Golden Crater being located right here in Honolulu?"

Nolan shifted again on his feet. "Well, sure, we have several places here — "

"Golden Crater is the very best. In the *world*. They'll give me the diagnosis I expect, and then we can proceed with meds and the proper treatment."

"No diagnosis is definite, Mrs. Flynn, that is not until the patient, er, passes — "

"Yes. I'm well aware of that. Thank you for pointing it out, but I don't accept that. It's too morbid, for one thing."

"And we can't allow the ugly head of reality to rear up in our face, can we, Mel?" said Martin.

Melody took a deep breath and closed her eyes. Hank knew she was counting to five. When she opened her eyes, she directed her gaze to Nolan, as if Martin didn't exist. Hell, for her, maybe he didn't. "Anyway," Melody told Nolan in her steel voice, "that's not why I've hired you. You're just a temporary solution to the overall problem. No offense."

"No offense taken." Nolan shook his head and edged closer to the door. "Hey, uh, Mr. Flynn, maybe I should give you one of my cards, too." Nolan fumbled in his pocket and pulled out a bent card with an ink smudge on it. "You know, in case you have any questions. You can call me. I always encourage the lines of communication to remain open. That's part of my service."

Martin took the card, gave it a cursory glance, tossed it onto the table with the white orchid, and rubbed the back of his head. "Sure. Got to stay up on the family."

Melody tittered. "As long as it doesn't interfere with your golf game, right Martin?" She pulled the door open for Nolan and released him. "We'll see you tomorrow. Be here exactly fifteen minutes early."

"Will do." Nolan sighed and darted outside. He jiggled down the sidewalk in his haste, and then Melody shut the door and bolted it, locking Nolan out and Rosie in.

Hank drifted back and forth, from the weeping fig to Rosie's side and back again. *Meds and treatment.* If Melody got her way, they'd end up drugging his Rosie until he couldn't reach her anymore. He couldn't allow that to happen.

"Martin, must you?" Melody said, following Martin to the liquor cabinet where he poured himself two fingers of scotch.

"Can't let this good stuff go to waste, Mel. We'll have to tighten our belts now that you're hell-bent on Golden Crater."

"My mother deserves the best, and anyway, after what I did for Barry today, we won't have anymore problems with money, no thanks to you."

"You're bringing Barry into this? Oh shit." Martin downed his drink and poured another.

"Martin! Watch your mouth." Then she turned to Rosie and pasted on her smile. "You'll never guess what I managed to do today for Barry. Is he ever going to thank me for *this*! He's never going to get a bigger break than this, and when he becomes famous, he'll have me to thank for it. He's going to owe me for the rest of his life. And if he doesn't take advantage of this big break that I just got him, I'm gonna kill him." Smile smile smile.

Rosie looked up from her thumbnails and opened her mouth. Her lips twitched, but no sound came out. A glimmer of recognition flared to life behind the opaque windows of her eyes.

"Mom! You know what I'm talking about, don't you? Very good! See, I knew all along that all was not lost. Maybe you'll even talk to us again one day."

Martin snorted, and scotch went up his nose.

"She *knows*, Martin."

Rosie glanced over Melody's shoulder, in the direction of the atrium entry, where Hank fluttered by the weeping fig.

"No, Mom, I'm afraid Barry's not here. Not yet. He comes next week. It would be so nice to hear your voice again. It makes me wish... Oh, but you have such a lovely voice, I just want you to know that. I miss hearing your voice, Mom. When you used to tell us all those bedtime stories when we were children, what I loved listening to the most was the sound of your voice. Not the stories. But your voice — oh! It always reminded me of folds and folds of velvet. Royal purple velvet. Did I ever tell you that before? Because your voice is vibrant like royalty and rich like purple, yet smooth and soft like velvet."

Melody fell silent, and the house fell silent around her. The air felt thick with memory, even for Hank. His life, their lives together, compressed into a single flash of memory, and the supernova of their lives dazzled the room in a brilliant explosion.

Melody glanced up at the brass and glass ceiling fixture that dripped over the dining room table. Its light had just shattered into darkness. "What did you do, Martin?"

"About what?"

"Never mind," she said. "We must've overloaded a circuit. Oh Mom, I wish you could tell me what that Nolan character did today. I'll bet he messed with my electricity to make it go out like that."

While she watched, the light came back on. "Isn't that odd?" She shrugged. "I guess we'll never know now what happened. We might as well have a cup of tea with Martin, so he doesn't have to drink alone."

Hank wondered how she could think of tea at a time like this. She was talking about putting her own mother away. For good. She might as well just put her down. Rosie'd be better off if some kindly injection put her down because then she and Hank would be together. They couldn't be together if she was drugged up. Once they got her on *meds and treatment*, they'd keep her there, hook her up to machines and tubes and force Rosie's old heart to keep on pumping, no matter what the brain was doing. Or not doing.

A gardenia-scented air current captured Hank and batted him around, back and forth, back and forth. He spiraled about the room, skimming from one end to the other, from the atrium to the dining L, from the sliding glass door of the lanai to the leather sofa, from the parquet floor to the white blades of the ceiling fan. He felt like one of Rosie's thumbs twirling and twirling round and round.

How could Melody do this? To her own mother?

Hank would have to stop her. He'd helped to change the

world by building a bomb that should never have been built, so surely he could do this one little thing. He would have to distract Melody from her course of action. That would buy him the time he needed with his Rosie. He only knew of one thing that was powerful enough to distract Melody from anything she set her mind to doing.

Love.

But...he was so very tired. Love. It was all about love in the end.

# ADELLE

**Adelle Somerset had** the patience of Job, but not even Job could've born the cross she had to bear: Daisy Somerset, Adelle's mother-in-law, living under the same roof. Daisy had come for Christmas a little more than two months ago and then never left, not now that Adelle's husband — Daisy's last surviving son — had gone from being the pastor of Dillon Falls to becoming a soldier, all in the space of a week. It didn't matter that George Somerset had a wife and daughter and an entire congregation who depended on him. Uncle Sam needed him more.

"Mommy, that's too tight," six-year-old Gloria complained. Adelle's fingers shook, tying the ribbons of her daughter's wool hat beneath her dimpled chin.

"Here, honey," Daisy said, watching them. Always watching them. "Grandma will do it for you." Wise, experienced, expert hands gently clasped either side of Adelle and nudged her out of the way.

Adelle sighed, relinquished her daughter's ribbons and stood up. She quickly turned away from her much more proficient mother-in-law, quickly, before her daughter could spot the tears budding in her eyes. The sound of "Don't be sad, Mommy" still echoed in her mind. The first time she'd heard Gloria's plea it had ripped her heart wide open that first night after George left, when she was putting her daughter to bed. It seemed that Adelle always remained on the verge of tears these days, and she couldn't let Gloria see them. There was already too much ugliness in the world, and she must appear strong, even if she wasn't. She *must*. For Gloria's sake. Little Gloria depended on her, but she suspected that even her own daughter was stronger than she. Adelle couldn't do anything right, not even the simple task of bundling up Gloria for the short walk down the road to the church.

"There we are," said Daisy in her candy voice. As Grandma, Daisy always sounded gooey sweet and artificially cheery, no matter that people were dying round the world, including some of their own people. "All done! Don't you look cute as a bug!"

As mother-in-law, Daisy scolded, at least that's how she sounded to Adelle, whose hands still trembled while she pulled on her gloves. "Now, when you get there," Daisy said, wagging her finger at Adelle, "don't you forget to properly thank all of the ladies."

"I won't, Mother Daisy." Adelle grabbed her pocketbook, took Gloria's hand, and yanked her with her toward the door.

"They've gone to a lot of trouble," Daisy called after them, "and they deserve a word or two of kindness in exchange."

"I know." Adelle trudged along the driveway, slipping on ice, nearly taking both her and Gloria down together. Daisy would've loved to see that — proof of Adelle's incompetence. She couldn't clean the driveway properly, either. Adelle never had been good enough for Daisy's son, and now she wasn't good enough to raise Daisy's granddaughter.

They were halfway to the road when Daisy called out again. "Don't be late coming home, you hear? I'm making George's favorite stew, and it'll be waiting for you when you get back."

Gloria tugged on Adelle's arm. "Is Daddy coming home?"

"No, sweetie, not for a long time."

"Then how come she's making Daddy's stew?"

"I don't know, I guess she misses him, too." At the end of the long driveway, Adelle didn't even pause as she hurried across the road. There wasn't much traffic these days, not that very many cars had ever come through Dillon Falls in the first place. It was such a tiny village, way up north in the hills, and George's first assignment after seminary. Tiny, yes, but Adelle liked it. She liked the sense of community, and she'd gotten along just fine here with her new neighbors, that is until Daisy had come to stay under her roof.

"Honey!" Daisy called. Adelle could barely hear her by now, but she didn't have to hear the words to know what Daisy was chiding her about this time. "Be careful on the road!"

Now she was glad that the pastor's house was down the road and across the sledding hill from the church rather than being adjacent to the historic wood building with its charming steeple. The distance between the parsonage and the church gave her a bit

161

of breathing room from her mother-in-law, even though she was still not out of sight from Daisy's watchful eye.

Daisy remained standing in the doorway of the pastor's brick home across the way. She shouted something more at Adelle, but now she couldn't hear, although she imagined it was something to do with staying bundled up. Don't let that muffler slip, goodness gracious no.

"Wait, Mommy! Don't go so fast!"

"Sorry, sweetie. It's cold out, and you'll catch your death if we don't get a move on." Adelle had become an expert liar. She'd had to, under Daisy's omnipresent presence.

They trudged along, past the sledding hill where children not much older than Gloria took advantage of their free time and the last days of snow. It was hard to imagine such a normal activity as kids playing outdoors was only a semblance of normalcy while the rest of the world was going mad.

Gloria tugged on Adelle's arm. "Can we go sledding too after church? Please, Mommy?"

Panic constricted Adelle's chest and throat. "I...I don't know, sweetie." George had always done the sledding with their daughter while Adelle stayed home and made hot chocolate. She wasn't sure she knew how to sled anymore. "It'll probably be too late by the time we're done with church. And Grandma will be waiting with her stew. You heard her."

Not that Adelle ever thought about giving up her daughter. No, no, she'd never ever do that, not for the world. The thought of it alone was blasphemy. And not that she wished either her husband or her mother-in-law ill, but the truth of the matter was that Adelle felt trapped. She was only 26 years old, and she might as well be locked up like the prisoners of war. They could go ahead and lock her away along with all the enemy aliens everyone was talking about. In fact, she *was* a prisoner. Another victim of war. The four walls of her world bound her as tightly as any cell. Responsibility for her innocent child made up one wall, and nagging from her well-meaning but domineering mother-in-law made another. The third wall consisted of the need to maintain normalcy on the homefront so that her absent husband would continue to have a worthy cause to fight for and come home to, and the fourth wall was his very needy congregation.

Somewhere along the way, Adelle had lost her youth, assuming she'd ever had one in the first place. The rest of the world spun on, dancing and singing with misplaced zeal here on this continent while the killing went on over there on that one. No matter the time of day or night. Such craziness didn't add up in her mind, and while she tried to make sense of the dizzy fervor that had gripped the world, Adelle found that she was left behind. Trapped. Cut off from everyone because of her four walls that closed in on her tighter and tighter. She could hardly breathe.

It was the latter wall that sent her off in a rush to escape her mother-in-law today. The congregation needed her. She didn't know anything about running a church, nor was it her obligation to do so during the pastor's absence. But this absent pastor also happened to be her husband, and he was counting on her. Daisy had told her so. It was as if George could reach out to the people of

Dillon Falls in spirit through Adelle. The Elders kept the worship services running, and Adelle's responsibility, as Daisy pointed out tirelessly, was to direct outreach, which basically meant doing everything else. It was expected of the pastor's wife. The duties of outreach were less clear than opening the doors for worship once a week, but Daisy was happy to interpret the endless examples of what Adelle's duties entailed. Today's task was to direct the scrap metal drive.

With a heavy heart, she turned into the little lane that carried them up to the front door of the church. Adelle didn't mind contributing to the war effort, and she didn't mind rounding up pieces of unused tin and dumping them into the collection bins. She just didn't understand why *she* had to spend the entire day supervising this effort when she could be out sledding with her daughter. Did it really matter if she nodded at Mrs. Wiley and thanked Mrs. Ingersoll and told Mrs. Boatman she'd be blessed in heaven? Would the Teasdale girl even care if Adelle praised her? Mother Daisy thought it mattered. Her mother-in-law thought Adelle's presence would encourage the townspeople to find even more scraps, and didn't she know? Every little bit would help bring the boys home sooner rather than later. Alive, rather than in coffins.

What Adelle would rather be doing was singing, but she'd learned long ago to suppress her own wants and needs.

She wouldn't have minded singing with the church choir, although she preferred to sing more joyous songs than hymns. Still, she would've taken the choir over nothing. But George had forbidden her. It was unseemly, he'd said, for the pastor's wife to be one unknown face among the choir. If she wanted to *direct* the choir, that was another matter and would've been perfectly acceptable. But Adelle didn't want to direct. She wanted to sing. She wasn't good at leadership, and besides, she couldn't read music. She'd never had any formal music training, but she had the gift of carrying a tune. People who'd heard her, had told her so.

"Yoo hoo, Mrs. Somerset," sang a woman's high-pitched voice from behind Adelle.

She'd just stepped up onto the first step leading to the main door of the church, and now she squeezed Gloria's fingers and turned to look for the source of the thin voice. A horse-drawn cart creaked along the ruts in the snowy lane and drew up behind them. The widow Mrs. Wallis Wiley perched primly atop the driver's bench with a purple rug wrapped around her lap. She pulled back on the reins, steering Jim, her old faithful workhorse, to a stop beside the church entry.

"Hello, Mrs. Wiley. Have you brought us some nice scraps today?"

"Oh, tish tosh. I don't see what good that'll do, what with all the battleships we've lost already. We can collect metal till we're blue in the face, but I'll tell you what. It won't make a lick of difference, not until we root out the evil from its den of corruption."

"Where's that?"

"Why, Mrs. Somerset, surely you remember? Your dear husband always delivered the nicest sermons on the dastardly vices of drink."

"Mommy, is she talking about booooooze?"

"There, there, sweetie, it's not polite to interrupt."

Wallis Wiley glared at Adelle. "It is a blessing," she said slowly, "that your mother-in-law is with you now to correct the misunderstandings in children such as what your little girl shows. Daisy is already making quite a difference with the language of the children now that she's taken over the schoolhouse. It would appear, however, that she's neglected the needs of her own family."

"Mother Daisy is keeping herself awfully busy," Adelle said.

"Because she's a woman who knows her duty," Wallis snapped. "As we know ours. Our work is never done, especially when we have the likes of that Kipp Lehnert in our midst."

"The postmaster? What's he done?"

"Well." Wallis paused to huff, as if gathering a head of steam. "He's trying his best to derail the Women's Temperance League of Dillon Falls, but he will not succeed. He's German, you know."

"But why would he do that just because of his German ancestors? Isn't he an American citizen?"

"You can't trust any of them. Not anyone who didn't come over on the *Mayflower* or shortly thereafter. But him, especially. Hasn't Daisy warned you? He's trying to subvert us from within. He's in a position to do that, being postmaster, you know. He intercepts our mail. We have to find another way to let our congressman know that winning the war is a choice we can make."

"A choice?"

Wallis snorted, and Jim answered with a whinny. "The disaster of Pearl Harbor wouldn't have happened if we'd made the correct choice back in 1933 and *not* done away with Prohibition. We're going to need a whole lot more than scrap metal if we want to avoid more disasters like that one. Pearl Harbor proved we can't defend our country until we get rid of the menace of alcohol once and for all. We have to do the job of defense sober. And we have to start the job of rooting out evil right here in Dillon Falls. Well, Mrs. Somerset? I assume I can count on the support of the pastor's wife?"

Adelle lowered her chin to hide the way she gulped. "Here? In Dillon Falls?"

"That's right. You want to keep this a safe place for your little girl, don't you?"

"Why yes, of course."

Just then, Jim stamped his feet and snorted. His restless shuffle jerked the cart forward, nearly throwing Mrs. Wiley off the bench seat. "Whoa, now Jim. What's that?"

"Did you hear it?" Adelle lifted her face to the storm in the sky and sucked in her breath to listen harder.

"Thunder," Mrs. Wiley said.

"No. Aeroplanes! And they're heading this way!"

# ELEVEN

Maybe there was something special in Melody's tea, for Rosie slept like a lamb that night. Today went smooth as trinitite, and now she sat attentively, watching Nolan arrange his cards on the table.

She would've made a good student, Hank had always told her. Over the years, he'd suggested — no, encouraged — her to take a few classes here and there, to take advantage of the free lectures offered by his colleagues in the various labs where Hank had found work.

Rosie would laugh that bewitching laugh of hers and say, "Oh dear, I promised instead to read stories for children's hour at the library."

Or else she'd say, "After I finish making our new curtains. I'll think about something else then."

Or, "But dear, we're moving again in a few months."

The closest she ever came was: "If it means so much to you,

of course I'll go to school. But where would I find my stories to tell you on our long walks every evening?"

Hank didn't ever want to force anything on his Rosie that she didn't want to do. He didn't think she avoided classes and lectures because of not wanting to *attend* them. He understood how limited her opportunities in this matter had been, coming from the coal-mining background she'd come from. He liked to think of education as enriching oneself, and he was sure his Rosie agreed. She always agreed. Besides, she was plenty rich enough. She didn't need anymore richness. So he didn't press the matter again. He only wanted her to be happy. To be complete.

But he knew that every once in a while she'd let in a shred of a thought about doing something for herself for a change. Then along came the kids and Girl Scouts and den mothering and PTA.

Face it, Rosie always preferred giving to taking. Even now, she was giving herself away piece by piece. God, how Hank hated this emptiness that devoured her soul, cell by cell. He wanted it to stop.

Sto-o-o-op!

But he was powerless. Helpless. In his netherworld of the unphysical. Realm.

He'd been wrong. What wasn't real *could*, in fact, hurt.

Goddammit to hell.

"We're on this picture right here, Mrs. Berryhill." Nolan raised his voice to be heard over the angst in the air and smacked his palm down on top of one of the cards. "Can you tell me what comes next in the sequence, Mrs. Berryhill?"

Rosie blinked a tired blink, a slow blink, so slow that its

outcome remained uncertain. Would she or wouldn't she reopen her eyes after the blink? And why should she? She'd heard his gawl-danged question, but she was mighty tired of his word games. Why was he doing this to her? Why couldn't he just let her be?

Why couldn't they let Hank be? He was tired, oh so tired of this world he'd helped create.

"Mrs. Berryhill? Are you okay?"

Hank wished he could tell Nolan to lay off, but his complaint was useless. He could glare all he wanted, but Nolan wouldn't even feel the scorch of Hank's disdain. Still, Hank's attention drifted upward to —

And he startled to see Martin standing there, both frowning and beaming at the same time, digging one fist into a pocket, watching over them. Well, not over Hank, of course. But how in hell had he slipped inside the house without Hank's noticing? Did this mean he was fading? Transitioning out, so to speak? Christ! He couldn't cross over yet to the other realm, not without Rosie!

"Of course she's not okay," Martin said. "She hasn't been okay for years. That's why you're here, as I understand it."

"Ah, Mr. Flynn. I didn't hear you come in."

Then, Hank thought, that made two of them. He felt better already. Maybe, he realized, it was *Martin* who wasn't real. Hank inspected him, taking in the golf shirt and creased shorts, the bare feet in loafers, the wind-tousled cowlick, and the pores of his tanned flesh, glistening with a fine layer of sweat.

"We finished early," Martin said. "Ten over par. My best game all year."

"Congratulations."

"Thank you. Damn, it feels good. It's about time, too."

"You should celebrate."

"Maybe I will. Are you a golfer, Nolan?"

"Me, sir? Naw. I played a little in college. P.E., y'know? Haven't been able to afford it in the real world."

"You know what it means, though, don't you? To have a good game? To feel like you've mastered the course?"

Nolan laughed. "Well, not personally, but theoretically, why sure. That's my job. Helping others find their way in baby steps toward the mastery of a goal. I do it every day. Helping others, that is. Not necessarily for myself, mind you. Do I understand?" He laughed again. "Sure do!" Then he wiped the moisture off his palms and onto his trousers.

Neither of them really understood, Hank thought. Mastery was what life was all about. You tried to master life until finally it mastered you. It always won in the end.

Martin nodded. "You do that, really? For your clients?"

Nolan, encouraged, went on. "Furthermore, I teach my clients that they matter. They should pick goals that mean something for *them*, not for others. Y'know? You gotta go after what you want, not what others want for you. After all, we've only got one chance to go around in this world, know what I mean? So we might as well take the best shot at it that we can. Go for broke, that's what I always say."

"Tell you what," Martin said. "You want to grab a beer and tell me more about that stuff?"

"Oh no, Mr. Flynn. That would be drinking on the job. I can't do that. Another time, though, maybe."

"Yeah. Another time."

"'Course, now's the time you need to celebrate, isn't it? I mean, tomorrow's too late, right? Well, seeing as how it's your wife's nickel, maybe I could just outline a few basic pointers for you while you pour yourself one. I mean, I'm here to listen, but I don't get too much of that from Mrs. Berryhill. No offense, seeing as how she's your mother-in-law."

"No offense taken, Nolan," Martin said with a chuckle. "Maybe I'll just do that. Pour me one." He waltzed over to the liquor cabinet. "'Cause, me, I'm celebrating. Yes, I am. It sure as hell isn't just any day that I score ten over."

"I can appreciate that, Mr. Flynn. This is your special day. You've earned it, and you deserve it. No one else."

"Not even Melody."

"She'll be proud of you."

"No, she won't."

Nolan tugged the already-loose knot of his tie. "That's what I said. That's why you have to own your own accomplishments. No one else can do it for you."

"No shit." Martin went straight for the scotch, poured himself two fingers, and downed it in one long swallow. "Ah, that's better." He slammed the glass down and poured another. "Sure you won't join me?"

"Ah... We're expecting Mrs. Flynn any moment. Perhaps I should just gather up my things and hit the road. That is, since you're home."

"Relax, Nolan, you worry too much."

"Yes, sir, I do, but I'm paid to. That is, I *hope* to be paid. And I won't be paid if...oh, never mind." Nolan scooped his cards together into a mass on the table, and then he slid the entire blob off the edge. Cards plunked like scattershot into his briefcase. Rosie's eyebrows arched in time with the crash of cards cascading against the vinyl bottom of Nolan's case.

Rosie knew the sound of cards. She'd picked up bridge at Los Alamos, played it every damn week over at the PX with the other wives. The shuffle, the snapping, the slamming of cards made a gay sound, a gay reminder of better times, uncertain times, back when the world came crashing down along with the cards and you had nothing, no one to depend on but each other, in a make-believe world of your own making. She didn't have to force the memory of those times, not really, for the times were ingrained within her, and they flowed through her veins and carried her away to another place that only she knew, a place that made her real again. Complete.

# TWELVE

Hank heard Lani's key in the lock of the front door before anyone else. The soft scratch probed, then hesitated, then dug again, more certain this time. Now Melody heard it too, and she paused on her stepladder, from which she was taping balloons to the metal rim of the sliding glass door out to the lanai. She jumped down from her perch, pasted on her smile, and flung out her arms to either side — *ta-da! Take my picture!* The front door swung open, and Lani stood there, staring into the atrium entry, not entering.

"Surprise!" Melody shouted from the living room. Her artful sewing hand traced an arc in the air, pointing out her arrangement of birthday balloons. But of course it was no surprise. Why else did Melody think Lani had returned?

"Where's Gran?" Lani asked, still not stepping inside.

"Silly! She's taking a rest, getting ready for your party."

"What party? You never told me about any party."

Melody laughed. "We always have a party on your birthday. It's about time you came home."

"I only came back to get my stuff. And to see Gran. I promised her."

Melody's smile slipped, and a dark look took its place, but only for an instant, and then she repaired her face. "We're not going to have any of that nonsense, not tonight. This is your party, and everyone's going to be happy. Understand? It's not every day that you turn sixteen. Everyone's coming to dinner tonight, so you just go wash up. I've made up the futon for you in my sewing room with your favorite sheets."

"Aren't you forgetting something, Mother?"

Melody fingered the scarf she'd draped round her throat to match her capris. She glanced at the dining room table, set for eight with the Flynn family china. A ninth setting of plastic for Rosie squeezed next to Melody's position at the kitchen-end head of the table. "No, I don't think so," she said. "Your father is supposed to be out buying charcoal for the barbeque. He of course forgot to check his supply."

"I'm a vegetarian."

"I know, that's too bad. Tsk, tsk. But don't worry. You're having a veggie burger."

"Couldn't we ever, like, have something I like? Like, pasta? It's *my* birthday."

"Yes, dear, I was there, too. That's why we're having a party. Everyone's coming. I've made sure of that."

"Everyone? Who's everyone?"

"Why, the family, of course, you silly girl."

"I'm not staying. Kapono's outside, waiting."

"Well, you just tell him to come inside. It's about time we meet him. What a lucky boy he is! He'll get to meet the entire family. Except for Silvia's children, of course. They think they're above such games, but they'll be sorry one day."

"Games? MOTH-TH-THER! You're joking, right? I'm not five years old anymore."

Melody laughed. "Don't tell your grandmum. She'll be so disappointed. You don't want to disappoint her, do you? She's already confused enough. Can't you just do this one little thing for her? Think of someone else for a change?"

Lani sighed and glanced over her shoulder. "I guess I'll just go tell Kapono not to wait for me."

Lani bowed her head and slinked back down the driveway. The front door remained open, letting warm, muggy air into the air-conditioned house. Melody gave a long sigh of annoyance, shut the door but did not latch it, then climbed back up onto her stepladder with another balloon and a fistful of tape.

Since Rosie was napping, Hank followed Lani, first outside. The slits of Kapono's eyes tightened as he listened to her. "Hey, it's the fam," she said. "It's not my idea."

Hank wondered if Kapono could even see Lani; he sure as heck couldn't tell. But he must've, because the boy reached out and cupped Lani's chin with his palm, tilting her head back to a kiss-me pose. Lani closed her eyes, waiting for the kiss, but instead he traced an outline of her lips with his other index finger and said, "See you 'round." Then he released her and slid behind the wheel of his dented Honda Civic. Lani's eyes popped open, and she watched with Hank as the car lurched away, like a bat out of hell. Lani muttered "Shit," then turned and strode up the driveway. Hank struggled to keep up with her furious pace.

Lani slammed the front door behind her. "Are you satisfied, MOTHER?" She stormed upstairs, taking the steps two at a time, and slammed the sewing room door behind her, too. By the time Hank caught up to her, Lani was face-down on the futon, sobbing.

Hank had never been good at consoling women. He'd simply had other things on his mind, which was probably the cause of the failure of his first marriage, if the truth were told.

The door rattled. "Lani! Unlock this door!"

"Go away, Mother."

"You don't have time to feel sorry for yourself. I have a list of jobs for you, and I have to go over my list with you."

"Go AWAY, Mother."

"All right, dear, I'll give you ten minutes to wash your face. No more, though. Our guests will be arriving soon."

Hank hovered above Lani, hesitating just an instant before slipping down into her space, reminding her. Maybe Lani could help derail her mother's intentions to farm out Rosie.

Lani jerked up, flinging Hank out of her head. She swung her feet over the side of the futon and wiped her eyes. She sprang to her feet and stormed across the room to a dresser, yanked drawers open, one by one, pawed through the neatly folded pieces of silk and cotton.

"All right, where is it, Mother?" Lani muttered to herself and to Hank. "Where'd you hide it?" She rummaged through shelves of pattern books and boxes of tracing paper. She pulled open the closet and riffled through garments under construction. She collapsed to her hands and knees and peered under an armchair, although it was not likely that Melody would stash anything valuable on the floor.

Lani stuck out her lower lip and blew out her frustration at a wayward piece of hair irritating her eyes. Then, inspiration lit her face, and she scrambled to her feet and ran to the door. Slowly, carefully, quietly, she turned the knob and pulled the hollow wood open a crack. She put her eyeball up to that slit, then opened the door further and stuck her head out into the hall, looking both ways, back and forth. Satisfied, she darted out onto the berber and tiptoed toward her parents' bedroom, where she replayed her previous pawing action through bureaus and night tables.

Finally, she scored. In her mother's lingerie drawer, amidst a mound of nylons, inside a neatly tucked pair of knee-high stockings, her fingers stumbled across a lump that shouldn't be there. She unfolded the bundle and pulled out a shark's tooth necklace. From the way her jaw dropped, Hank could tell that wasn't what she'd been looking for. Still, it caught her interest. Such necklaces were a dime a dozen here in Hawaii. Why had Melody carefully hidden an inexpensive tourist curio?

A smile tugged at the corners of Lani's lips. She pocketed the necklace, then refolded the pair of stockings and fluffed up the mound in a semblance of Melody-order. She continued her search, opening drawers, sifting through shelves, the closet.

"Ah-ha!" she cried when she flipped off the lid to a shoe box. A shudder rolled through Lani as she pulled out a pocket-sized book with a bent, black cover. She clutched her journal to her bosom and leaned her forehead against the door of the closet. Then, as an afterthought, she fanned through the pages. Yes, the book appeared to be intact.

Hank noticed that Lani forgot to replace the shoe box lid. She was careful to restore everything else to its pre-search appearance, but that one thing she forgot in her relief to reclaim her treasure.

Back in the sewing room, Lani hid the journal under the dresser, a place Melody wasn't likely to search. She fastened the shark tooth necklace round her throat, then bounced downstairs.

Rosie was shuffling back and forth from the door of the kitchen, across the living room, to the hall by the front door, and back again. She lurched to a stop when Lani and Hank flushed down the stairs, and her eyebrows arched.

"Hi, Gran. D'you have a nice nap?" Lani bent down to kiss Rosie on the cheek.

"Well," Melody said, appearing from the kitchen. "You seem to be in a better mood. Good thing, too, since you don't have much time to fill the water glasses. They'll be here any minute. Your father showed up, and now I have him working on the grill. Remember, two ice cubes per glass, no more, no less. Got that?"

Lani opened her mouth to reply, then decided against whatever retort she had in mind. Her head jerked in a sort of indifferent nod of acceptance as she helped Rosie down onto the sofa. "Comfy, Gran?"

Rosie focused her empty stare on Lani, the vacuous look that told Hank she was working hard to remember her granddaughter. She knew she should know her. Her own flesh and blood carried a certain Ayres-Berryhill scent, after all, but she just couldn't quite recall the details of who when and where. Lani didn't notice, and she headed for the balloon-rimmed door to the lanai. She slid the glass open and called, "Hey, Dad, what's going down?"

Martin was wrestling with a bag of charcoal. "Can't get the goddamned thing to light."

"I don't think it'll help to throw more charcoal in."

"What the hell do you know?" he shouted, dropping the bag and snatching up a can of lighter fluid. "How many of these goddamned grills have you ever lit in your life?"

"Martin! Not like that!" Melody hurried out of the kitchen and shoved Lani aside. Just then, the doorbell rang. "Oh dear, they're here already. Lani, go answer that, while I help your dad."

"Whatever."

Vanessa and Silvia stood side by side on the front stoop, each bearing gifts, while Caleb stood behind them, shuffling his feet and digging his hands in his trouser pockets.

"Surprise!" Vanessa said. She thrust her department-store-wrapped gift (the bigger the better, and it would be impractical, knowing Vanessa) at Lani, pecked her on the cheek, and breezed inside.

"Happy Birthday," Silvia murmured, handing over her home-wrapped gift with the uneven taping job (probably a practical watch, judging from the cube shape of it). She folded Lani into a bear hug, nearly smothering her with the extra rolls of baby fat she'd built up with each of her pregnancies.

Those two sisters were as unlike each other, Hank thought, as Melody and Barry, who at least had the excuse of gender for their differences.

Caleb padded inside after the women and waggled his eyebrows at Lani. "I have a gift for you, too, but it's at the store. You ought to come by after school one day."

"Okay, Unca Caleb, thanks!" Lani adored him, Hank could tell from the smile in her eyes. As for her aunts, well, they were another matter.

Melody stepped in from the lanai and swiped her hands together, then examined her nails for traces of charcoal dust. "Welcome!" she sang. "Where are Mom and Dad Flynn?" She glanced around the room with anticipation, as if in search of a surprise, one especially for her.

"They're coming separately," Vanessa said. "You know how they are."

"They'll be here any minute," Silvia said.

"That's perfect, because we've had a little delay." Melody dipped her head in the direction of the lanai and gave a rueful grin (if Hank ever saw rue, this was it). She perked up, switching a switch. "But we'll be ready soon. Won't we, Lani?"

Lani ignored her, in favor of shaking her gifts.

"Anything I can do to help?" Silvia asked in the tiny voice that did not go along with her physical size.

"Yes you can," Melody said, showing off her famous smile. "I have just the job for you. Come with me, and I'll show you." As she turned for the kitchen, she stopped and added, "That's good, Mom. You sit right there on my nice sofa, where I can see you from the kitchen, and you can see everyone."

Silvia waddled after Melody, and they disappeared together into the kitchen.

Vanessa headed for Martin's liquor cabinet. "I'll help myself. Don't mind me. Kay, what can I get you?"

Caleb scowled and twitched, as if a pesky fly buzzed his face. In this case, the pest was his sister-in-law's nickname for him. His declaring that he didn't like the name only fueled her persistence in using it, so he'd learned long ago not to mention it again. Instead, he twitched.

"Nothing?" Vanessa said. "But Kay, this is an important occasion. It's not every day that a girl becomes a woman. How 'bout you, Lani? What'll you have?"

"Diet Coke."

"Hon-n-n-ney!"

Lani popped the ribbons off the over-sized package Vanessa had handed her. Caleb glanced at Vanessa, checking her reaction, but she was busy pouring vodka into a tall glass. Then he cast a worried glance at the kitchen door. Still, no Melody.

"Hey," he finally said, "are you supposed to be opening your gifts already? Your mom probably has a schedule."

Lani shrugged and ripped the paper down one long side of the box. She tugged at the lid, tearing it as she pulled it off. She stared at the fluffy thing inside, "hot pink" Rosie would call the color.

Lani grabbed the thing by its neck and pulled it out of its nest — a stuffed flamingo dressed in a tuxedo coat with a stove-pipe hat. She hooted.

"Did you win this at some fair?" she asked, plopping it onto the sofa next to Rosie. The glint in Lani's eyes cooled way down. Rosie arched her eyebrows and leaned away from the flamingo.

*Don't worry, old girl, it's not real. What's not real can't hurt you.*

Vanessa handed Lani a can of soda. "It made you laugh, though, didn't it?"

They giggled together, and Caleb sauntered out to the lanai. Men had to gravitate together in a house full of women, Hank understood. Melody emerged from the kitchen with a platter of raw meat.

"What's going on out here?" she said, smiling in anticipation of the game. "Where'd you get your friend, Mom?"

Rosie turned and stared at Hank, who perched atop the coffee table and murmured sweet nothings in return. Her eyebrows settled back in place.

Vanessa laughed louder, but Lani fell into a silent sulk, mad, apparently, at having been coaxed to laugh against her will.

"Did you remember about the ice cubes, dear?" Melody asked.

"Yep."

Melody nodded in the direction of the table. This time her smile showed the tips of her incisors. "But where are they?"

"I dunno, in the freezer, I guess."

Silvia, who'd followed in Melody's wake, did a U-turn and scuttled back into the kitchen. "I'll get the ice." Squeak, squeak.

"I hear you've got a boyfriend," Vanessa said, gliding over to Lani's side and staring deep into her eyes, as if she could read her fortune there.

Lani stared back. Her face went dead-pan, obscuring whatever information Vanessa searched for there.

"That's right," Melody said-sang, sailing toward the door to the lanai with her platter of meat. "I had *so* hoped Kapono would join us for dinner tonight, but he had other plans."

"Kapono?" Vanessa said. "Hawaiian, is he? Is that where you got that shark's tooth you're wearing? He probably gave it to you for your birthday, I'll bet."

Melody sucked in her breath, sucking the warm ambience of this family gathering right out of the air. Hank floated off the coffee table and squeezed between Rosie and the flamingo. The three of them shivered together.

"*What* shark's tooth?" Melody's face paled as she slunk away from the lanai door and tiptoed closer to Lani. "Where'd *that* come from?"

"Why, Mother? Don't you like to have your stuff searched? Imagine that!"

"What are you suggesting? You think that necklace is mine? I'm sorry, you're mistaken. *I* would never wear anything so tacky."

"That's why you hid it, huh?"

"I don't know what you're talking about."

Hank, Rosie, and Vanessa watched their exchange as if it were a Ping Pong match. Then the sound of the door swooshing open, admitting a puff of burning charcoal, brought the match to an abrupt halt.

"What who's talking about?" Martin asked from the doorway. "And where in hell's the meat? I'm ready. You want the goddamned fire to go out?"

"Nothing important, dear," Melody said, recovering. "They just surprised me, that's all."

Sure, Hank thought. Melody didn't slip often, but when she did, it was a sure-fired signal of a tsunami approaching.

# OCEAN CITY, 1983

**To celebrate Hank's** birthday each summer, the family always took a beach vacation together. Rosamonde had a bad feeling about this one. She and Hank had taken lovely trips since his retirement nine years ago this coming September — goodness, had it been so long? Not that the vacations before retirement had been so bad, either. It's just that ever since that gold watch dinner party, she and Hank had done special things. Extravagant things, like riding the gondolas of Venice, things no one could any longer do, like climbing the pyramids at Chichén Itzá. It was as if they searched for a blaze of glory before their lives would eventually go out.

They'd always loved the beach, but really, there was nothing extravagant about it, at least not on the east coast. It was a quiet, restful place, not too far from home in case one of the kids needed them. They never needed them these days now that they were so far away — Melody in Hawaii and Barry in Colorado. She wondered sometimes what was the use of having children if they moved so

187

far away from home?

Of course, no one even knew where home was anymore. Home had been lots of places over the course of their lifetime. Home was where the family was. Home *was* family. But she missed the idea of home being centered on a place. Maybe she'd missed an important piece of her life by giving that up to the gypsy way of life with Hank.

On the beach, Rosamonde saw lots of families. None of them were hers, however. Seeing other families together, playing together in the waves, laughing together under their beach umbrellas, running together with paddleballs or volleyballs or kites, building sand castles together — all of it made Rosamonde miss her own family all the more.

They used to take the kids every summer to one of the beaches up and down the east coast after moving to Maryland. Before that, when they lived in New Mexico, the kids had never even seen the ocean. What was the ocean without the kids? Ocean was kids, same as home was family. It was endless water, stretching to the horizon and beyond. As far as she could see. And it went even farther than that. She'd never known that any space could be so empty. Sure, the beaches were crowded, and the line of waves filled with tumbling bodies. Beyond the surfers there were a few fishing boats. After that, an occasional freighter outlined on the horizon. And miles of nothing.

Nothingness unsettled her. It left her with a weak feeling in her knees, reminiscent of vertigo when she peered over the edge of the tippy top spire at the cathedral of Salisbury.

Renting the cottage should've been Rosamonde's first clue that this vacation was doomed. Duh-DA-duh-duh duh-DA-duh-duh, Jaws was on the prowl. Not even their fifth choice of cottages had been available because Rosamonde hadn't phoned at the right time to make the reservation. She was only one week late. So they'd gotten stuck in a cottage that no one else had wanted, old and run down with peeling linoleum floors and sticky casement windows and no air conditioning. The wood on the deck was splintered, and there was no awning, making it less than desirable to sit out there, and there were only plastic chairs, anyway, not the wooden rockers she always liked. At least their cottage was beachfront, as she specified, although a tall dune blocked their view of the waves, but the sea oats were fun to watch swaying in the steady breeze.

She wasn't complaining. They hadn't *had* to take the cottage. Being in this one was better than the alternative of being a block or more off the beach, where heat rolled over the rows and rows of bungalow rooftops and blistered up from pavement, suffocating everyone caught in between, and all you could hear was the purr of air conditioners, not the rolling surf.

No, she wasn't complaining. It was just a sign, that's all, and she should've paid better attention.

The next sign was when the kids decided not to come. It was too far to travel, Melody complained, and anyway, why should she leave her perfect beach there? Why didn't they all go to Hawaii, instead, where it was a paradise? And Barry couldn't get off work from the bar, not even to go see his family.

Rosamonde should've known that this vacation was doomed.

Hank had said, "Why the hell should we change our plans because of the kids?"

And so they went. Playing gin rummy with just the two of them was not the same. Strolling the boardwalk, munching roasted peanuts and salt water taffy wasn't the same with just the two of them. They tried to absorb the energy radiating from the boardwalk like waves of heat, but they'd taken in too much sun instead and they couldn't absorb more.

They sat alone together at a Formica table in a crowded fish place eating their fried flounder. Silence hung over their dinner, damped by a smell of frying grease, although the place bustled around them with noise. Customers rushed in to take out meals to their sunburned families. She and Hank could've taken their flounder back to the cottage, too, but eating in a lively place was one way to grasp at a bit of outside contact.

The cottage was too quiet. And empty, like the ocean.

Rosamonde read both of the books she brought with her in the first half of their week, and she had to go to the little pharmacy, which carried more beach balls and sunscreen than actual drugs. The single rack of paperbacks contained bestsellers and romances. She'd already read half of them. The bestsellers, that is. She wasn't desperate enough yet to read romances. And the other half were too feel-good for her reading tastes. Not that she didn't want to feel *good*. She already felt great and thought she must be the luckiest woman alive. But she wanted more in a book than that. She wanted something to chew over. A puzzle.

She loved puzzles of all types. Jigsaw puzzles were her favorite type of puzzle, not for the sake of moving pieces around, fitting shapes together, but for the pictures that developed. Her favorite picture puzzles were landscapes populated with people that unfolded a story.

The pharmacy had an array of puzzles, but they were all ocean vistas or gardens. They were nice, but this was the wrong time of year to work a jigsaw puzzle, anyway. That was a better activity for being closed in during the winter, best beside a roaring fire in the hearth and mugs of hot chocolate for each member of the family. Puzzles were not for outdoors at the beach. This was the time of beachballs.

Next to the shelf of puzzles was a wire bin of colorful balls in all sizes. She was particularly drawn to a cobalt blue ball, a nice pumpkin size. Blue was her favorite color, and cobalt her favorite shade of blue, like the sky over a New Mexico desert before night descended, and she imagined a spaceship settling down and E.T. taking her for a ride. But you had to have two to make a ball worthwhile, and she and Hank had slowed way down for that sort of activity. She moved on to the shovels and buckets and thought about building a sand castle and imagined the good king who would live inside her castle and the neighboring bad king who wanted to steal away the lovely princess...

She ended up settling on *The Hotel New Hampshire*, which she'd already read, but it was worth another read.

Why oh why had they come to the beach? Neither Rosamonde nor Hank particularly enjoyed swimming, although they did enjoy strolling along the water's edge. That must be where she lost her cameo. The clasp must've broken, and that beautiful wedding gift must've slipped off the chain and fallen unnoticed into a wave that swept it out to sea, lost forever. That's what happens, she told herself, when you take precious things to a place like the beach — you lose them.

Once a day, she and Hank would venture into the surf, no farther than up to their waists, and they let the waves wash over them, bouncing them off their feet, then depositing sand in the crotch of their bathing suits. If the tide was going out, Hank would push farther, just past the line of breakers, and he would swim back and forth, parallel to shore among the swells while Rosamonde watched, getting her knees battered. She wouldn't be able to rescue him if he needed rescuing, but she watched anyway, as if her watching kept Hank safer that way.

But she couldn't keep him safe. She couldn't keep the world safe. Life — but mostly death — went on (AIDS, and cyanide-laced Tylenol, and embassy bombings) and there wasn't a darned thing Rosamonde could do about it. She focused her effort on Hank, on reassuring him that the state of the world wasn't his fault. If he and the others at Los Alamos hadn't opened Pandora's Box, someone else would've. The Russians. God forbid, the Nazis. And then what would the world have been like today? No, it wasn't Hank's fault. Life and death were beyond their control. It was their job to make do the best they could with what they had. Lord, they'd come a long way from their origins in coal-mining hills. She wondered how many bastards on welfare back there shared her genes while she played decadently in the waves. There was no way to tell, but she bet she had secret family, still hidden away in the hills. She and Hank had had to escape when they had. The cost of their escape was world destruction. Those were the demons that drove Hank. Rosamonde knew it wasn't true. The demons were all in his head.

Hank felt driven by the ticking clock of the world's imminent destruction, and for that, he felt driven to experience life and the world before it would self-destruct. They knew it would all come to an end one day, but Rosamonde hadn't expected her world to end while on vacation. Vacations were for resting, loving, living. Not dying.

So when Hank awoke her one night after a day in the surf, on the sand, reading, eating fish, boardwalk walking, and playing cards, at first she didn't understand. Her mind refused to uncurl from the residue of the day, refused to let go of the sense of peace and contentment that filled her, refused still to recognize the warning signals that she'd ignored up until now. Pains in his left arm? Whatever did he mean? He'd swum too hard that day in the swells, against the current. Perhaps he was too old to pretend to be a young man anymore. His youth was taken from him with Trinity. He'd stopped being a young man when the Enola Gay opened her bay doors.

But the pains didn't pass, and Rosamonde knew it was up to her. She had to do something. She had to save him. She had to forge farther into the surf and pull him back from the brink of death.

Should she call for help? She didn't want to wait for an

ambulance to show up. Hank could be dead by then.

Why oh why hadn't Melody and Barry come along?

No, it was up to her. The car. Yes, the car. She would drive Hank. She could do that, even though Hank had become the driver, her chauffeur, since his retirement. He had nowhere else to go any more, nothing else to do with life other than cart her around to her bridge games or the grocery store or the hairdresser or the library.

Could she even drive anymore?

Where would she take him? He needed a hospital, but where was it? Hank could die while she floundered around, searching.

Go. Just go. Now.

She slipped a housedress over her head. It ended up backwards, but she didn't care. She grabbed her pocketbook and guided Hank, still in his pajamas, outside to the car, a Buick.

"No, you can't drive," she told him, and she opened the passenger door and nudged him gently into the seat.

Her fingers fumbled with the keyring. Which key was it, goshdurnit? This one looked right, and she stabbed it into the ignition and managed to start the car. Now where?

She'd seen a little clinic, which probably mostly treated sunburn and scrapes, but they'd know where she would have to take Hank.

The paramedics took one look at Hank, then took him by ambulance to the nearest hospital. So Rosamonde had to wait after all. Wait, as they wormed through traffic, and she squeezed Hank's hand.

"Can't you hurry a little faster?" she said through the tiny window to the driver. "Maybe turn on that siren of yours?"

"We're doing the best we can, ma'am."

After an eternity, they pulled into the hospital driveway, pushed Hank's gurney through the sliding doors of the emergency entrance. Rosamonde stumbled down the brightly lit hallway behind them and felt like a wave rushing to shore, rushing to engulf its victims, sweep them away.

Rosamonde hated hospitals. The antiseptic smell crept through her being like a poison. Hospitals reminded her of death, not a place that saved lives. She still shuddered from the memory of her brother's death in a Zanesville hospital so long ago — more than forty years, she thought. He'd died a long, drawn-out, painful death years after his mining accident.

*Please, God, don't let Hank die!*

Rosamonde wasn't ready to be a widow. She was far too young to be cursed with the loss of her life's soul-mate. If Hank survived the stroke, she swore she'd never ask for a thing more. Why oh why had they chosen this particular time to go on vacation? Away from their own doctors. She hadn't known where to take Hank when he'd awakened her with pains in his left arm.

At the beginning of the week, when they moved into their rental cottage on the beach, she'd thought it so grand here. Now she thought it hell. She only wanted to escape. Break out of the hospital with Hank and run away where no medical problems could ever touch them again.

She'd had a bad feeling about coming here.

# THIRTEEN

No no no no no! I know what you mean to do, but there's nothing wrong with me. Not at all! I am not stupid. You think you can fool me, but you cannot. I know that long word Melody said. Ap-ap-ap-ap...poing? The word sounds funny, but it's not funny. It means "doctor" and I hate hate hate hate going there not at home.

"Damn godamnit fuck you to hell!" I say, and Melody turns her neck in slow motion to show me the color of her eyes. Yes, maybe she has heard me this time. Goodie! I cannot be sure, so I wave my arm over my head. Something flies out of my hand. I think it is that flowered thing she gives me to drink with. The lighting thingie on the table on the other side of the room suddenly wobbles and falls and crashes apart into splinters all over the floor. Oh my. How did it break like that, all on its own?

She is running. Melody is afraid. But she is not as afraid as I am afraid.

You tell her, Hank. You tell her no no no no.

"Martin," she says. I do not know anyone by that name. She is trying to confuse me, but I am not stupid. "Martin, go get Nolan."

"Damn godamnit fuck you to hell!" I say. I am always a player of words, yet I do not know what a Nolan is.

"Quick, Martin, go after him. He can't have gone far."

Hank! Where are you? Why don't you tell her? Tell her to stop. Stop! Stop! Stop!

The thirsty one snarls and shows his teeth, the way old Blue used to do long long ago. How I miss old Blue. Blue, where are you? Are you hiding from me? I am coming for you, Blue, oh yes I am. Here I come. I'll bet you're hiding in one of my rooms, just like all the rest.

The thirsty one is gone, and now Melody is running again. She runs to another thing, the talking thing. "Caleb?" she says into it. How can someone be inside that little bitty thing? She does not sound afraid anymore. "We're home, and we could sure use a bit of help."

"Damn damn damn damn you!" I tell her again. *I* am not home, and neither is the person in the talk thingie.

But she does not hear me. "Yes, yes," she says, "but Martin is useless, you understand?"

So I raise my voice. "Fuck you damn damn goddit!"

She is not listening to me. She still speaks to the person inside the talk thing. No one hears me. No one listens anymore. "Caleb, I need your help..."

Hank, I need your help.

You tell her about... Oh dear, I shall have to go through the rooms of my mind for that. But I don't want to hurt. I shan't go there. No.

Hank? Where are you, Hank?

Are you hiding from me again?

I think I must hide, too. That way I'll find you. Hah.

#

**Hank didn't need** the elevator at Jewell's high-rise condominium. He shot up through the elevator shaft to the ninth floor, and then stepped through the closed door of Jewell's unit. She and Lani sprawled on their backs on the floor and stared up at the clacking ceiling fan. Their feet rested atop the glass surface of the coffee table, and they appeared deep in conversation.

"Nice necklace," Jewell said. "Birthday present?"

"Sort of."

"Don't tell me. Let me guess. It's from Kapono, am I right?"

"Naw, he split."

"How come? You didn't...?"

Lani shook her head.

"So what'd you tell him?"

"I'm not ready for that," Lani said.

"Smart girl. You've got plenty of time to get serious. Besides, there are lots of fish in the sea."

"Now you sound like my mom."

"That's not too surprising after all our years together. How old are you, kiddo?"

"Sixteen."

"Then that's how long your mom and I have known each other."

Lani swung her long legs from the table onto the floor and rolled over to sit upright. "What I don't get is how come you and my mom ever started hanging out together. You guys are so different from each other."

"We had a mutual friend. And then... Hell, I don't know. Sometimes we don't always pick our friends. Love happens."

"You mean, you didn't *want* to become friends with my mom? I can believe that. Who would?"

"Don't be so hard on your mother."

"She treats me like a baby."

"What do you expect? You'll always be her baby, in her eyes."

"She's not the only one."

"There are others? Who else?"

"Like, everyone."

"Not your dad."

"Dad doesn't treat me like anything, 'cause he doesn't even know I exist."

"Um, well... He may not be so good at saying what he feels."

"Yeah? How do you know?"

"Men are often that way. Besides, your mom tells me a few things from time to time. Don't underestimate your mom, kiddo. She's a very talented woman, and she knows how to handle people, besides. She usually gets what she wants. Try not to let the way she is bother you too much. That's what I do, and we get along fine."

"You mean, you give in to her. Yeah, I thought so. She always gets her way. Just ask my dad."

"Martin?" Jewell swung her feet from the table and knocked over a glass of iced tea in the process. "Oh, darn, now look what I've done." She jumped up and ran into the kitchen for a tea towel, then returned to mop up the mess. Lani followed along, going through the motions of helping, but anyone could see her heart wasn't in being very helpful.

"What did you mean about asking your dad?" Jewell said when they were done cleaning up and settled cross-legged on a goat-skin rug. "Why do you want *me* to ask him?"

"Not you. Ask anyone, I mean. Dad's never around anymore. I think he can't stand her nagging him all the time. She's good at that. I wish he'd just argue back sometimes, y'know? Instead, he lets her walk all over him, and then he goes away and plays golf or something. Isn't she like that with you, too? Doesn't she try to run over you, too?"

"I'm her boss, remember."

"Oh, yeah. But I'll bet there's not a single other person on the planet that she listens to, besides you. She'll never listen to me, never ever."

"Have you tried talking to her?"

"I don't have to. She snoops in my diary."

"That's not acceptable. No wonder you're upset."

"Yeah."

"No wonder you needed to get away."

"Yeah."

"Well, kiddo, you can stay here for a while, but not indefinitely. You'll have to go back sooner or later. Your grandmother needs you."

"Yeah, I guess she does, doesn't she?"

Hank flitted through Lani's head and deposited a picture of Rosie, waiting... Alone... Yearning for her family...

Lani cocked her head and stared at the ceiling, deep in thought. "Gran needs me to protect her from Mom."

*That's right. You got it.*

"'Protect'?" Jewell said. "Isn't that a bit dramatic?"

"Now you're sounding like Mom again." Lani frowned.

"Sorry, kiddo. I don't want to be one of the evil adults. We can't help who we are."

"You're not like the rest. How come you're so cool, unlike my mom?"

Jewell laughed. "You think I'm cool?"

"Sure. You let me stay with you. Most adults would've told me to go home."

"You'll go home when you're ready."

"Well, if I lived with you, I bet you wouldn't treat me like a baby the way Mom does, snooping in my diary, would you?"

"I believe in a person's right to privacy, but I can't say what I'd do if I had a daughter."

"Do you ever wish you had? A daughter, I mean?"

"I don't have to. I have you."

"But I mean, don't you ever wish you'd gotten married and had a family?"

"I don't have time for that. I have the store instead. The store is my family, and all that comes with it. You... Your mom..."

"I wish I could live with you instead."

"Then we couldn't have our nice little chats like this, could we?"

Lani snorted. "No one wants to talk with me now that Gran's here. Gran is like all Mom can think of."

"Maybe your mother feels guilty about something."

"Mom's never guilty. She never makes a mistake, not ever, so how can she feel guilty about anything?"

"Good point."

"You think she's got something to feel guilty about?"

"Kiddo, *everyone* is guilty of *some*thing."

"Yeah? Like, what'd you ever do that was so wrong?"

"Plenty. We don't need to go there."

*But you will,* Hank thought, stepping into Jewell's space with an image in mind of his wronged daughter. It was time Melody found out. Time to let something else preoccupy Melody enough to interfere with her plans to commit Rosie. That's why he'd come here.

Jewell must've gotten Hank's message, for she sprang to her feet, tumbling Hank's presence out of her. She paced back and forth, rubbing her arms as if suddenly cold. Her brow creased with a frown.

Lani watched her, her head moving back and forth. "Something wrong with your guy?"

"No. There's no guy. That's over."

"How come? I mean, it hasn't even started yet, has it? How can it be over after a first date?"

"It wasn't a first date."

"Oh. So, it *was* a date, after all. Like, how long were you going out?"

"You ask a lot of questions that aren't any of your business, don't you? No wonder your mom kicked you out."

"Hey, if you don't want to talk about it, just say so."

"Okay. I don't want to talk about it."

"Okay."

"Okay, then." Jewell sighed. "Look. Sometimes you find out guys aren't who you think they are. Only then, it's too late."

"You mean...he *lied* to you? What a creep! Just like my mom. Except Mom lies so smoothly she doesn't even know when she's lying."

"He knew, all right, but it doesn't matter, because it's over. And so is this conversation."

"How can anyone expect me to learn about guys and all if they won't talk to me?"

"Okay, you want to talk? I'll tell you what you need to know, kiddo. We can't always do what our hearts want us to do."

"I'm never going to be like that. Why shouldn't I do what I want to do?"

"Because then you might end up hurting other people you love. Nothing — no guy, no one person — is ever worth that, making it so that you end up left all alone, without your loved ones surrounding you."

"Are you telling me you have to give up what *you* want just to keep from hurting someone else?"

"Yeah, I guess so."

"That sucks."

"Yes, it does."

"Well, I don't care if I hurt my mom. What about the way she hurt me? I'm not gonna let her run my life for me, no way. *Every*thing I do is wrong, according to *her.*"

"No, kiddo, that's not true."

"Even if I tried to do what Mom wants, it'd still be wrong. How do I know if I'm ever doing anything right? Can't you, like, talk to her for me or something?"

Jewell stopped pacing and sighed. Her chin dropped in a defeated nod. "It's time, isn't it? This can't go on any longer. Love happens sometimes. You don't ask for it to hit you when it does. Then you have to be strong enough to know whether or not you can accept it."

*Are you going to be strong enough?* Hank thought. *Strong enough to do the right thing?*

#

**The bell jangled** over the main door to Caleb's Corner, and Lani strode inside, into the dim interior of the store. Right on schedule. Just as Hank had planned.

"Unca Caleb?" she called.

205

"Back here, Lani," he said from a leather armchair in the far corner of the store. Rosie sat in Hank's lap, and together they rocked a platform rocker, creaking it back and forth. Her gaze focused on the oak table before them as Hank whispered sweet nothings in her ear.

Lani's sneakers thumped along the wooden floor as she raced through the store. "Gran!" she said, bursting upon them. They might've made a Norman Rockwell painting the way they sat there, so together, so big-time family in the center of Caleb's mock lounge a la turn of the century. The previous century, that is.

Rosie didn't look up. She and Hank kept on rocking.

"I skipped the beach today to go home and spend some time with you, Gran," Lani said, "but Mom said Unca Caleb brought you over here. What's going down?"

Caleb answered, as if he understood the question. "Nothing much. Your grandmother needed a little outing, I think, so I went over there to get her."

"You? But how could you leave your store? Why didn't Mom bring her?"

The ends of Caleb's mouth turned down. "I don't think she could this time. She tried to reach your dad to help, but I guess he was away, so she called me — "

"What do you mean Mom *couldn't*?"

"Just that. I guess each of them, your mom and grandmother, had their own ideas about what they wanted to do, only those ideas mixed about as well as oil and vinegar."

"Oh, I get it. Gran, you had a fight with Mom? Cool! Looks

like you won, too."

"I'm glad you came by, Lani. Now I can show you your present." Caleb pulled himself out of the armchair and padded around the oak table to the opposite perimeter of his lounge area. He'd created a boundary that separated his lounge from the rest of the store by wedging together odd pieces of wooden cabinets. He patted one of them. "Here it is. This is why I couldn't bring it to your party. You like it?"

Lani gasped. "You're giving me...*furniture*?"

His face twisted with a smile of pain. "Not just any 'furniture'. This is a genuine, nineteenth century secretary, all maple. See? This little door pulls down and becomes a desk. Inside there are little pigeon holes and shelves for your private writing materials. And best of all, Lani, it's got a key. You can lock it up. Keep your important stuff private." He held up a tiny skeleton key between his fingers, then tossed it up and down in the palm of his hand.

"No way!" Lani raced to Caleb's side and folded him into a bear hug. She buried her face against his shoulder and sniffled.

"You like it?" he asked.

"Do I like it?" She pulled away from him and stared at him through the tears streaming down her face. "It's the best. You're the best. Thanks, Unca Caleb! But... Where am I gonna put it? I don't have a room anymore."

"You will, Lani. I'll keep it here for you until you're ready." He placed the key in her hand and closed her fingers around it. "Now, if you don't mind sitting with your grandmother a bit, I'll just go back to my business. Traffic always picks up over the holidays."

"Okay, Unca Caleb." She wiped her face with the back of her hand and sniffed again.

"Your grandmother sure looks happy now. Guess she likes it here. No place like home for the holidays." Caleb smiled at Rosie in the rocker and headed back to his cash register toward the front of the store.

Lani gazed like a loving parent at her new writing desk, pocketed the key in her jeans pocket, then danced back to Rosie, where she knelt beside the platform rocker. "Hey, Gran, I bet all this old stuff reminds you of home, huh?"

Rosie stared straight ahead. The table before them was filled with the pieces of a partially assembled jigsaw puzzle.

"We don't have any antiques at home. Mom won't allow them. What am I gonna do?" Lani glanced back at her uncle's gift. "I think they're kinda' nice. Cozy and comfy nice. I guess they're not antiques to you, are they?"

Rosie finally blinked.

"You were alive when this stuff was new. Well, not all of it, but lots, I'll bet." Lani scanned the crowded contents of the store around her. She turned back to Rosie. Awe shone from the coal-black depths of her eyes. "It's probably still new to you, huh Gran?"

Rosie's lips twitched.

"I know what, Gran! Maybe you can help me. I have to do a research paper on World War II for my history class, and I'll bet you can tell me what it was like living back then, huh? I'll list you as a source, okay?"

Rosie's lips moved faster and faster.

"What's that, Gran? Are you saying something? I can't hear you."

Rosie stood up slowly from the rocker, releasing Hank. She stepped cautiously the few steps across to the oak table.

Lani sprang to her feet, catching her grandmother by the elbow and following her to the table. "Hey, it's the puzzle! You been working this, Gran? Looks like more pieces have been worked. You can see some of the picture now. Hey! What happened?"

She backed away from the table and peered through the store in the direction of the cash register. "Hey, Unca Caleb! What happened to the other puzzle? This one's different."

"No, it's the same one, Lani."

She rubbed her brow and frowned. "That's funny. I could swear... Oh well. I guess we can work this one, too."

Lani returned to Rosie's side and peered over her shoulder at the spots of developing picture. "Remember, Gran? Remember how you used to always make up stories about the puzzles when we worked them together? Where'd this little guy in the yellow jacket come from? He's on crutches. I wonder what happened to him?"

Pulling away from the table, she surveyed the clutter of the store and called out to her uncle. "Where's that boxtop, so we can see what the picture's supposed to be?"

"Oh, it's around somewhere, Lani."

She gave up and turned her attention back to the jigsaw pieces displayed before her. "Funny, I don't remember seeing anyone on crutches before. Did they even have crutches back then? Maybe

I could put that in my report. You'd know, Gran. Did you ever break your leg when you were a little girl?" Lani laughed. "Naw, I can't picture you doing anything dangerous. I bet you never broke your leg. I wonder what the guy in the yellow jacket did to break his leg?"

"He betrayed his best friend," Rosie said.

"No way! And Mom thinks you can't say more than a word or two."

"Of course I talk."

"Tell me more, Gran, please?"

But Rosie stared down at the table. Her gaze fixed on the puzzle.

# ARNIE

**Arnie wasn't as fast** or agile as Lyman. He half galloped, half slid, half tripped over his snowshoes, following Lyman down the hill to the blue bundle. It couldn't be a body. Where on earth had Lyman got such an idea? Lyman must be *expecting* bodies, that's what. On account of his being a spy.

Good thing Arnie wasn't as fast, because he decided all of a sudden that this was a booby trap. Whoever, whatever was under that blue blanket wasn't meant to be out here, and these freezing temperatures and snow drifts were sure to keep lookey-lous away. Lyman must've known all along. His contact was meeting him, yep, that's what Arnie bet. Lyman saw this as his chance to eliminate Dillon Falls's Civil Defense by luring Arnie out to this isolated patch of woods. That's why Lyman didn't talk much. He'd known all along what he was going to have to do. Get rid of Arnie, and you pave the way for a Nazi invasion. Arnie hung back.

Lyman bent over the blue bundle and called up the hill to

Arnie. "It's a girl! She's still alive, but just barely. C'mon, help me get her out of here."

Arnie didn't move. So that's how Lyman meant to do it? With a fabricated girl. But of course that wasn't right. Arnie was too smart to fall for that trick. Why, there weren't any footprints other than Lyman's and his that broke the snowy expanse surrounding them. How on earth could anyone else have gotten here ahead of their breaking out the sugar sap trail? Let alone some girl. It just didn't make sense. There weren't any tracks of any sort, even if a sled had been able to get through the tall drifts. How had a girl gotten here? Nossiree, this was a trap, all right. Probably it wasn't a girl at all but only Lyman's stash of rifles under that blue blanket. There was no body, not even the body of Lyman's contact. Yes, that was it. His contact had left rifles here for him a couple days back, then fresh snow had covered up the tracks. No one could survive long out here, especially not a Nazi far from home.

"C'mon, what're you waiting for?" Lyman shouted. "Are you yellow, or something? She's already half dead. She ain't gonna bite you or nothing."

Arnie felt his blood stir. What did the summer man know about him that he dared to call him yellow? Yellow he wasn't. He'd show him. Even if it meant walking into his stash of contraband. Arnie moved first one foot, then the other, even though they felt like lead weights attached to his snowshoes.

Then he spied a lock of blonde hair. Slipping out from under the blanket. Arnie's legs gave out from beneath him, and he fell down flat on his butt. Cold numbed him right through his coveralls.

How... How could it be? All he could think of was his little girl Peggy, who had blonde hair and wasn't so little anymore. What if the girl under the blue blanket was his very own Peggy? Coming home from that bomb factory and somehow lost her way? Oh, Lord, Lord...

Arnie pushed his numb joints to action, forced himself up to his feet, and stumbled the rest of the way to Lyman's side. He folded back one edge of the blue blanket. It wasn't Peggy, but this girl didn't look a day older. Oh, Lord. "You sure she's alive?"

"Barely. Help me get her up."

"What's she doing here?"

"Hell if I know. Between us, we can carry her back to the horses. You got a doctor in town we can take her to?"

Arnie laughed. For a city boy, Lyman didn't know much. "Naw. Nearest clinic is thirty miles away. We'll take her to the church. Pastor's wife will know how to take care of her."

Lyman snorted. "I seen her. She's not much more'n a kid herself. What does she know?"

"You got a better idea? Look, this girl's gonna freeze to death if we don't get her out of the snow and get her warm."

"What about your trail? You still want to break it out?"

"We got to get her out of here first, and then we'll see how much daylight we got left."

"Maybe none, not if that storm comes." Lyman nodded vaguely in the direction of the thickening cloud cover.

"Son, I reckon the storm has already arrived."

# ADELLE

**Idle hands were the** devil's hands, Adelle thought. She already knew it was so. Mother Daisy didn't have to remind her, but still, her mother-in-law did. At least a hundred times a week. Enough times that now Adelle had to listen to Daisy's nagging voice in her head while she polished the church silver in the Sunday school room. Nearby, little Gloria served a tea party for the church dolls that represented Mary and Joseph.

Worse than idle hands was an idle mind, but luckily those aeroplanes she'd heard had filled her mind this last hour. She'd heard them. And then they'd vanished. That is to say, the machines that made the sound of engines in the sky simply never materialized from across the hills. But she *knew* she'd heard them. Mrs. Wiley had scoffed. Said it was thunder. Even Jim had heard the planes.

Where'd they gone? More importantly, where were they *from*? Mercy in Heaven, she hoped the planes were *theirs* and not...

She chided herself and rubbed harder with her polish until her muscles ached. That's why they had Civil Defense, wasn't it? Oh dear oh dear, maybe Mr. Trimble was right about their need for blackout curtains.

But it was broad daylight when she'd heard the planes. Had they crashed? Somewhere up in the hills? Was that why she never saw them?

Already, Adelle was nearly done with her task, and she'd only been at it for the last hour. How on earth was she going to pass the remaining hours of the day? Not as many folks were coming in with their scrap metal as Adelle would've hoped, so there'd hardly been any interruptions. The collection bin had a long way to go before it would be half full. After word got out about the aeroplanes, folks around here would realize the urgency of their situation and come rushing in to fill the bin past full.

There was one of them now. Footsteps scuffed in the entryway, and the sound of rattling cans broke the sense of calm Adelle always felt here in the house of the Lord. She wiped her hands and stepped across the airy room to see who was there. Kipp Lehnert, in his yellow jacket with dirt stains on the cuffs, stood in the hallway peering into the big, mostly empty box. He carried a bag over his shoulder that reminded Adelle of Santa Claus.

"Why, Mr. Lehnert," Adelle said, moving briskly down the hall toward him, "how nice of you to bring us a contribution."

"You'd be surprised what we find at the post office."

"Well, it's nice of you to collect it and bring it over on your day off."

"It's the least I can do since you ladies moved the collection site over here. I never complained having it over at the post office, you know."

"I know, but it wasn't my idea to change things. It was my mother-in-law's. She thought that since you're closed on Saturdays, it would be better to offer a place people could use on weekends."

"A sensible woman, your mother-in-law, and smart, to boot."

"Oh, yes." Mother Daisy never missed an opportunity to let Adelle know how much more competent she was, and Adelle seethed with silent resentment.

"What would you do without her," Lehnert asked, "now with the pastor gone?"

"I'm not entirely sure."

"You must worry about your husband a lot. Maybe with all the hits our boys are taking, even the pastors will turn into killers."

Adelle clutched her throat in a demonstration of horror. "Oh no, not George. George would *never* follow that path. He's there for the morale of the men, not to be a real soldier."

"You just never know in times of need, times like these, what folks will turn to. They'll do more than an innocent woman like you can possibly imagine, all in the name of stopping that evil incarnate, that Hitler." Lehnert turned his bag upside down over the collection bin, creating a din of clatters.

Adelle backed away from the postmaster. His remark sounded like a warning to her, but she had no idea what he was warning her of. "Do you have news, Mr. Lehnert? Has something gone wrong on the front line?" Perhaps he had news of those aeroplanes.

"What hasn't? That Jap sub attacked California only yesterday.

That was only the beginning. There's worse yet to come, you mark my words. They'll be here before you know it, and we've got to be prepared. Everyone says that. It's not just me. Why, the folks were talking about it over at Boatman's. Being prepared, I mean. No one knows what to expect anymore. The war is turning everyone into killers. Look at us. You know what this scrap metal is going to be turned into? And we have the little lambs of children collecting it for us. Killers, all of us, that's what we've become."

Adelle gasped. "Hitler started it. And besides, he's evil. You said so yourself."

"Is that any excuse for making us into killers, too?"

"I...I don't know. He must be stopped at all costs. He *must*. Then we can go back to being who we are. Or were, that is." Or never were, Adelle thought but didn't dare voice. She could've been a singer.

Lehnert wagged his head. "Ah, but that's the rub, Mrs. Somerset. We can never go back. We just have to make the best of who we are now. We're still trying to figure out who we are, 'cause we don't know ourselves anymore. Me, I'm not complaining. Don't get me wrong. See? I brought you all this metal just like I was supposed to. It's not mine. Folks have left it behind over in the post office. I'm just cleaning house, that's all."

Adelle edged farther away. "And we're glad you did. Our boys would thank you if they could, so I have to thank you in their stead. Good work, Mr. Lehnert."

Thudding sounds against the door outside drew Adelle's attention away from Lehnert, and she breathed a sigh of relief.

She felt uncomfortable alone in the presence of a man who wasn't her husband, but specifically this man Lehnert. She couldn't tell whose side he was on.

Heavy footfalls clumped in the entryway, and a man's voice called out, "Hello?"

Adelle scurried to the door, giving Lehnert a wide berth along the way. Just inside the door stood Arnie Trimble, holding a grown woman in his outstretched arms. She looked to be sleeping, or dead perhaps. A blue blanket draped from her backside to the top of Trimble's rubber galoshes. Another man, one she didn't recognize, stood awkwardly behind him.

"Why, Mr. Trimble! What is it?"

"We found her out there on the other side of the falls, half frozen to death. Thought maybe you could help."

She stifled a gasp. Now was not the time to fall apart. "Of course. There's a cot back here where you can put her. I'll get the first aid kit." If this mysterious girl had fallen out of one of those aeroplanes, then she was going to need a lot more than iodine, but that was the best Adelle could offer right now.

"She doesn't have any broken bones or cuts on her, at least nothing obvious that we could see without looking where we shouldn't. I think she just needs to get warm and get some warm food inside her, then she'll be good as new."

"This isn't the best place for her to warm up. It's so drafty in this old church. Maybe you should bring her over to the parsonage. Can you carry her that far?"

"We brought her here, didn't we?"

"Who is she?" Lehnert said, creeping closer, craning his neck for a look at the girl in Trimble's arms. "What was she doing out there?"

"Don't know. Never seen her before. She can't be from around here."

Lehnert turned to Adelle. "Maybe you can check, Mrs. Somerset, and see if she's got any identification on her."

"Who she is is the least of our concerns right now, Mr. Lehnert."

"Thing is," Lehnert said, "maybe I've seen her somewhere. She looks kind of familiar."

"What were you doing out in my sugarbush?" Trimble said.

"Nothing, of course. A lot of faces pass by my window at the post office every day."

"So you're saying you've seen her in town? How come no one else saw her?"

"How do you know no one did? I'm telling you now that I might've."

"If she's already been to town, then, what was she doing out in my sugarbush?"

"Gentlemen! There's plenty of time later to sort all that out. Right now time is of the essence to see to her needs. Mr. Lehnert, will you stay here in my absence to watch over the scrap metal drive?"

He nodded, and Adelle turned to Trimble. "You men go on ahead to the house with her. My mother-in-law is over there, and she'll let you in. I'll just get my coat and bundle up Gloria, and we'll catch up to you. Go on, now. There's no time to lose."

Just then, the girl moaned. She mumbled a few guttural sounds, or maybe she coughed. Maybe she uttered words that Adelle didn't understand. *Ich friere.*

"Sounds like German," Lehnert said.

# FOURTEEN

"**I**'m in love with him," Jewell said.

*Oh Christ*, Hank thought, *not like that! Tell her, but don't rub her nose in it, for chrissakes!*

Melody jumped up from her teak chair on the lanai and ran around the matching table to Jewell's side. Shade cast a mottled pattern from the canopy of trees, too crowded in the postage-stamp sized garden behind Melody's house. It was as if Melody had flipped a switch, and now the birds sang from above. She slid her arms around Jewell's shoulders, carefully, so as not to snag the flowery silk of her muumuu, one of Melody's island collection "Because Someone Cares," and hugged.

"Well, that's wonderful news, my friend! This calls for something more special than iced tea." Melody released her friend and made a flitting fluttering motion toward the sliding glass door.

"No. Mel. You don't understand." Jewell caught Melody by the arm and pulled her back.

Melody smiled. "You're right. Sherry or champagne?"

"You really don't know what I'm trying to tell you, do you?"

"Of course I know. You're in love, and it's about time, if you ask me. Love is just what you need."

"I never asked for it," Jewell said. "It just happened."

"That's usually the way. I'll go see what Martin's left us in the liquor cabinet, and I'll hurry right back — "

"No... Mel, please..."

"I'll only be gone a minute, then you can tell me all about it."

Jewell's voice broke. "Sit down. Please."

"Oh. I see. You don't want to waste a perfectly fine glass of my iced hibiscus tea that I've already poured for you. I understand. Well, all right. We'll have our celebration drink later. You can be thinking about which you'd prefer, meanwhile." Melody sat down, leaned forward, and folded her hands across her knees. She smiled so hard that her ears stretched. "Go on. I'm listening."

"I... I thought it was innocent at first. And that you knew. And you didn't care. I... I thought it meant nothing to you. It meant nothing to me."

"Of course it means something, silly. Why do you think either of us shouldn't care about your happiness?"

"I didn't mean for it to happen."

Melody laughed. "That's exactly why real love is so dangerous. You can't control it. Believe me, I know that well."

"But it's the other way around. Love controls *you*. I mean, me. You can't help yourself when love finds you. Or, rather, *I* can't. I didn't. And there you are."

"You're having trouble with this, aren't you? Is this your first time in love? Let me tell you about love. There are two kinds of love, one is like a weed that pops into your garden uninvited, and the other kind is the rose. You may think the weed is pretty at first, but it's wild and doesn't belong in our rose gardens." Melody shook her head with vigor. "You may be attracted to something so wild at first, something that's not real and just happens without anybody controlling it or explaining where it came from. But you and me, we know better than that. We're adults, and we have to be in control of our lives. We need the kind of love that you can cultivate, like all these beautiful flowers that I've chosen for my garden. You see the difference? Chosen. That's the kind of love you want. The kind that doesn't come looking for you. Not the weed. You have to go out and find the rose you want, cultivate it, toss out the weeds that can leach all the nutrients from it."

"No! It's not like that. I would've never done it that way."

"But why on earth not? You're not a young girl anymore. That is, you're a mature woman. You're like a fine chardonnay that gets better and better with age."

Jewell didn't respond. Melody gave a little gasp and went on. "You're not trying to tell me that you're unlucky enough to have fallen for a weed, are you? Jewell, honey... That kind of love is for teenagers. Not for someone like you. You'd make some man a very lucky catch."

"Mel... He's... not just anyone. He's...a married man."

"Oh. I see. Well, that puts a whole new light on things. Does the wife know?"

Jewell groaned and rubbed her forehead. "Apparently not. I don't want to hurt...her."

"Well, of course not, Jewell. You'd never hurt a fly. You couldn't. You're too good of a person."

"Oh, stop. Just please stop."

"But it's true. Maybe your problem is that you're too hard on yourself. You should let yourself go sometime. I mean, not that you should let yourself *go*, you're too pretty to do that, but I mean, set yourself free. Let your hair down, you know what I mean? You deserve happiness, don't you?"

"Maybe not at that cost."

"You have to decide what's most important in life. Is it your love for *him* or your consideration for *her*?"

Jewell wiped the corners of her eyes. "You're right."

"I know. I only wish others realized that occasionally. Lani, for instance. But she can't help herself. She can't help it that her brain hasn't completely formed yet. She'll come around — Hey, this is supposed to be a happy time for you. Why are you crying?"

"It's just that... Oh, Mel... It's not easy to do the right thing. You go along in life, and you think you're being good, and then when your defenses are down, bam! You screw up royally good, and then, how do you fix it once you've screwed up so bad? Maybe it's impossible to fix. Ever. Oh, God!"

"Jewell! Of course you can fix it. It's just a mistake. Everyone makes them, even me sometimes. Some people make mistakes more often than others, but you're not like that. You're far too smart. Whatever's wrong, you can fix it. I know you can, because

I'm going to help you. Now all you have to do is tell me what it is, then I'll come up with a plan."

"No. You can't." Jewell sniffled and sat up straight. She stared glumly at the thick greenery surrounding the lanai. "You see, I... I... Oh, God, you're going to hate me."

"That's silly. Of course I won't. Go on. You can tell me."

"You're going to have to remove your collection from my shop."

Melody fell silent for several, long heartbeats while the birds around them chattered from the treetops. "What do you mean? What collection? My herbal teas?"

"I'm talking about your designs. We can't show your designs in my shop anymore."

The birds' chatter increased to a roar. "My *design* collection? You can't mean that. Why don't you take a deep breath, get in control of yourself, and start from the beginning."

"Mel. You and me. We've got to split."

"Oh. I think I see. My designs have grown too large for the venue."

"No, you don't see at all. You never — "

"Well, you surely can't think that you're giving me notice. That's just too crass. No, you can't fire me, if that's what you think you're doing, because I quit."

"You never have seen, not really. You've always been in your own little reality, and you've never seen what's going on around you. Like the way it is with Martin. And now Lani. You've driven them away, don't you see?"

"That's not true, and how dare you — "

"It is true. And where do you suppose your daughter came when she needed someone to talk to? To me, that's who. That's why you can't work with me anymore. Don't you see now? I didn't ask for it. It just happened. Chemistry, or something. Oh, Mel, I'm so, so sorry." Jewell jumped to her feet, ran into the house, snatched her purse, and sprinted for the door.

Melody staggered to her feet under the weight of the bomb. Her lips tightened into a thin line, and a flush colored her high cheekbones as she stared after her former best friend. She lifted her glass of hibiscus tea and aimed it as if she meant to hurl it. Hank cringed. Then Melody set the glass down and sank back into her teak seat.

The puff of emptiness that had been Hank's heart ached now for his daughter, who slumped in her seat like a deflated balloon. What else could he have done? He'd helped create this disaster. He was good at that, helping create disasters. He'd had no choice in the matter. Melody and disaster were like two speeding trains on a collision course, and there wasn't a dang thing he could do to stop the impact.

# MARYLAND, 1980

**Her daughter's wedding** day dawned as sunny as Rosamonde felt. Who wouldn't love to see one's daughter as a real, living, breathing princess, if only for a day? There was always a magical air about weddings, and this time the central player was the very own creation of Rosamonde and Hank's union. Through Melody, Rosamonde experienced the magical transformation herself, and since it was a vicarious experience, Rosamonde didn't have to own any of the stresses that had shattered Melody's usually placid disposition over the last nine months.

Yes, Rosamonde thought, creating a wedding was rather like creating a baby, and today their baby had come due. All the hard work and planning finally came together in one big pay-off. Today should be the happiest, grandest day of her life thus far, having built on all the happy, grand days leading up to this one.

It wasn't.

Rosamonde couldn't pinpoint exactly what was missing, other

than her cameo, which she would've dearly loved to have worn for this special day. Outwardly, everything seemed perfect, right down to the seed pearls and satin ribbons Melody had hand sewn into rosebuds on the silk gown she designed for her crowning moment.

At first, Melody had wanted her wedding day to be the same Saturday that Barry graduated from high school. She argued that the graduation would be over by noon, and besides, that was only high school. Cheesy nice, but who cared, really? Graduations weren't as important as weddings, and her wedding wouldn't take over until late afternoon. Her wedding could feed on the festive spirit that Barry's little affair would generate. It was convenient planning, too, for the guests, who could attend both. Really, without Melody's help, poor Barry could hardly expect to have very many, if *any* guests in attendance.

But that line of reasoning didn't fly with Hank. The resultant argument was the only time Hank ever put his foot down and actually won. Barry would have his own separate day to shine, by god, the whole damned day and night. Melody would have to wait another week.

The wedding was the following Saturday. Out of town guests would have to choose between attending a high school graduation or a wedding, since it was impractical to think of their staying over a week, or heaven forbid, making the trip twice.

None of that really mattered, because there were no out of town guests besides Martin's family, and why should they be interested in Barry's graduation?

All of Rosamonde's family was dead, and all of Hank's family had disowned him long ago. Their New Mexico friends were scattered to the four ends of the globe, and everyone else — those who actually came to the wedding — lived within a couple hours' driving distance.

The Flynn party, with the exception of Mr. and Mrs. Flynn, arrived throughout the day on Friday, settled into their hotels, and arrived late for the rehearsal. Rosamonde wouldn't have cared, but she could see that Melody was upset by their tardiness. Not just upset but offended. As if the traffic that had tied them up getting to this lovely Methodist church had been an excuse they'd given instead of outright rebuffing her. Perhaps she wasn't good enough for the Flynns' only male heir to the line?

When Melody became upset, her smile tightened into a thin line, showing no teeth at all, and her voice rose in pitch. A flush smudged her high cheekbones, so that someone who didn't know her might think she was merely excited, as a bride should be, but Rosamonde knew her daughter, and she recognized the flush of offense. Melody didn't just get mad. She got offended. Everything was personal to her. Everything that could go wrong, went wrong deliberately to spite her. Because she wasn't good enough.

Rosamonde could sympathize with those feelings. She'd experienced something similar, although hers had been more of an inferiority complex, which was something she'd worked hard to overcome, rather than feeling singled out as Melody felt, the target of persecution. Rosamonde had come from a community of coal miners, who were hard workers and dedicated, but hardly on top of social protocol. Then, with her and Hank's elopement, she suddenly found herself in the social circles of scientists, many of whom were from Europe and all of them with educated backgrounds. While Rosamonde was no dummy, she'd only completed high school. Most of her education came after that, self-taught by virtue of her favorite pastime of reading. But in the company of those scientists, she didn't even understand the same language. After that, she'd spent a lifetime learning and compensating for her inadequacies.

Mr. Flynn was expected the next day, driving down from New York where he'd been attending meetings all week, which had something to do with his coffee business. Rosamonde hoped he would allow himself enough time for the drive so that he wouldn't be late to the wedding.

Mrs. Flynn didn't travel, so she wasn't coming. Not at all. Not even for her own son's wedding. Rosamonde thought this outrageous. Couldn't the woman make one exception to her silly rule once in her life for an occasion as special as this? Her absence was more like a boycott. But the woman didn't travel. Period. There was some story or other about how she'd been scheduled to fly on some plane once upon a time that ended up crashing, and after that she'd always traveled by boat whenever she had to leave her island. Over the years, she left the islands less and less. To travel to the continental United States, then across its breadth of seemingly endless mountains and plains by a combination of bus and train was more than anyone could possibly expect from her.

But the simple fact of the matter was that she was missing her own son's wedding. Her only son. Maybe this wedding didn't matter to Mrs. Flynn. Maybe weddings only mattered if the child being married was a daughter, not a son, and since Mrs. Flynn had already gone through her daughter Silvia's wedding, she could skip her son's. Rosamonde wouldn't know, but she thought perhaps this was a reasonable guess. Certainly, Melody's wedding mattered to *Rosamonde*.

"Now, Mom," Melody told her, ushering her into a pew at the front, "this is where you're going to sit. Barry will seat you, and you won't have a thing to worry about."

What she meant was, Rosamonde wasn't to be trusted with a special task, like lighting a unity candle. Of course, there was nothing to unite without the groom's mother present. Yes, Mrs. Flynn's significant absence stuck in Rosamonde's craw. There were already enough absent people who weren't here and never intended to be. They didn't also need the absence of a player who was *supposed* to be here and could be.

Rosamonde slid around in her pew, its wood slick from centuries of wax and polishing bottoms, and watched the rehearsal begin. Silvia was the first bridesmaid, so she'd had to arrive today, unlike Mr. Flynn. And since she had two children, ages three and one (Silvia had only been married a little over three years, and that thought made Rosamonde's heart flip over, unable to stop herself from wondering if the same accident could possibly have happened to Melody who might already — oh joy joy joy! — be carrying Rosamonde's grandchild in her oven), Silvia had arrived without her husband. Caleb Rothschild stayed behind in Hawaii to look after the babies, since he'd only been given a job to do and not a role in the wedding. He wasn't allowed to be an usher or a groomsman with a white baby rosebud in his lapel, and Rosamonde couldn't help but wonder why. She suspected that she would like him. His name conjured up old wealth and aristocracy, yet he'd stayed home, giving his children piggy-back rides. Rosamonde liked that inconsistency. She liked life to be unpredictable. He was a sensitive man, apparently, or else too broke to afford three more air tickets. Yes, Rosamonde definitely decided she liked him.

Silvia, a baby-making machine, was pregnant again. Under Melody's direction of choreography, Silvia waddled down the aisle, clutching Barry's arm while Barry's facial expression suggested that Silvia had cooties. His attention wandered across the pews to his cute little blonde girlfriend, sixteen years old if a day. Kitty, was that her name? Kitty, like a kitten sharpening her claws, sat there watching Barry sharply as if he might at any moment make a pass at the pregnant sister-in-law-to-be.

Silvia was oblivious to the dynamics going on around her. She clung to Barry's arm for support, looking as if she'd tip over at any moment without having something to cling to. Considering how fast Barry was navigating the aisle, Rosamonde supposed it was possible that Silvia could fall right over. She had no balance, thanks to her watermelon tummy, about which she'd assured everyone, including Braniff, that she wasn't as far along as she appeared. Still, her size threw her off balance, and Barry fairly dragged Silvia along, who clearly had in mind a slower, more rhythmic gait. In *mind*, perhaps, but not in actuality. The step that came across was clumsy, stumbling, and off-balance, reminding Rosamonde of a pinball machine flashing "tilt," when Barry tugged too hard.

"No, no, no, Barry," said Melody, sweeping down the aisle to her brother's side. "This is not a race to the finish line. Look, haven't you practiced your walk the way I showed you?"

Kitty giggled and covered her mouth.

"Step...pause...step," Melody said, demonstrating a gliding motion as she flashed her smile in a *take my picture* pose. "I'll bet you can do it. It's easy."

Silvia coughed, looking doubtful.

"Whatever you do," Melody said, wagging her finger at Barry, "don't leave your partner behind. It's like a dance. The two of you have to coordinate your steps together. Got it?"

Barry rolled his eyes, and without offering Silvia his arm again, he skipped the remainder of his aisle navigation and edged over to his final position in the groomsmen's line. Silvia tottered along to the bridesmaids' side and shifted on her feet. Either her shoes pinched her swollen feet, or her feet ached. Probably both.

If Silvia weren't noticeably pregnant, she'd fade away unnoticed into the woodwork. The woman radiated plainness: short and squat with mousey brown hair, a sallow complexion, and undersized facial features. By contrast, her sister Vanessa was drop-dead gorgeous. When it was Vanessa's turn to breeze down the aisle (too fast by Melody's standards but graceful, like a swan), Barry came to attention and stopped fidgeting. All eyes in the church were fixed on Vanessa. The groomsman whose arm she was offered was a friend of Martin's, a fraternity brother or some such, Rosamonde believed, she hadn't caught his name, but whoever he was, he might as well have been the invisible man while in Vanessa's presence. Tall and lithe, Vanessa was blessed with Mother Nature's gift of perfect proportions. She was a woman who made her surroundings come alive. Her passage down the aisle was an entrance of sorts, for someone accustomed to being noticed, like a movie star acquiescing to doting fans.

"Vanessa, I'm glad you're enthusiastic," Melody said, "but really, you can tone it down a bit. Take it down a notch or two, okay? This isn't the runway for a beauty queen competition."

Vanessa ignored Melody's instructions, winked at Barry, and sailed on to her position beside Silvia, taking a small bow as she pivoted in place.

Melody frowned, but only for an instant. Then she blinked her scowl away and turned with a smile to her maid of honor, a gal from the fabric shop where Melody worked. Bev and Melody weren't especially close friends. They'd only known each other four or five years, but still, Bev was the closest concept of a friend that Melody had since they left New Mexico and lost touch with everyone.

Rosamonde blamed herself for that, for their nomadic life. She'd always thought her children would be more adaptable than they'd turned out to be, but no. Both of them had always had a hard time making friends, ever since they moved east. So Rosamonde was glad when Bev entered Melody's life as someone with whom she could share an occasional movie or cocktail or an entrée to a party.

Bev was the sort of gal who'd been born for the part of second fiddle. She would always be a bridesmaid, never a bride.

In the fabric shop, she would always be a clerk, never a manager or designer. As a seamstress, she would always go for Simplicity patterns, never Vogue.

But she made a cute bridesmaid, even if her home-made dress looked home-made with its crooked zipper stretching like a chain of teeth up her back. She showed too much gum when she smiled, but her smile came from her heart and reflected a certain smugness, a self-satisfaction from her role as matchmaker.

It was Bev who'd introduced Melody to the politician's wife, whose house she cleaned in her spare time, and who became Melody's best customer of tailor-made clothes, and it was the politician's wife who inadvertently brought Melody and Martin together. Martin had accompanied his father to D.C. for the committee meetings discussing the import of Hawaiian coffee as opposed to South American, and Melody's customer was the wife of the chairman of the committee. As a favor to the politician, Mr. Flynn volunteered Martin to pick up the politician's wife's package from Melody.

And the rest was history, as they say.

But Rosamonde could imagine it, even though Melody always remained secretive about those early days with Martin. Rosamonde imagined the fireworks that instantly ignited when Melody and Martin caught each other's glance over a bolt of fabric. It would've been close to Melody's quitting time, and Martin wouldn't let her alone until she agreed to have a cup of coffee with him. Over coffee he probably impressed her with the story of how her cup had come to be, starting with a fragile plant that he lovingly tended, then eventually collected the beans one by one, and the process of sorting and drying and roasting, and finally coming to Melody in this liquid form, a nectar filling her cup that Martin himself had personally provided for her. Oh, yes, Rosamonde could imagine the way Martin must've overflowed with charm.

The coffee would've led to wine, which would've led to dinner, followed by more coffee, and then all the caffeine would've kept them awake long enough to sit through a movie together, then a nightcap, then...

Melody never said, but that's how Rosamonde imagined it. Martin, charmed by Rosamonde's talented daughter, and charming in return, had swept Melody off her feet. She'd been swept, all right, because Rosamonde knew that Melody had had plans of her own that she'd had to give up for Martin.

And was he worth it? The dumping of one's dreams. He stood now, in place beside his best man, another fraternity brother who looked interchangeable with Vanessa's partner. Rosamonde couldn't recall his name, either. They were Martin's boys. Friends on the surface. No more than drinking buddies, she feared. She wondered if they ever dug deeper, if they knew each other's secrets, hopes, and fears, if they knew anything besides each other's golf scores or who would host Saturday Night Live this week. For instance, Rosamonde wanted to know who Martin thought would win the presidential election this year? When she'd asked Martin whom he supported, he'd been evasive, indecisive, and uninformed, all of which shocked Rosamonde considering the many Flynn trips to committee meetings in D.C.

Rosamonde had an opinion. Not that she cared much for the peanut farmer from Georgia, but the alternative frightened her. The alternative had the power to bring to reality the deepest darkest fears from Los Alamos days. Oh, they were headed down a dark path. And all Martin seemed to care about was his golf game.

At least he made Melody happy. Just look at her now, radiating her bridely happiness, gliding on air down the aisle with eyes only for Martin. And this was only the rehearsal, not the real thing at all. Hank led their daughter on his arm, and Hank's face was nearly bursting with all the pride a proud father should have.

Yes, maybe Martin was worth the sacrifice of dreams to create such exhilaration.

Melody had worked her way through college with her job at the fabric shop. When she finally finished her business degree, she planned to open a design shop of her own, using both her skills with fabric and her business expertise. She wouldn't accept any help from Hank, and she saved for the down payment for the shop that she would need. She was almost there when Martin arrived on a politician's errand. A favor, that turned out to be much more.

Sometimes one's plans turn around with a strong enough sweep. Rosamonde knew. That had happened to her, too, when Hank swept her off her feet back in Zanesville all those years ago. She hadn't really thought, back then, what her life would be like, not as Melody had her business plan, but never in a hundred years would Rosamonde have been able to guess back then how her life would turn out.

Weddings were magical in that they made you look forward to

mythical grandchildren and backward to your own wedding, your life, and what had been. If Rosamonde could've changed her life...

Maybe she wouldn't have sold the family farm. She hated losing those family connections. Because she'd severed the family ties when she buried her mother back in forty-six, there weren't any Ayres here for Melody's wedding. Rosamonde had no one else older than she, no one to turn to for wisdom. They'd all predeceased her. So she hadn't exactly severed the family ties. But there were a few cousins still in those coal-filled hills, cousins who didn't know she existed. Cousins who should be here today representing the Ayres side of the family. Cousins who didn't care.

If she hadn't sold the farm, she wouldn't have lost touch with them. She wondered what her life would've been like if she hadn't lost touch with the few remaining souls of the Ayres clan.

Then there was Hank's side of the family. Although to be fair, Rosamonde had no control over that. They were the ones who'd rejected Hank, unlike Rosamonde's self-blame for losing her cousins. She was still bitter about that, and so she wouldn't have wanted any Berryhills here for Melody's wedding. But it was too bad that it had come to that. Too bad that they hadn't accepted the fact that sometimes marriages fail, as Hank's first marriage had failed. Sometimes you just have to dissolve it and move on. If Hank hadn't gotten out of that first marriage...

Oh. Rosamonde shuddered to think what her life would've been like without Hank. She couldn't imagine. Nossir. That was the limit of her imagination. Not even she, story-spinner extraordinaire, could spin the tale of life without Hank.

She shivered in the cold, slippery pew and tried hard to concentrate on the proceedings around her.

# FIFTEEN

When Hank returned to Caleb's Corner, Rosie and Lani were still bent over the puzzle, just as they were when he'd left them there. He'd had to leave, once Lani arrived, because he had to make sure that Jewell followed through. She hadn't, but anyway, she'd given Melody something else to worry about. Losing her job was enough of a distraction. He hoped he'd bought Rosie some time.

She looked content, pinching a piece of the puzzle between her thumb and index finger. She stared at the developing picture of old-fashioned maple sugar tappers and listened to Lani's stream of chatter. It was almost as if Rosie hadn't noticed Hank's absence. Rosie'd always had a special soft spot for her only grandchild. Lani was the only person alive who could settle Rosie's mood. Rosie didn't even look up, away from the snowy scene, as Hank slipped back to her side.

"So, Gran, want to try your piece over here? Look, it might

243

fit in this little grocery store. No, wait. Your piece is blue, isn't it? That won't work. The store is yellow. Except for the sign. What does it say?"

Rosie laid her piece down into a snowy hillside.

"No, Gran, there's nothing blue in the snow."

"She comes home," Rosie said.

"Who? You, you mean? Are you ready to go home now? Want me to take you?"

Rosie clutched her piece again and touched it to the woman waving from her yellow grocery store. The worked pieces fell apart, crumbling the store. "No!"

"That's okay, Gran, we can fix it again."

Then Rosie's fingers tripped over to the church, where a woman approached, clutching a little girl by the hand. She tried to fit her blue piece there, but the church scene broke apart. "No!"

"I don't think it goes there, either, Gran."

Rosie moved her blue piece across the village scene to a woodcutter's shed where a woman watched a man carrying a load of wood. She dropped her blue piece there, and the woodcutter's woman split apart, taking the shed with her. "No!"

"Nope, not there."

Rosie moved the piece to the frozen pond, where a trio of youths ice skated. "No!"

"Your blue is too big for that."

Rosie shifted to the foreground where the sugar tappers worked over their buckets hanging from pegs that stuck out of the barren maple trunks.

"But the snow's not blue, Gran. Oh. Look at that. I think you've found where it fits. Good on you, Gran! Way to go! How'd you know? What is that blue thing, anyway, in the snow? Where'd it come from? I don't remember any blue bundle lying on the ground."

She looked up. "Unca Caleb, are you absolutely, positively *sure* this is the same puzzle?"

But he was busy with a customer, and Lani returned to the puzzle. "Who put something blue in the snow? What is it?"

"My sister who died."

# ADELLE

**By the time Adelle** returned home, fairly dragging Gloria along by the hand, Mother Daisy had already taken charge. The blue blanket that had been wrapped around the strange woman now hung on a peg by the door. Mr. Trimble and his hired man sipped coffee in the kitchen while Daisy tucked the stranger into Gloria's bed.

Adelle hurried to the open doorway to Gloria's bedroom and stared at the strange, blonde woman filling out her daughter's little bed. Mother Daisy bent over the woman, inspecting her.

"She's soaked through," Daisy said without looking up, as if she could scent Adelle behind her. "Go get one of your flannel nighties, and we'll put it on her. And bring back a hot water bottle and an extra blanket or two."

Adelle sent Gloria off to wash up for lunch, then did as Daisy bid. Fury fueled her race through the house as she searched for the necessary items. When she returned, Daisy had already removed the woman's penny loafers, slid down her woolen slacks, and worked at the buttons on her cardigan and blouse.

"You rub her feet," Daisy said. "We have to warm her up slowly." Then she added, "Gloria can sleep with you tonight."

It was another of her mother-in-law's unnecessary reminders. Where else would Gloria sleep?

All the same, Adelle wasn't sure she liked the idea of a stranger in her daughter's bed. Not only that, she felt just a little nervous about having the stranger in her home. She wasn't sure why. Normally, she wouldn't be suspicious like this, but these were such uncertain times.

She felt uncharitable, and that left her feeling as if she was betraying George. But her first duty was to her daughter. If Adelle didn't stand up for little Gloria, who else would?

Oh, she wished George were here. If he were here, the world would be normal. Ordinarily, Adelle wouldn't be afraid of a tiny blonde woman in the house. But nothing was normal these days.

Maybe the strange woman wasn't really unconscious. Because she'd whispered words. *Ich friere.* Incomprehensible words. No matter. Adelle had *heard.*

German, Mr. Lehnert had claimed. He would know.

But why would the woman *pretend* to be unconscious? Perhaps she was playing some sort of game with them. Or worse. She'd been dropped by aeroplane to gain entry into Adelle's home. Oh no, Adelle and Daisy mustn't turn their backs on this woman, not even for a minute.

What if the blonde died?

Adelle shuddered and helped Daisy lift the unconscious woman. She was definitely unconscious now, whether or not she'd pretended before. Adelle could tell from the way they had to roll her upward, off the pillow. The woman flopped forward as if she were a life-sized rag doll. Poor thing didn't weigh much more than a doll, either, and Adelle had a fleeting image of this wafer-thin body actually stuffed with rags.

Together, she and Daisy peeled off the woman's wet clothes. They couldn't help but notice the red welt across the taut flesh of her belly — a scar? Beneath the woman's collar, a thumbnail-sized cameo dangled from a silver chain round her throat. They left the necklace fastened on her as they slipped a flannel nightgown over her head. No point removing a personal treasure like that and risking distress when the woman would awake to notice her cameo missing. But oh, Adelle would've liked to inspect closer the fine details of that delicate face of carved stone, as mysterious and unknown as the real-life woman herself.

Dressing her was not an easy task, but finally they did it. When they were done, Daisy stood up and stretched her back. "Come sit down to lunch before you head back out."

Adelle tucked another blanket around the blonde and whispered. "You go on. I'll sit with her a while."

"Honey, she won't go anywhere, that one won't, not yet at any rate. Come on, you've got to keep your strength up. Besides, I've invited Mr. Trimble and his helper to stay to lunch, and you need to be a gracious hostess."

Reluctant to leave, Adelle gazed at her guest. "I wonder who she is? Did Mr. Trimble say anything when he brought her here?" She suspected that he would've told Daisy more than he was willing to tell Adelle, since Trimble and Daisy were of the same generation. "Does he know who she is?"

Daisy clucked her tongue and sighed, clearly impatient. "She had no business being out there in the sugarbush. Must've been on her way somewhere and got lost. Whatever was wrong with her mind to make her go and do such a tom-fool thing?"

That did it. Adelle backed away from the side of the bed and put a finger to her lips. "She'll hear you."

"Honey, she's dead to the world."

"There are stories all the time about unconscious people who understand what's being said around them. We don't know what she can hear and what she can't."

"*I* have nothing to hide," Daisy said. "Besides, I know a thing or two. That's why George thought it best that I come take care of you while he's away."

Adelle pulled Daisy out into the hall and closed the bedroom door, separating them from the stranger in Gloria's bed. "She's not from around here. She doesn't even speak English."

"That's nonsense. She can't be responsible for what came out of her subconscious. Did you look at her? Of course she's one of us. What would George think if he could hear you talk like that?"

There it was. Her unworthiness.

Just then, the sound of a slam erupted from the kitchen, as if something heavy had fallen onto the linoleum tabletop. Dishes clattered. A chair scraped against the floor.

"No, I won't settle down," said a man's voice that wasn't Trimble's. "You're wrong, that's all there is to it."

Footsteps pounded across the room, and then Mr. Trimble's hired man exploded into the hall. When he saw Adelle and Daisy standing there, he hesitated and lowered his chin, as if embarrassed by his outburst.

"G'day, ma'am," he said, then rushed to the door, grabbed his coat from the peg, and stormed outside without even slipping it on first.

# IMOGENE

**Let's get out of** here," Paul said, tumbling off the sled.

"We've got to take cover," Troy said, scanning the terrain. "Over there! Behind those big rocks! C'mon, it's not far!"

Imogene, abandoned in her giving birth position on the sled, harrumphed and plopped her mittened hands against her waist. "I'm going to see what it's all about. Who's coming with me?"

"Don't be crazy, Imo," Paul said. "You want to get shot at?"

"No one's going to shoot me. They wouldn't dare. Besides, it's just hunters."

"Not this time of year."

"Target shooters, then."

"You want to get eaten by wolves?" Troy said.

Imogene aimed a scathing look at the boys, meant to make their little pricks wilt. She scooted off the sled, stood, and brushed snow from her woolen coat and matching leggings. She hated the home-made outfit, but what else could she do but wear it? Freeze?

The boys didn't notice fashion; only her girlfriends did. Imogene was careful never to wear anything little-girl-goofy like leggings when her competition might be around. No respecting girl would be caught dead out here on the hill above the skating pond, so Imogene figured she was safe. Her girlfriends were such ninnies. They actually listened to the grownups who warned that this hill was too steep to be safe for sledding. Look at all the fun the other girls were missing.

Imogene marched on toward the woods, where they'd heard the gunshot clear as day, although today was far from clear. Still, the gunshot was what had caused all this commotion in the first place. The wolves the boys thought they'd heard were another matter. There were no wolves around here, that is, none of the four-legged kind.

Snow crunched behind her, and Paul caught up to her and grabbed her by the sleeve. "Don't worry," he said, breathless, "I'll protect you."

She swung her arm up high and twisted out of his grip. "I'm not worried, and I don't need your protection. Why don't you save it for Troy?"

"Ah, honey, he don't count."

"Don't 'honey' me." She turned away from him and marched on. A thrill coursed through her, whether from the unknown ahead or from the consternation she herself was inflicting on Paul, she couldn't tell. It didn't matter. Nothing could happen to her but triumph. She was confident that Paul would follow along like a puppy dog and that Troy was now creeping out of his hidey hole, unable to bear being left behind.

She lifted her chin high into the air and felt a grin tug at her lips, threatening to ruin the mad face she put on for show. Snowflakes brushed her cheeks. Criminy, it was snowing already. It wasn't supposed to snow again, not with spring around the corner. The endless snow was another reason why Dillon Fell was the most boring place on earth.

She was tired of sledding. She was ready to go skinny dipping. Not here at *this* pond, of course, which was way too small and too close to town, but at the lake, way up in the hills, which was big enough that the fishermen never bothered you.

Then she saw a flash of red through the wall of tree trunks ahead. A man wearing a red coat emerged from the woods, moving swiftly toward them. He carried an armload of wood, but where was he going with it, Imogene wondered? Where was his sled?

"Dad!" Paul said from behind her shoulder. "We weren't doing nothing wrong."

"Where's your rifle, Mr. Ingersoll?" Troy asked, running up behind them. "We heard shots."

"No, kids, you didn't hear nothing. What are you doing way out here all by yourselves?" His gaze fell on Imogene, sweeping her up and down, as if he knew all about it. As if he knew the way Paul touched her all over, leaving her feeling all goosebump prickly and breathless.

"We weren't doing nothing wrong," Paul said again. "What are you doing out here, Dad?"

"Working, boy, what else?"

"We heard wolves, Mr. Ingersoll," Troy said. "Did you hear them, too?"

"Nope. I told you. You didn't hear nothing. Got it?"

Paul's dad scowled, and he looked rough with his unshaven chin. Hatred gleamed from his eyes. Imogene could almost see the steam rising off his puffed-out cheeks. Yes, hatred, that's what the big scary lumberjack felt. Imogene was certain. Well, her parents didn't exactly love her, either, so she supposed that was possible. But, hatred? That was a bit strong for a parent. All the more reason why she had to get out of Dillon Fell.

Imogene broke away from the boys and Paul's dad. She ran on through the snow toward the woods, toward the point where Paul's dad had emerged from them. "Hey!" one of them shouted behind her. "Come back here!" That shout was from Paul's dad. He scared her, and she ran even faster. He would have a hard time catching up to her, as fast as she ran. Besides, he had that armload of wood, and he would either have to drop it first before giving chase to her or else run with it. The load would slow him down, like a ball and chain, and Imogene could outrun him. She took advantage of her head start and plunged on. The boys might follow, but she didn't care if they did or not. She could handle them. It was Paul's dad who frightened her. Maybe she would just keep on running. Leave Dillon Fell behind her for good, once and for all.

# BALTIMORE, 1974

**Rosamonde dragged her** feet getting ready for Hank's retirement party, which would be held later that night. It was supposed to be a festive affair, a private dinner at their local Elk's Club. It was to be a celebration of all of Hank's accomplishments. It should be a time for Rosamonde to bask in the glory of her husband, but instead, she felt as if she were dressing for her own funeral.

Her fingers shook as she painted her nails. Drips of her favorite shade of red polish, a red as deep as a poppy, splattered her flesh, contrasting sharply with the deathly pale of her skin. God, even her fingers were pale, drained of blood. Icy cold, her fingers froze the splattered polish to red ice crystals upon contact.

Her fingers, useless.

Spreading her fingers apart, she recapped the bottle of polish and chunked it into the wastebasket. She gave a loud sigh, then soaked a cotton ball with remover and scrubbed the crystals from her fingers and the sticky polish from her nails. Tears streamed down her face as she worked. It was the pungency of nail polish remover that made her cry, she told herself, nothing else. Breathing in the vapors fired her throat, like inhaling splinters of glass. Not that she ever *had*. She could imagine. Thank goodness she would never need to do her nails again, not now that she and Hank were being put out to pasture.

He was only sixty-two, and she, fifty-one. Much too young to stop being useful. To end their purpose in life. To stare death in the face. Retirement was nothing more than an admission of death. Tonight's banner at the Elk's Club might as well read "Welcome, Death!" Retirement parties were an oxymoron. *Her* parties, the ones she'd hosted throughout Hank's career, were always festive affairs. Rosamonde had thrived on her duties as hostess while Hank toiled away, uncovering those secrets of the universe that allowed humanity to self-destruct. Parties were supposed to be festive, but there was nothing gay about dying, whether the dying was physical or emotional. Death was all the same.

Without her nails done, she felt unfinished in her beige chiffon, a smashing dress that showed off her legs and cleavage. The neckline would've been perfect for her cameo if only she hadn't misplaced Hank's necklace somewhere. Melody had made the dress for her last Mother's Day, much to Rosamonde's astonishment. She suspected it was some sort of atonement after the disastrous first year of college Melody had suffered through.

She wouldn't think about that. No, not tonight of all nights, a night of honor.

Click-clacking in her high heels, she prepared a tray of

Manhattan cocktails and carried them out to their glassed-in porch, where they'd acquired the habit of enjoying a few moments of solace at sunset. They were oh-so-lucky to own this charming house, which overlooked the bay. This was their sixth home in the last seven years since they'd come back east, but all those previous moves had been worth it to end up here. This home was finally a keeper.

"Drinks are ready!" Her voice sang as she called Hank. And when he appeared in the doorway, winking at her with that devil-may-care look in his eye, she felt her heart leap into her throat. Bogie could take lessons from her Hank, who cut a handsome, dashing figure in his double knit suit. Navy anything was certainly a lot sharper on her husband than that old used-to-be-white lab coat he usually wore. The more stains the better. Stains were a badge of honor.

Well, he didn't need his stains to be honored tonight.

They settled down together on the love seat to watch the spill of salmon and rose and orange seeping across the still waters at the foot of their sloping lawn. Each day the show changed slightly with the appearance (or not) of clouds above or the amount of ruffles in the water below. Hank propped one arm along the top of the cushion behind her, and she lowered her head onto his shoulder. She lifted the hem of her skirt above her knee and crossed her legs, rubbing her nylons against his pants leg. Electricity zinged between them, literally and metaphorically.

"Know what I think?" she said. When her fingers danced upward, tracing around the mother-of-pearl buttons of his dress shirt, her bare nails glared back at her.

"Hmmm?" He kissed her forehead.

"I think we should stay here."

"Okay." His lips brushed the arch of her eyebrow nearest him, the side of her nose, her rouged cheek, while his hand slipped around from the cushion's back to probe the V-neck of her chiffon.

She kissed him, then laughed and pulled away. "Hank, listen to me. I'm serious."

"Me too." He pouted and leaned over, snatching his drink from the aluminum TV table beside them.

"I think we should cancel our trip next week."

He choked and set his glass down, spilling drops of whiskey. "You what?"

"You heard me."

"But the reservations are all made. The tickets are bought. Don't you want to see Paris in the spring?"

"Of course I do. I'm just not sure that the time is right, that's all."

"Honey, at my age I can only retire once in my lifetime."

She felt her eyes water at the sound of that word — damn! — and she willed the tears to dry up. It would be a fine kettle of fish if her mascara ran now. "It just doesn't seem right. Not now. It's too soon."

"Too soon? What are we waiting for? The time isn't going to get any better. We don't have as much time left as we used to have."

"That's the point. It just seems wrong to celebrate a thing like this. Your retirement. Now that you're retiring, what's left for us, except to die? It's hardly a thing to celebrate, is it? We're going down like the sun goes down, except that we'll never come back up again. It's over for us, Hank."

"Aw heck, no. It's not over. It's better from now on. Don't you see?" He nodded at the bay, where fiery colors washed across from shore to shore. "Everything's better in the sunset, including us."

She wiped her cheek.

"What's really worrying you?" he asked. "The kids? Is that it? They'll be fine. Melody will take good care of Barry while we're gone."

"No," she said, sniffling. Although it was a worry, to a certain extent. Twelve-year-old Barry was so clever, so unpredictable, and Rosamonde couldn't help but wonder what sort of tests he'd put his older sister through, testing her authority during parental absence. "Maybe it's too much responsibility for Melody. Maybe we're asking too much of her. We've always asked too much of her."

"It comes with being the first-born. Don't worry about her. She'll handle him."

"She has enough on her plate, working and trying to figure out what she wants to do about school."

Hank stiffened. "There's nothing for her to figure out. She's making her life harder than it needs to be. We can count on her. That's all that matters."

"Yes, we can count on her, but..."

"But what?"

261

"Hank, I...feel so alone."

"Alone? And who am I? Chopped liver?"

"I should never have sold the farm when Mom died."

"You want us to become farmers now in our old age?"

"Don't say that, Hank! We're not old."

"It's a joke, Rosie, just a joke. Have some more of your drink."

Dutifully, she tipped her cocktail up to her lips with her undone nails and sipped. She'd always known her duty, or so she'd thought. Now she wasn't so sure anymore. With Hank's retirement, her known world was colliding with the unknown. If she'd truly been dutiful all her life, she'd never have let go of the family property.

"Granddad built the house," she said. "That would've been about a hundred years ago. Dad farmed the land when he wasn't mining. And I just let it go. After all the hardships they went through, fighting to keep the place going. Just like that. How could I have done such a thing? I lost my heritage. And now I have nothing to pass on to our children when the time comes."

"You did the right thing," Hank said. "The kids wouldn't have wanted that old place. Look at us. We're better off here."

"Are we, Hank? Maybe we should never have left Los Alamos. That was our happiest time, don't you think?"

He grunted. Rosamonde could tell that he agreed with her, but he didn't want to admit to it. "We left New Mexico," he said, "because we thought we could be even happier here. Every time we've left a place it's been because of our dreams. Now the kids have their own dreams, and they're different from ours. You can never go back. Why would you want to?"

"I don't know. Those places are familiar, I guess, and what's familiar feels comfortable."

"Honey, Los Alamos isn't familiar anymore. We completed our purpose with the end of the war. And Ohio sure as heck isn't familiar, either, not without all the family. They're dead and gone, and so is the family farm."

She sighed and smiled a thin smile. "You're right, as usual."

"Me? Hell, no. I'm a walking textbook of mistakes. Just ask anyone. They'll tell you. If we hadn't built the bomb, then hell, we wouldn't have tricky Dick today, either."

"Oh, Hank, that's absurd — "

"Is it? Our mistakes have made a new world for us today. Because of our mistakes, they're letting me go."

"No, Hank, that's not true — "

"Of course it's true. They can't get grants with someone with my kind of history on their payroll. Why do you think they've bounced me around from lab to lab the last ten years? Hell, Vietnam is my fault, too."

"I'm sorry I even brought it all up," she said, flicking the air with her colorless nails. "I'm sorry to go on like this."

"I'm sorry, too. The world's gone crazy, and none of it's familiar anymore. That's why you and me, we matter. We got each other, Babe."

"Tonight is your special night and I've ruined it for you with my silly regrets."

"There's nothing silly about regrets. If it weren't for regrets... Why...we wouldn't be getting ready for my retirement party tonight."

There was that word again. A shiver crept along her spine.

"It's just that... Hank, I'm scared."

"I know, honey." He took her in both his arms and held her tightly until her trembling stopped. "I'm not retiring. I'm getting released. We're finally free, don't you see? We're the ones who'll have the last laugh."

"I don't feel much like laughing."

"You will, once you get used to the idea. Honey, your laugh lights up the world. Retired life will be a new time for us, but it'll be even better than everything that was before. You'll see. Things just always keep getting better for us."

"How can it be better when we have no future left? There's nothing anymore, except for us to die. That's our future."

"Then every day we get from now on will be a gift. We'll find something else to drive us. We'll live life to the hilt while we can."

Before death, that's what he meant, when everything would all come to an end. Their work. Their life. Humanity. She just hadn't expected the end to come so soon, that's all. Yes, Hank was right. They would have to find another purpose. Quickly, before their private world came to an end. And it would. It was only a matter of time. She and Hank would have to find a safe place, a place where they could ensconce themselves from the rest of the world gone mad.

The search for their new place in the world would start next week on their whirlwind tour of Europe. Hank called it a continuation of the celebration that surrounded his retirement, but Rosamonde thought of it as a search for their destiny.

"Don't worry, honey," he said, nuzzling her ear, "you don't have to laugh tonight. If it's any consolation, I don't want to go either. It's a formality we have to get through. They don't want to honor me anymore than I want their gold watch. Tell you what, we'll pawn it. Use the money to buy us some mussels in Paris."

"Oh, Hank! You can't do that! It'll be something tangible, a trophy, to remind you of all the amazing accomplishments — "

"Mistakes, you mean. I don't want anything around to remind me of all the mistakes I've made in my career. Mistakes I can't undo. You and me, that's the only thing I ever did right. Now you'd better go wash your face so we can get this last sham over with."

Yes, Hank was right. He was her rock in the quicksand of her world. Retirement wasn't death, and death wasn't the end. It was the beginning. All that mattered was that she and Hank were together. He was her world. And family. Family trumped death.

# SIXTEEN

He's a nice enough looking young man, but I do not know why they bring him to me. They forget that I do not like strangers. Strangers fill the pages of my life. Strangers frighten me. I do not remember why exactly. I think because I am lost. No, *I'm* not lost. I've only lost my way. I used to know the way. The strangers around me are lost. Not me. Hank, I'm afraid...

#

**Rosie didn't recognize** her own boy. *Their* boy, Barry. Not such a boy anymore but a man heading into middle age. He breezed into the atrium of Melody's house as if he'd never been gone, shrugged off his backpack, and dropped it on the slate floor.

Hank, Rosie, and Doc Nolan (he wasn't really a doctor, but that's how Hank was beginning to think of him) were sitting outside in the heat on the lanai, counting butterflies when Melody returned from the airport with her brother. They watched the sibs' entrance through the sliding glass door.

All the way from the lanai you could see Melody's grimace at her brother's slovenly habits. Good God, you'd think they'd gone back in time to when Melody was a Miss Priss fifth grader and Barry was a clumsy toddler.

"You can keep your things in the coat closet," she said, nudging Barry's backpack with her toe. "You're sleeping on the pull-out sofa down here." She strung her car key on a hook by the door. "Go on and tell Mom hello. She's been waiting for you a long time."

"What the hell's up with the wheelchair, Mel?"

"Lower your voice. She's not deaf, you know."

"Can't she walk anymore? When'd that happen? You didn't tell me there's anything wrong with her legs."

"Well, if you spent a little more time helping to take care of her, you'd know."

"I can't just pick up and leave L.A. whenever you want me to. I have deadlines."

"What's more important? Your deadlines or hers?"

"The wheelchair, Mel. Why's she in a wheelchair?"

"It's easier this way. You don't know how hard it is to get her around where she needs to go."

"You want her legs to atrophy? You have to encourage her walking as long as possible."

"You're telling *me* how to take care of her? Oh, sure!"

"Just be reasonable for once in your life." Barry stalked around his backpack, still on the floor, and strode across the living room to the sliding glass door. He yanked it open and plunged out onto the lanai. "Hey, Mom, how's it going?"

Rosie shrank even lower in her wheelchair. If she kept on shrinking, she'd blend right into the fabric of the chair. She arched her eyebrows high, an old signal of alarm, and rubbed her thumbnails as Barry approached her. She cringed when he planted a kiss on her cheek, and her mouth opened wide in a silent "oh!"

It was at times like this that Hank's ghosthood was a goddamned nuisance. He could neither assert himself with the living nor find peace from them. Christ.

Barry stuck his hand out in Doc Nolan's direction. "So you must be the new guy my sister hired to watch my mom?"

"That's right. Nolan Penrose." Doc Nolan scrubbed his palm on the threadbare khaki of his rumpled pants, then shook Barry's hand. "We've been getting to know each other, your mom and I."

"She tell you all the family secrets?"

"Barry!" Melody stepped out onto the lanai and scolded her brother. "We don't have any secrets."

"Every family does, Mel."

Nolan cleared his throat. "Actually, your mom doesn't talk much."

"Not to you, maybe," Barry said. "Usually, you can't shut her up, right, Mom?"

"Oh, Barry." Melody sighed. "If you only knew."

"Well, that's what I'm here for. To find out."

"And I thought you came for the turkey," said Nolan, chuckling. Barry and Melody didn't laugh along with him, but Hank thought it was kind of funny. Hank appreciated Doc Nolan's sense of humor. Sometimes you had to look for it, but it was there, waiting to trip you.

Barry tugged at the bristles of the narrow strip of beard that decorated his chin like a flag. "So where's the kid?" He looked around himself, as if she were here somewhere, hiding under a man-sized leaf, and he hadn't spied her yet.

"Lani has a boyfriend," Melody said with another grimace of distaste.

"No way. What is she? Fourteen?"

"Try sixteen. How could you forget?"

Barry shrugged. "I dunno, Mel. I guess I forget lots of things these days. None of the things I'd like to forget, though."

"Barry, Barry, when are you going to find yourself the right girl and settle down? You can't wait forever."

"Why not?"

"Well, folks," Nolan said, sweeping his hands together in a single clap, "I think I'll just be running along now."

"Yes, you do that," Melody said, pasting on her smile, suddenly aware that someone outside of the family was present and privy to what he had no business being privy to. "You'll be back tomorrow, just like we discussed already. My brother and I have an important appointment tomorrow, and we can't take our mother along with us. Lani and Martin, of course, are too busy to help out. That's why I needed to hire someone like you, Nolan. You've been a godsend to us. Really."

Doc Nolan beamed. "Glad to be of help. Well, hasta la vista, then." He scurried so fast to the door that he tripped over the runners of the jam.

No sooner had he slid the door closed behind him than Melody turned on Rosie. "Mom, look who's here! Barry's come home, just like you hoped he would. Aren't you glad? And I picked him up at the airport just now. He's come to spend Thanksgiving with us, haven't you, Barry?"

"Sure, Sis."

"And he's going to stay with us through New Year's, too, aren't you, Barry?"

"Uh... That's still under negotiation."

"There's nothing to discuss. It's your filial responsibility. You do want to earn a share of the estate, don't you?"

"Um, Mel, maybe we should continue this conversation another time, okay?"

"You can't avoid it, Barry. You men are all alike. You avoid your responsibility."

*Now, wait a minute*, Hank thought. *That's just not fair.*

"We women have to take care of everything," Melody continued. "Just as I've done for you, getting you that appointment with Lacey Glade. You did remember to bring a copy of your script with you, didn't you?"

"I'm not sure she's right for the part, Mel. I sorta' had in mind someone a bit, er, more mature. More solid on the character actress side. A bit less, uh, fleshy. Oops, I meant 'flashy'."

"Well, it's not for you to decide, is it? Beggars can't be choosers, can they? When someone like Lacey Glade says she wants to do your script, you have to be grateful for the lucky break that comes your way. You're in no position to dictate anything, little brother. Anything."

"She wants the part? Really? You didn't say that before."

"Because she hasn't actually said so in so many words. But she will. Just you wait and see."

"Mel, the whole world doesn't bend to what you want it to do, y'know."

"Maybe it should."

"God forbid."

Maybe the world would be a better place, Hank thought, if women ruled. Would The Bomb have been built if women had been in charge, both in Los Alamos and Washington? Throw in London, too? Fat chance for the russkies, but you could dream, couldn't you? He could see it now: The world's newest secret weapon was unleashing the power of women's wishes.

"I'm only doing this for you, Barry. You want me to call off the appointment?"

"God, no."

"Then you should show a little more appreciation."

"Whatever."

Melody looked him up and down, took in the soiled jeans and the fraying tee shirt. "Did you bring anything else to wear in all that luggage of yours? Anything, shall we say, more presentable?"

"Got my trunks and my laptop. What else do you need here

in Hawaii?"

"Maybe some clean underwear?"

"You got a washing machine, don't you?"

Melody's eyes opened wide with surprise, and she folded her arms against her boob-flat chest. "You know about washing machines, do you? Bet you don't know how to operate one."

"Cut it out, Mel. Don't start on me. Where's Martin, by the way? Can't get your rocks off?"

"Martin doesn't live here anymore."

"Whose choice was that?"

"He has other interests right now. That's all you need to know."

"Don't tell me, let me guess. He's got something going on the side, and it ain't coffee?"

"Barry! You shock me. Why are you being so cruel to me? We have Mom to consider, and you're making up lies about me. Well, I won't have it."

"You don't have to, Mel. I didn't think old Martin had it in him. I guess I was wrong."

"It wouldn't be the first time."

"That Martin got caught?"

"That you're wrong, you jerk. Anyway, I have no intentions of discussing my married life, so you can just drop it right now. Got that?"

"Damn. And I was hoping to cash in on the soap opera market."

"Just keep your mind on your own business. You'd better shape up if you want to sell yourself to Lacey Glade."

"It's my script, Mel, not me. Although, if it'd help my chances, maybe I could get a little piece, too."

"Barry! You're not in L.A. anymore. I have an impressionable daughter, so you watch your mouth in my house."

"Aye, aye, cap'n." He saluted, then turned to Rosie. "Mom, what're you up to these days?"

"She escaped one day last week," Melody said for Rosie. "Scared me half to death."

"Still got your old spunk, eh Mom? I don't blame you. I'd want out of here, too."

"Be serious, will you?" Melody said. "She could've gotten herself killed. Lani found her in time, thank goodness, but she was wandering in traffic. We can't let that happen again."

"Well, it shouldn't, not now that you've got that quack on your team."

"If you're referring to Nolan, you're completely wrong. His credentials check out. Nolan is a big help, yes, but he's not here all the time. First of all, I couldn't stand to have him around anymore than absolutely necessary. He's so...so...I'm not sure how to describe it."

"He's not your type, is he, Mel?"

"Well, that's putting it mildly. But that doesn't matter. He does whatever I ask him to do."

"Can't stand chewing him up and spitting him out?"

"Barry! The point is, Nolan's not here all the time, and when he's not, the rest of us have to watch Mom. We have lives, you know, even if you don't, and sometimes our backs are turned.

That's when Mom can escape."

"Ah. So that's why you put her in a wheelchair, huh? So you can strap her in when you have to go pee?"

"When are you going to grow up?"

"Never, I hope."

"That's apparent. Will you stop your clowning long enough to help me get her over to Golden Crater? I have an appointment for her. We're so lucky. We got in."

"Lucky, yeah. That's us."

So Melody had gone and done it. Despite Hank's efforts over at Jewell's apartment, efforts that had led to her split with Melody. That little business should've given Melody something else to think about, but it hadn't. As if Hank didn't exist. As if he didn't matter. Time was passing him by.

Hank whirled out of control, spinning on an air current, stirring the air stronger and stronger into a whirlwind of his fury. His helplessness. Hibiscus leaves rattled. Flower petals dropped. Birds screeched and got the hell out of Hank's way.

"I think a storm must be blowing up," Melody said with a worried look to the sky.

No shit. Hank, co-conspirator of The Bomb, would come up with another plan, and it would be an even bigger bomb.

# NEWARK, 1971

**"Okay,"** **Hank said,** embracing Rosamonde. "Everything is going to be okay once we get to Baltimore."

Rosamonde's body fit perfectly against Hank, and she melted in his arms. She didn't think it would be all right — it never had been, really — but she believed Hank. She always believed Hank. Without Hank, there was no light.

She was just tired of moving, that's all. She'd lost her precious cameo in one of the moves, a misplaced box inside a misplaced box. And she was tired of not having roots. It was as if The Bomb had blown up their tenuous roots to smithereens.

"I feel bad for Melody, graduating next year from yet another new school."

"Don't worry about her. She's strong."

"Still. Five high schools, Hank? You think that's easy for a girl?"

"Maybe if she'd've studied more it would've only been four, instead."

277

"Hank! You're awful!"

"You going to trade me in? Get yourself a new model? No one would blame you."

"Never! And don't talk like that, either. It's not your fault, and it never has been."

# HUNTSVILLE, 1969

**"But we just got** here, Hank. They can't want us to move already."

"Honey, it's where the grant needs me. It's not up to me."

"Why didn't they know before they sent you here that we're not going to stay?"

Hank shrugged. Rosamonde didn't like the way that vein stood out on his temple and throbbed. She'd never noticed it until two moves ago. Hank was being punished, she suspected. Still punished for those missing notes. Well, that wasn't his fault!

Still, Rosamonde didn't really mind moving back north. Here among the ladies of her new bridge club, she heard more chatter than ever about The Bomb and how it had rung in the Nuclear Age as if that was some of world-wide Black Death. Didn't they know? It was only meant to destroy evil, not goodness. No, the tension in the air down here wasn't right for them. Besides, the kids had found no friends, and the library had no room for Rosamonde. She sighed. Time to move on. She'd go anywhere with Hank. Yes, it would be okay.

# SEVENTEEN

T hings changed after the wheelchair entered the house. It was as if something disappeared from Rosie's person, not just her spirit. She wasn't the same old girl anymore, and Hank was having trouble reaching her.

He was a barometric drop in air pressure. His time was running out, and there was still much to do.

He'd grown to trust Nolan, mostly because Melody found the doc pathetic, but also because nothing ruffled the doc. If the shenanigans in this house didn't move Doc Nolan, then Hank felt confident that Rosie was safe enough with him. And so Hank didn't mind leaving Rosie for short periods in Nolan's gentle care.

Because there was still so much damage to undo.

That's how Hank found himself here, fluttering around the stale airspace of the Koa Mo'ole. No smoking ban could purge the years of cigarettes this place had seen. The smell of smoke lingered in the crushed velvet of stage curtains, the burn holes of the tablecloths, and the mold that thrived in crevices where floor met wall.

No wonder. It was dark enough in here to chill Hank. The place had no windows to let in the light of day. The only way you'd know it was day outside was because there were no customers and the metal chairs were stacked upside-down atop tables. Only one table was set up with a candle-shaped lamp glowing in the dark. Lani and Vanessa sat there, the only live ones in the room. While they chatted, Hank checked out the sound equipment. Hell, if they'd only had half a smidge of this technology back in his day...

Lani sipped her diet Coke and Vanessa dug with her fingers for the olive in her martini. "She couldn't remember where I work?" Vanessa let out a squawk of laughter.

"Maybe she just forgot," Lani said.

"Don't believe that for a minute. I wonder what she's up to?"

"Why does she have to be up to anything? She stays awfully busy with her store."

Vanessa sucked the juice from her olive. "Yeah, too busy. We used to hang together some, back then, did she tell you that? She was always too busy even then to have any fun. God, I haven't seen Jewell Mattingly in years." She scrunched up her eyes in thought. "Let me see. God, it was before you were born. Then your mom got in the way. She's good at that, isn't she? Jewell and her friends used to come in here pretty often, and so did Martin and your mom. I introduced them all, and then we went our separate ways. Shit happens. I have no idea why Jewell would suddenly bring it up again after all these years. But I'll tell you this. She's definitely up to something. Believe it."

"Why don't you like Jewell?"

"Did I say that? God, I thought I got over that years ago. How'd you know? What are *you* up to? I know, this has something to do with your mom, doesn't it? And that shark's tooth necklace, too, I'll bet."

"Why do you say that?"

Vanessa shrugged and lifted her glass to her lips. She drank a while and thought a while, and the alcohol seemed to oil the memory parts of her brain. "Well, it's that necklace," she finally said. "I'd forgotten all about it, but now that you bring it up..." She narrowed her eyes, as if that would help her see through the dark into the shadows of her memories.

"See, Jewell had a friend, a surfer dude, but that's not all he did. He'd find shark's teeth and bring them in to shore to sell them on necklaces. God knows how he found the teeth. He'd tell you a different lie every time you asked. Huh." She snorted, thinking about it.

"So, you think my necklace is one of his?"

"Well, I dunno, let me take a closer look at it. He used to paint his initials on tiny shells that he tied on to hold the tooth in place."

Lani unclasped her mother's necklace and passed it over to Vanessa, who held it close to the tiny lamp on the table. She aimed the claw of her little finger at the shells. "There it is. JH. That's him. Jimmy, or was it Johnny? Something-or-other. Where'd you get this? Did Jewell give it to you?"

Even in the dark Hank could see the ruddy flush on Lani's cheeks. "Uh-huh," she said.

It was a lie. He knew that for a fact. He'd been there when

she'd found the necklace hidden in her mother's stockings.

#

**I want...I do** not know.  I want full.  I look for something...
I cannot remember what...  Who...  Something, someone...who
matters.

Who matters?  This place...  Not right.  Where is this place?
Where am I?  Where are you?  Who are you?

I used to remember.  Who...?  There is...so much...  Everything
is...nothing.  Empty.  Nothing.  No one.  Around me.  In me.  Me in.

All is white.  White is empty.  Empty is all.  All is not full.

# EIGHTEEN

Rosie watched Doc Nolan keenly the next day as he laid out his cards on the dining room table. Hank almost thought he detected some of Rosie's old spirit from the glint in her eyes. Either she was growing used to Nolan's presence, or else she wore him like a broken-in house shoe.

She let him go through his game of cards without complaining or losing interest. Not that her attention was really fixed on the doc, but she let him think it was. She was a mind adrift, slumped in her wheelchair. As if the advent of the wheelchair took the rest of the fight out of her. Even Hank was having trouble getting through to her with his old love notes. He wasn't sure she felt his presence anymore. Rosie, Rosie, Christ Rosie, where are you?

The front door burst open and Martin slammed through. "Melody?" he yelled. "Where are you?" Then he spied Doc Nolan and Rosie at the table, and his voice dropped. "Oh, it's you." He strode across the room and bent down to Rosie's level. He peered into her eyes. Her brows did not arch. "How are you, Mom?" His voice wavered and his eyes squinted. Hank thought Martin was going to cry.

Rosie ignored Martin, pretending interest in Doc Nolan's card game instead.

Martin stood, shoved his fists into his pants pockets, and rattled some coins. "God, how fast does it go? She doesn't remember me, does she?"

"Not necessarily," Nolan said. "Some days her memory comes and goes, along with awareness. At least she's not reacting violently at you."

"Violent? Has she been violent?" Martin withdrew a hand from his coins and finger-combed his hair, pushing it from his eyes. "I haven't been gone so long."

"Away on business, I imagine? You'll probably notice more changes each time you come back from a trip."

"I've been at the club, and no, I won't be back. Not here. I only came today for my things."

Nolan's elbow knocked some cards off the table. "Oh." His voice squeaked. "I see. Anything you care to talk about? Professionally, I mean. It's, uh, your wife's nickel."

Martin sighed. "Where is she this time?"

"Mrs. Flynn and Mr. Berryhill have gone to the Beach Towers. I believe they have an appointment with some actress about Mr. Berryhill's movie script. Mrs. Flynn phoned a little while ago saying they're on their way home now. They should be back any minute."

Martin sighed again and headed for the stairs. "Then I guess there's no chance I can get out of here with my things before they return. I guess Melody will have to hear me out once and for all." He shook his head. "Except she won't listen. I might as well talk to her goddamned orchids."

"You could, uh, do a practice run on me if you like."

Martin paused at the foot of the stairs. Resting one hand on the banister, he turned and eyed Doc Nolan. "Where did she ever find you, anyway?"

"One of my neighbors referred me. I believe she works with your wife?"

"Jewell?" Martin's voice cracked. He released the banister and fled up the stairs.

*Nice try, Doc.* Hank had always known that Martin was a coward. He couldn't face down anyone, least of all his wife. Hank always suspected that Martin would never amount to anything. If he ever managed to get control of his dad's coffee business one day, he'd run it into the ground. And the family empire ends with one set of weak genes engendered from a night of passion and hope.

In the beginning, Hank always had high hopes for his son-in-law, and now he wasn't fond of having to manipulate him this way, turning on Melody. It was all for Rosie's sake. Hank would do anything for Rosie.

Once Melody and Barry returned home, Hank thought, she'd run all over Martin, and he'd go cowering back to his club and his seven-iron.

But Hank couldn't predict the future now any better than he'd taken care of the future through his nuclear work of the past.

Martin was still upstairs, sounding off with periodic thuds and stomps across the floor and slamming doors and drawers when Melody and Barry breezed into the atrium. "Is that Martin's car outside?" she said, her face flushed.

Doc Nolan shrugged. "Maybe. I don't know what car he drives, and besides, Mrs. Berryhill and I haven't been out front to see any car at all."

"Well, is he here?" Melody's voice rose in pitch. She dropped her purse and keys on the valet table rather than carefully putting them away. She stepped into the living room and glanced down the hall to Lani's former room, then to Doc Nolan and Rosie sitting at the dining room table. "Where is he?"

Just then, as if in answer to her question, Martin descended the stairs with two suitcases in hand. "You're back," he told them, then set down the suitcases next to the kitchen doorway.

"Hey, Martin, what's up?" Barry said, striding past Melody toward Martin. Hank didn't miss the snide grin on Barry's face, pointedly noticing Martin's suitcases that were going, not coming. "Missed you last night, you devil you. I thought you were out of town on business."

"Is that what she told you?" Martin said.

"She didn't have to tell me anything. I just figured." Barry stroked his chin, which must itch, given the sparse bristles of the beard he was trying to grow.

"All right, everyone," Melody said, "you will have to excuse us. Martin and I have some things to discuss. Nolan, I'll expect you back here tomorrow, same time. Barry, you can take Mom out for a stroll on that beautiful sidewalk along the beach. You *can* handle her wheelchair, can't you?"

Doc Nolan obediently swept up his cards and stuffed them in his briefcase. Barry grinned and punched Martin in the bicep.

"Sure you don't want me to stay?" Barry asked. "You and me, bud, we can take her on together. That should make the match almost even."

"No one has to go anywhere," Martin said, "because there's nothing to discuss. I'm leaving, that's all. You're all going to know about it sooner or later, so you might as well hear it from me first."

Melody gasped. "Martin! Of course you're right that there's nothing to discuss. What's there to discuss? There's nothing to discuss. There's no problem, so how could anyone have a discussion?"

"Wake up, Melody."

"Where are you off to this time, dear? When will you be back?"

"You know where I'm going. And I'm not coming back."

Doc Nolan lingered over the sorting of his cards, dropping them first in one compartment of his briefcase, then pulling them out to find another slot.

"Of course you'll be back," Melody said with a little laugh. Then she turned to Barry. "That Martin is such a jokester," she explained.

"This isn't a joke, Melody," Martin said.

"Mom, how's your day been so far?" Melody turned away from Martin in a swirl of chiffon gathers and flounced toward the wheelchair. "Ours has been just grand. They're going to make

Barry's movie! Mom, your son is going to be famous! Can you imagine that? And none of us ever expected Barry would amount to anything, did we?"

"Melody," said Martin, coming up fast behind her and catching her by the arm, "listen to me."

When Melody turned to meet Martin's gaze, Hank chilled from the flash of frost in the air. "Let go," Melody said between her teeth. Her jaw locked into place.

Martin turned loose and fell backwards a step.

"That's better," Melody said with a slight grin of triumph, not a happy face. "You wouldn't want to do anything to compromise the family business, would you, dear? Does your father know about your plans? He wouldn't approve, you know. Have you thought about that?" When he didn't answer, she went on. "No, I suppose not. Well, you have to realize that appearances are everything. If you can fool people into thinking you're important because of the way you look, then you're successful. Just look at *me*. That's why I design my creations for my clients. That's what they want. The appearance of success, of confidence. Isn't that what you really want, dear? We all want approval, don't we, really? Well, if you bring a disgrace to this family, you'll never have that, and it's time you realized it. Too bad that Barry has to hear this, but you forced me to tell you the truth. So now you'd just better think twice about what you want to do. Think about it. Now, dear, when did you say you'd be back?"

"I won't be back, Melody. Some things are more important than appearance." He gave her a sad look of pity.

Melody laughed again. "Like, what?"

"The truth. It's time to face the real truth, not your invented truth."

"Truth? If you're referring to those people whom you thought you could trust but they end up stabbing you in the back, that's not truth, Martin. I would've thought that you, of all people, would've understood about loyalty, after all your years working with your family's business. Loyalty is right up there with appearance in terms of importance, Martin." Her tone of voice chided. It was the voice she reserved for Lani, whom Melody thought needed constant guidance.

"I know you know the truth," Martin said. "I know Jewell told you about us. I never intended to hurt you, Mel — "

"Know?" The sound Melody made was a cross between a laugh and a sob. "I'll tell you what I know. I know that a knife in the back isn't the end of everything I've ever worked for. There are plenty of other shops where I can display my designs. But there's only one family."

"Family," Rosie murmured.

All eyes turned on Rosie. The air in the room, heating up, held its breath.

"That's right, Mom," said Melody, "you've taught me well about the importance of family." Then she turned on Martin again. "See? Even Mom understands your foolish little joke. Here's the truth, Martin: You can't throw away your family. You can't throw away everything you've worked for. Not for some...some *harlot*."

Martin's arm reared back, as if he meant to strike Melody.

Hank had never seen him so animated. He guessed he was wrong about his son-in-law. His arm fell useless to his side, and then he bent over to pick up his suitcases one by one.

"You wouldn't understand about real love, would you, Melody? I'm not talking about flings. Is that what you had with him? The man who actually fathered Lani? Stud service? A one-night-stand?"

Melody gasped. "Martin! That's not...not true!"

"Truth, Melody?" Martin strode toward the door, suitcases in hand. "I'm talking about wanting the stuff that lasts. You wouldn't know about that, would you?"

"But...how...how did you...find *out?*" Her cry was a wail piercing Hank's soul.

"Did you really think I wouldn't know? Goodbye, Melody." He struggled with the door while the folks inside held their breaths, all except for Rosie, who tuned out, and Hank, who had no breath to hold. Barry studied his sister thoughtfully, and Nolan's jaw hung open.

Melody turned to Barry, gave him an imploring look. She inhaled a gulp of air. Her voice shook, but the flame of her guiding light never wavered. "I...didn't let that little accident...get in the way of the family. You can see that, can't you? Don't worry about Martin. He'll come around to his senses in a day or two."

Barry reached for Melody and embraced her. "It'll be okay, Sis."

She leaned her head against his shoulder. "I'm just so tired. So tired of it all. That's all. God forgive me, but some days I...I wish she'd die. So it'd be over." She closed her eyes and sobbed.

*Me too, honey. No one's going to fault you.*

# ARNIE

**"Dagnabbit,"  Arnie** said, listening to the parson's front door slam shut behind Lyman. "Beg your pardon, ma'am," he quickly added when he saw the two Mrs. Somersets standing there in the hall, both of 'em wearing bewildered looks. "Lyman had to rush out 'cause he wants to get back to work before the storm hits. Looks like we're in for it later on this'afternoon."

"Well, in that case, Mr. Trimble," the parson's mother said with a harrumph, "you need to get a hot lunch into your tummy, since I expect you'll be wanting to get back out there, too. You too, honey," she told the parson's wife. "You can't expect Mr. Lehnert to do your job for you all afternoon."

The older woman led the way into the kitchen, where she bustled and fussed, and the younger one flitted about like a shadow. As they filled the place with the warm smells of fried eggs and buttered toast, they reported about the stranger, still unidentified, who was resting as comfortably as possible for a girl who nearly froze to death. They refilled Arnie's coffee cup, and then they all scraped their chairs, pulling up to the metal rims of the table.

"It worries me that she's still unconscious," Arnie said. "That girl might'a been Peggy. What was she doing out there? It's as if she come from nowhere, dropped smack dab out of the blue."

"Didn't you hear the planes this morning?" the parson's wife asked.

"Planes? What planes?"

"It was earlier this morning," she said, "on my way over to the church. We heard aeroplanes heading this way from the north, but then they never came. They must've turned around and gone away. Maybe they dropped the woman into the sugarbush before they turned around."

"Oh, honey," the parson's mother said. "You've been listening to too many radio programs."

"Mrs. Wiley heard them, too."

"She was telling us about booooze," the parson's daughter said.

Daisy Somerset gasped and patted her bosom. "Young lady, I'm sure you misunderstood. If you're finished with your lunch, you may go play in the front room as a special treat. There's a good girl."

Gloria skipped away, and Daisy refilled Arnie's coffee cup again. Her hand shook.

"Well," Arnie said, once the child was gone, "falling out of a plane would explain how she come to be there in the sugarbush with no tracks. But how come she didn't break every bone in her body?"

The three of them shook their heads in silence. "Because," Daisy finally said, "everything has a purpose. *She* has a purpose.

It's a purpose so big that *that's* what kept her from breaking any bones."

"But what could be her purpose for coming *here*?" Adelle asked. "Nothing makes sense in this world anymore."

Arnie finally spoke, drawing out his words long and slow with thought. "She's got to be in cahoots with someone."

Both women shrieked. "Whatever do you mean?"

"I have a theory," Arnie said, and then he told them about his idea of a German invasion through the back doors of the Lawrence and Champlain. "The sugarbush girl must be part of it. She's got a contact person here, someone helping her from the inside."

"Here? Mercy sakes!"

"Why, what you're proposing...you must mean to suggest that... We have a spy in our midst? Right here in our own backyard?"

Arnie nodded. He didn't like the idea any better than they did, but in wartime, you had to expect such a possibility. You couldn't be too cautious.

"So...the planes I heard...they were *German* planes? Oh my. Oh my."

Arnie shrugged. "They're building new machines all the time. Better machines, and they can reach farther afield. Just look how far they come to hit Pearl Harbor."

"But...how would the Germans get their planes all the way over here undetected?"

"No one expected they could hit Pearl, either, and then they went and did it." Arnie paused while the parson's mother uttered a prayer. "Look, they can't do it without some help. That's why I'm saying they got someone working on the inside for them. One of us. Someone from Dillon Falls."

"Who could it be?"

"We must remain vigilant."

"Well, I suppose the sugarbush girl *could* be German. She was speaking German, that's what Mr. Lehnert said."

"It doesn't mean a thing, honey. German Americans aren't so uncommon round here."

"We got too many, if you ask me," said Arnie. "Kipp Lehnert's one of 'em."

"Do you suppose Mr. Lehnert knows her?"

"Didn't act as if he did."

"Well, he wouldn't let on, not if they're in cahoots together."

"So that's why Mr. Lehnert showed up at the church at the right moment."

"Then you're assuming Mr. Lehnert is our spy?"

"No, I can't believe it." Adelle covered her mouth with her hand, and her eyes opened wide. "He's our postmaster."

"There's a war on, honey."

Adelle frowned. "Don't I know it?"

Arnie sighed. "As an officer of Civilian Defense, it's my duty to turn in Kipp. Unless... That's exactly what our spy hopes I do. Keep me occupied while he — or she — or both of 'em — go about their real business and pull off their operation, whatever it is, probably paving the way for a bigger invasion along the coast. The girl must be one of them. But what I can't figure is why did they send a girl to do a man's job?"

"Less suspicious that way," Daisy said with a knowing wink.

Arnie came to a decision. "I'll tell you what we're going to have to do. You got to let her stay here with you. Let her and her partner, Kipp, but Lord I hope it's not he. Anyway, let 'em think we don't suspect. Let 'em go about their business. Let her lead us straight to their operation, then bam! We break it up."

# KANSAS, 1967

**Oh, glorious day!** After twenty-three long, long years of detour, they were finally on the right road!

Rosamonde and Hank were leaving the west. Now the world would forget them and forget what they'd done. Forget, maybe, but forgive? Never.

Ah, well, they'd never be back west again. They were finally heading east to Bethesda. East had always been their dream. Their mental make-up aligned with the east. They'd never been birds of the west.

Not that they detested the west, no. New Mexico would always hold a fond place in Rosamonde's heart as the birthplace of her miracle babies. But now it was in the past. Along with all those other brief assignments to places like Berkley, Denver, Seattle, and finally back again to Los Alamos.

The kids' patience hadn't even made it out of New Mexico. The first squabble came in Taos. They had to go potty in the mountains where there was no filling station where they could stop. Five-year-old Barry didn't care about using a roadside bush, but twelve-year-old Melody refused to consider such an option. They'd finished their bags of Cheetos and were hungry again at Raton Pass. Barry threw up in Pueblo, and by the time they made it to Limon and Interstate 70, Hank had rearranged the luggage to erect a barrier between them in the back seat of the station wagon. Who would've ever thought the miracle babies would fall apart like this?

Rosamonde laughed. They'd scarcely begun their journey east. They were like pioneers in reverse, and she spun stories along the way for everyone's amusement. What would it have been like if the west coast had been settled first and people had migrated east?

Rosamonde felt her heart soar along with the descending altitude as they traveled east. She loved adventures. Yes, she could've been a pioneer if she'd lived during that time period. For the adventure alone. Not necessarily for the destination. She tried not to think of this trip as leaving New Mexico, because she'd liked their life there. But it was temporary. They'd always known that. Los Alamos never felt like home. Home was a permanent place, not temporary, and one day she *would* go home. One day she'd be ready. Not this time. Now they were headed for their next adventure, bigger than the last one. Hank had been offered a spot in one of the Bethesda labs.

They stopped for the night inside the Kansas border, where the flat prairie looked like it would go on forever. It was a place, Rosamonde thought, where time had forgotten. A nice place to stop over for the night, no more. She felt the gathering storm around them, had felt it for the last few years in Los Alamos. They were living in a bubble of false innocence, or maybe that was the west, a place that struggled to catch up with the rest of the world.

It was naïve to think they could go back to the way life was before the war, and she knew these times of false innocence couldn't last forever. They were headed into storm central, back east, the vital hub of the nation. She longed for the vibrancy. She longed for a place of change, where important decisions were made that could change the face of the world forever. But for now, for one night, they basked in the innocence of a small, western Kansas town whose name she did not know.

They had a nice steak dinner in the café next door to their motel — amazing what only a few dollars would buy you in this place — and then they collapsed into bed. In the morning they emerged from their motel room to find their station wagon gone.

Hank was more upset about losing his briefcase than the car. He chastised himself for not having brought it inside with them overnight. What kind of fool was he? Notes... Transcripts... A life's work... All gone.

It was Rosamonde who held the family together, who marched inside to the reception desk, who told the clerk to phone the police. She didn't care about Hank's notes half as much as she cared about her cameo. Why oh why had she packed it in the big suitcase they'd buried at the bottom of the pile and left in the wagon? The cameo was too precious to wear, just for a car ride, and now it was gone. The wedding present from Hank was gone.

Even when the sheriff recovered their car—found it abandoned after an apparent joy ride — the cameo remained missing.

"Are we going to make it, Hank?" Rosamonde asked. They were on the road again, and for once in her life, she'd run out of stories to tell the kids. Nothing in the flatness of the forever landscape inspired her imagination. She couldn't imagine the pioneers, who'd crossed this plain on foot and in covered wagons. She'd save those stories for the next day.

"Honey, you'll see. It'll be worth it. We've always wanted to go back east, haven't we? It's just a little bit farther."

"Bull."

"Rosie!" Hank's eyes widened. The top of his balding head bobbed in the direction of the back seat.

"I wonder if they brought bulls with them? The pioneers, I mean. I feel like a pioneer, Hank."

"You want to get out and walk? You'd melt in five minutes."

"How'd they do it?"

"They were motivated. Motivation lets you do anything. We proved that at Los Alamos, didn't we?"

"What's next, Hank?"

"Trying to put the genie back in the bottle, that's what."

"Maybe he wants to stay out."

"Then we have to learn how to live with him."

"Yes... Who would've ever thought we'd end up here on this road? The road to our future is through our past."

Hank snickered. "Well, we'll be going through Ohio in another day or so. Want to stop and take a look at our past?"

"Not on your life. I don't ever want to go back there. I could never live there again. We've come too far. Los Alamos broke our ties with our past. Maybe that's the best thing it did for us. We were happy in Los Alamos, weren't we, Hank? And it'll be even better where we're going next."

# NINETEEN

No, I do not like this place. Bad bad bad. I do not want to be here. I must move on. I must try again.

# IMOGENE

**The woods closed** around her. Once the boys followed her, and she was confident that they *would*, it wouldn't be hard for them to see her tracks through the snow. She wasn't ready to be caught yet, so she raced on. But despite her efforts, she had to slow down a bit. The snow was deeper here in the woods. She wondered why that was, since less snow could penetrate the treetops, even if they were bare of leaves. It didn't make sense to her, but still, that's the way it was. Branches scratched at her face, and she had to slow down long enough to bat them out of her way. Then the wool of her mittens snagged on a thorn, and she had to pause again, but ever so briefly, to yank her mitten loose. The whole thing wanted to slide off her hand, and slivers of snow slipped inside, along her wrist. She paused to shake the snow from her wrist and glance over her shoulder.

No one followed her.

She pouted a little, wondering why they hadn't given chase

yet. What if she got lost out here in the wilderness? Who would find her? Troy, she hoped. He'd know how to survive. On the other hand, Paul would keep her warm. Omigosh, what if it was Paul's *dad* who found her? The very idea sent a chill through her, energizing her enough to plow on.

She didn't trust that man at all. He was so mean to Paul. No wonder Paul couldn't wait to graduate and enlist. Paul didn't say much about his family, but she knew his dad was definitely up to no good. His mom was okay, though, because she let Paul do whatever he wanted, which meant whatever Imogene wanted.

She surfaced from her thoughts long enough to realize that she didn't know which way she headed. Every direction around her looked the same, except for her tracks, which disappeared not too far away. The land sloped this way and that, and the snow looked like a blanket rolling across the slope. The trees before her looked exactly like the trees behind her. She stood in the basin of some sort of gulley. The land sloped up in each direction. For all she knew, she was circling around and would emerge back at the very same spot where she'd entered the woods, instead of forging ahead. What she'd intended to do was cut through the woods, come out on the other side, to the road. She knew the road wound through here. She had an aunt and uncle who lived on a farm on the other side of the woods, and she supposed their farm was where she was subconsciously headed. If she cut straight through the woods, she'd intersect the road eventually, which wound like a snake through here.

Now she wasn't sure if her course wound as snake-like as the road. Maybe she'd end up going in circles.

She couldn't see the sun, hidden behind a thick layer of clouds. Even the clouds were hidden from her view by the webbery of the branches above her head. She just had no idea which way north was. This gulley got her all turned around. *Don't be stupid*, she told herself. She studied her tracks coming down into the gulley. It was a simple matter to continue up the opposite side of the gulley, wasn't it? But what she couldn't be sure of was where that direction would take her. Had she inadvertently doubled back? The layout of the slope, with that old dead tree lying whopperjawed, looked kind of familiar. Maybe she'd already passed it. Now that she studied the snow, she saw lots of tracks. Paw prints of animals... Wolves? There were bigger areas of tromped-down snow. She couldn't tell which of the tracks were hers, or whether any of them were hers. She picked a direction free of tracks and headed up the slope.

Over the sound of her breathing, she heard another sound, one that didn't belong to the woods, as her own gulping breaths didn't belong. She heard the soft clack of wood bumping against wood. It was a distant sound muffled by snow drifts, the density of the woods, and the rabbit fur of her ear muffs. Had she circled back? Was she hearing Paul's dad with his armload of chopped wood? She slowed her pace and crept up to the top of the ridge. She fell to her knees, felt the cold numb her through the wool of her leggings, and crawled on. Using a bush for protection, she peered through its bare branches for a view of what lay on the other side of this ridge.

At the bottom of the hill was the snowy ribbon of the road. She could tell it was the road because a truck sat there, parked. A blue blanket covered a lumpy load in its bed, and a woman stood behind the truck, tucking in the ends of the blanket. Effie Boatman! What was she up to?

Imogene stood up and plunged down the hill toward the truck. "Mrs. Boatman, can you give me a ride to town?"

The grocer's wife jumped at least a foot. She turned around and gaped at Imogene. When she saw who was crashing down the hill through the underbrush, her look of guilty surprise turned to alarm. "What on earth are you doing out here, child?" She moved away from the truck, as if trying to steer Imogene away from the mysterious load under the blue blanket. "Why, you're hurt, aren't you? Look at you, all covered in snow! Does your mother know where you are?"

"No-o-o-o!" Imogene worked up a good sob. "Mama sent me out to...to...um, to mark the trees for tapping, and I got lost."

"You'd better climb in." Effie lifted the tail gate into place. Imogene hurried to help her, but Effie pushed her away. "Just get in the truck."

"What've you got back here?"

"Never you mind. You want a ride or not?"

"Yes ma'am." Imogene stumbled along the side of the truck to the passenger's door, which gave off a loud, tinny creak as she opened it. Paul's dad was sure to hear it and come running. Even if he caught them before they could get away, Mrs. Boatman wouldn't let him hurt her.

Still, Imogene scrambled up into the cracked vinyl seat and felt the warmth of the cab's interior wash over her. That's when she realized how numb she really felt. She didn't think it was entirely from the cold outside. Mrs. Boatman sure was acting strange.

"Lucky for me," Imogene said once Effie hauled herself up into her seat, "that you stopped right here in the road when you did. What made you stop here, anyway?"

"You sure are curious, aren't you, girl? How come a smart thing like you got lost?"

"Must be all the snow. I got turned around."

"I'll say you did. Seeing as how your family's sugarbush is way over on the other side of town."

# TWENTY

"**M**om?"

Melody opened her eyes and pulled away from Barry's embrace. "Lani?" Her eyes continued to widen, and she sucked in her breath. "What are you doing home?"

"So it's true?"

"What's true, honey?"

"Nice, Mom," Lani said, her olive complexion paling to a weak café au lait. "Real nice."

"Hey, kid, whassup?" Barry said, hurrying over to Lani. He held out his palm, waiting for a high five that Lani ignored.

"You didn't hear anything, did you," Melody told her. It wasn't a question.

"When were you going to tell me?" Lani asked, jutting out her chin.

"Tell you what?"

"What I didn't hear. About my dad."

"He was just here. You missed him."

"No, Mom, not Martin. Martin almost knocked me over on his way out. Martin didn't see me, but then, Martin never has, has he?"

"Don't talk about your father that way."

"So it's not true?"

Melody's gaze flickered away from her daughter, onto her mother, and back to her daughter again. "Honey, did you leave Kapono out in the driveway again?"

"Mom, answer me, goddammit!"

Barry rubbed his chin. Hank could almost hear the tapping of the mental typewriter taking notes about the unfolding drama.

"You don't talk to your mother that way, young lady," Melody said. Then she turned to her brother. "Barry, isn't it time to take Mom out for her walk today?"

"No, I don't think so," Barry said, rubbing away.

"Do it anyway, there's a dear." Melody smiled.

"*I'll* do it." Lani flounced across the room toward Rosie in her wheelchair. "That's why I came home, anyway. To be with Gran. Gran's the only one around here who wants me."

"Now, Lani, that's not true," Melody said.

"How would you know, Mom? You have your own idea of what's true. Doesn't matter if it's real or not."

"Barry, go with her," Melody said. "She's in no state to take care of Mom."

"Sure, Mel. Anything you say, Mel. You always know what's best for everyone, don't you? The rest of us, we're just here to follow orders."

Hank was torn between staying with his daughter in her time of need and following the trio outside into the golden sunshine. Rosie would be in capable hands, after all, and Melody had no one.

No one.

So. A little marital indiscretion, eh? She couldn't very well blame Martin for *his*.

In the end, Hank chose the walkers' company, because, well, Rosie was what mattered the most in his world. They weren't to the end of the driveway when they heard the sound of shattering glass behind them. Barry stopped and looked over his shoulder.

"What was that?" he asked.

"Nothing," Lani said. "She has to vent by herself. She won't do it in front of anyone. When you go back, you won't find any evidence, either. She will have swept up all the pieces of broken glass, and she'll be smiling again. You wait and see."

"Where are you going to be?" Barry asked.

"Not here."

"Y'know, kid, your mom may be a bit high strung, but she's not all that bad."

"You could've fooled me. I've heard you and Mom argue. Every time you're together."

"It doesn't mean a thing. It's just the way we talk, that's all. She has your best interests in mind. She loves you."

"She doesn't love anyone except herself. And maybe my dad. Whoever that is. Do you know?"

"Me? Naw. Thinking back, though, that explains a lot. I always thought she made a mistake marrying Martin. She must've realized it, too. She went through a period of depression sometime before you were born. I thought it was to do with her little sewing shop at the time, that place she couldn't make much of a go at. She was just doing alterations, and she hated that. Then suddenly she got all happy, and I thought it was because she'd met Jewell and found her niche and quit her former shop all in one stroke. I guess it was someone else she met, instead."

"Yeah, and maybe Jewell knew about it. That must be what Jewell meant when she was talking about mistakes and such. Jewell must know who he is. My real dad, I mean."

They fell silent, lost in their thoughts. Traffic whizzed past them, as life had done for Rosie. Where had it gone? How had it come to this? Barry and Lani slumped as they walked, taking turns pushing the wheelchair. But if they only knew. Then they'd have a real reason for their slump.

No one had intended to end up at Caleb's Corner, Hank could tell from the sudden way that they halted their desolate march and gaped with surprise at the sun-bleached, sand-blasted awning. But there they were. It was the same with life. How had they gotten there? They'd followed their course blindly, as if they'd known all along where they were going, but no one does, not really. Life had carried them along to this point. They'd known the path so well between Melody and Martin's house (Melody's now, Hank supposed) that their feet had carried them here. To this moment.

Rosie leaned forward in her wheelchair with anticipation, poised to spring out, but before she could do so, Lani held the door open while Barry pushed the chair inside.

"Unca Caleb?" Lani called. "Gran and I brought my other uncle with me. You remember Barry?"

"Sure do," Caleb said, scurrying out from behind his cash register. "Come on in. Make yourselves at home. Have some lemonade. It's hot as blazes out there today."

"No kidding," Barry said, but Hank didn't think he was referring to the temperatures.

The wheelchair made a rubbery, thudding sound as it rolled along the wooden floor. Rosie's eyes were wide with interest, and her long fingers gripped the arm rests tightly. She blinked at everything rolling past her, more absorbed in things rather than Hank's presence. "Go home," she said.

Lani led the way to the back of the store, to the comfortable grouping of furniture that felt like down home. She already stood beside the big oak table, gleaming with a coat of new polish, when the wheelchair arrived, along with Rosie, Barry, and Hank.

"Where is it, Unca Caleb?" Lani said, standing on tippy toes, looking past the furniture and into the dim recesses of the store.

"The pitcher of lemonade is in the little fridge, like always," Caleb called back through the darkness.

"No. I mean the puzzle. Where is it? It's not on the table anymore."

Floorboards creaked with Caleb's passage through the store, following the wheelchair. "Someone bought it. Just this morning."

"What?" Lani said with an explosion of pent-up frustration. "But that was Gran's favorite."

"Well, honey, we have other puzzles. Go pick one out. They're all the same."

"No. You don't understand. It was *that* one she wanted."

"Mom?" Barry said, bending over the wheelchair. "Are you all right?" He caught Rosie as she tipped forward, collapsing in his arms. Then he yelled over his shoulder, "Someone call 911! I think she's passed out."

Caleb rushed back to his phone by the cash register with Lani hot on his heels. "You have to get it back," she said.

"Not now, honey. Can't you see that your grandmother needs help?"

# LOS ALAMOS, 1944

**Sometimes Rosamonde** wondered if she'd made a mistake coming here. This high mesa was nothing like Ohio. It was so remote that it was practically wilderness, for one thing. And for another, the air was so dry that it cracked her skin and made her lungs hurt, just to breathe.

She wasn't allowed to leave the compound, not even to visit Mama and Papa, whom she'd left back east, ailing of the lung disease. Worse than that, she couldn't even *tell* the Ayres where she was. (Or the Berryhills, for that matter, but they didn't count, since they weren't speaking.) Separation from family was the worst possible fate of all. She was as good as a prisoner.

But of course none of this was a mistake. She'd come here because of Hank, and she'd do it again in a heartbeat. She'd go to the ends of the earth with Hank, and by golly, that's exactly what she'd done by coming *here*. This place was surely the end of the earth. She knew it was important, his being here, important for the entire world. She could sacrifice her comfort for a cause bigger than herself, couldn't she? Besides, this assignment was only temporary, as long as the Nazis ran rampant over Europe. Hank would help to stop them. He had to. What was more important than that?

Well, family, of course. Little good family served if the Nazis were in control of the world. The Nazis separated thousands of families each day. They had to be stopped at all costs, and she was proud of her Hank for his part. He may not be in charge of any lab, but his role was not so insignificant. Everybody contributed to the cause, and the end result of victory wouldn't happen without everyone's contribution.

Rosamonde's included.

It was Rosamonde's job to ease Hank's burden by making him forget how the world stank at the end of each day. And that wasn't easy, because sometimes Hank's days didn't end. Then Rosamonde was stuck with the other wives, whose focus wasn't as much on their husbands as it was on chasing their children, and somehow they thought Rosamonde wasn't quite one of them because she didn't have a babe of her own. There was plenty of time for that. Besides, she wasn't sure she wanted to bring children into a world under siege by a madman who never combed his hair. And she was certain she didn't want to have a baby without her own dear mama around for support.

She reached into her basket for a freshly laundered sheet and fought the wind to haul the wet cotton up to the line. Hanging laundry always reminded her of her mama and home. Her eyes brimmed with tears, but she blinked them away and pulled a wooden clothespin from her mouth to clamp down over the sheet. Mama never had to fight such wind, just to hang her laundry. Sometimes she thought the wind was Hitler spitting his contempt on her. Well, she wouldn't give in to that monster. No. She wouldn't. She sniffed away her tears, then reached for a sock.

The other job she had to do was keep an eye on her next-door neighbor. Had the woman no decency? Her necklines were too low and her hemlines were too high. Her lipstick was too thick and too red (for serious times such as these) and her fingernails too well matched. She wore silks in the middle of the day with no slip beneath to hide the outline of her legs, which by the way, were encased in nylons with no runs. Where did she get them in these days of doing without? Furthermore, when her neighbor's husband worked in the lab, the woman left their hutment. Not that leaving was so suspicious, for there were plenty of places within the compound to go, such as the commissary, the dispensary, the PX, the community room, the chapel. But Rosamonde noted from the chit-chat of the other wives (not her friends) that Natalia (her neighbor) never showed up at those places, at least not a decent enough amount of visits. At least Rosamonde wasn't ostracized on that account, for she knew her Christian duty. Her mama had taught her well.

The creak of a car door made Rosamonde look up now from her basket. She knew that sound, followed by a slam. Natalia was leaving again. She drove everywhere, and by the way, where did she get the fuel coupons? Not that the compound was large enough to use up that much fuel. But that brought Rosamonde back to her earlier point: why didn't Natalia walk when she went out to Lord knows what places?

Rosamonde laughed. Of course she couldn't walk in those spike heels she liked to wear, to show off her nylon-encased legs under the silk dresses which were inappropriate enough for daytime wearing. Didn't the woman have a housedress? Who did she think she was? Jane Russell?

A chill tickled Rosamonde's spine. Maybe the woman was deliberately making Rosamonde crazy with jealousy, and yes, a little bit of island fever, they called it. Maybe the woman Natalia, Rosamonde's neighbor only *pretended* to be a floozy. Rosamonde felt the blood drain from her head, as if she'd stood up too fast and now she was going to faint. She swayed a bit on her feet. She'd been on her feet all along, but still, she felt faint. Oh, lordy. She understood now. Natalia's behavior was a cover-up. She wasn't a floozy, not really. She only wanted the other women to *think* that about her. Lead everyone astray. Let something else distract everyone, when the truth might be... Could be... Surely... She was a spy. That's what.

Rosamonde should've guessed sooner. Not even Natalia's name was American.

Rosamonde cradled her forehead in her Clorox-scented hands and thought. What could she do? She couldn't worry Hank about this. He had enough on his mind. Could she go to the general himself, the man in charge of their confinement?

No, he'd laugh her right on out of his office. And what's

your evidence, he'd ask. Because the woman Natalia wears nylon stockings? No, it'd smack of jealousy, that's what the general would think.

Okay, maybe Rosamonde *was* a little jealous. Just a tiny bit. She'd had no idea that marriage would turn her into such a dullard. Such a spiteful plain jane, fast becoming a shrew, that's what she was. It'd be different if she had a baby, but she and Hank hadn't been able to conceive yet.

Rosamonde would have to gather her evidence herself, and what the heck? She had nothing but time. Her endless, empty days stretched ahead of her, with no sunset anywhere close to a horizon for her and Hank to walk into. She wiped away her tears with the back of her hand, streaking them across the grit the wind had blown on her face. She glanced over the socks on the line and watched Natalia's red coupe back out of the driveway. With the top down, Natalia's out-of-the-bottle blonde hair flapped in the breeze and stuck to the edge of her mouth, glued there by the paste of her red lipstick. Natalia lifted a white-gloved hand from the wheel to wave as she roared away. Rosamonde felt her cheeks flush. Natalia had known Rosamonde was watching. Had given her a show. Why would she do that, unless she was guilty of something?

Rosamonde unclenched her jaw, and the clothespins dropped from her mouth and plunked atop the wet clothes in her basket. One pin tumbled away into the patch of dirt they called a yard down here on the high desert, but she didn't fetch it. She wiped her hands on her apron as she ran out to the rutted lane and peered after the red coupe. There it went, making a right turn.

Rosamonde took a deep breath and plunged across the dirt tracks. She knew a short-cut around the side of the barracks that would take her to the next road over, where she could spot the red coupe's progress. She paused beside a pinyon and shaded her eyes, following the streak of red. Even under the glaring light of a desert sun, Natalia's car showed up like a smear of blood on Hank's lab coat. Her heart beat sped up and hammered against her ribs. She gulped air, but she could never get enough down here to fill her lungs, to replenish her soul.

The red streak faded away in the distance, washed away into the parched soil as if it had never existed. Rosamonde blinked, but she couldn't settle the rippled air that seared her horizon. She knew a gate was that way. Natalia was leaving the compound. That meant she had a special pass. Because of her husband? Or some other connection?

Natalia must be reporting in.

Rosamonde pondered this as she retraced her steps across the dirt. There was nothing she could do. But she couldn't let it go. It was imperative... Betrayal was the worst enemy... For the safety of the homefront...

One of the wives Rosamonde knew volunteered her secretarial skills over in one of the administrative offices. Rosamonde wondered if they kept records of passes over there. Maybe...

Rosamonde reached for the next sock in her basket and pegged it up to the line. She stared blankly at Natalia's empty hutment across the way. Her head filled with possible stories, possible ideas. The wind whipped her wet laundry and danced across their yards and fluttered the curtains in Natalia's window. Open window.

# TWENTY-ONE

*Rosie, I'm here*, Hank called, but the love of his heart didn't respond. It took the paramedics to reach her, to find her pulse, to bring her back. He'd never felt so helpless, not even with Trinity, when the sequence of explosions spread beyond scientists' control. His team had only initiated the sequence, and then nature took over. As now. All Hank could do was wait.

Hank had never done so well at idleness, at waiting. That's why retired life hadn't agreed so well with him. And being bounced from lab to lab. Waiting, always waiting. He'd had nothing to wait for anymore.

Now he was waiting for his Rosie.

So he decided that Lani needed him more right now. He followed Lani, once the paramedics wheeled Rosie away in the ambulance. Lani wandered from Caleb's store, along the beach, stopped to chat with some surfers, and eventually ended up at

Jewell's apartment building, conveniently around the dinner hour.

"Hey, Jewell," she said when Jewell opened the door a crack.

"Hey yourself, kiddo. Where you been?"

Jewell didn't step aside, didn't make any moves to admit Lani.

"What's for dinner?" Lani asked, ducking to one side to peer around Jewell.

Jewell stepped quickly to block her view. "Nothing left. I thought you were going to have dinner at Kapono's."

"I broke up with him."

"Oh. I'm sorry."

"I told you. Mom always gets what she wants. Is that my DAD inside? What's he doing here? Looking for *me?*"

Jewell sighed, pulled the door open wide, and stepped aside, inviting Lani in. "I could fix you a sandwich if you're hungry."

"Dad?" Lani rushed inside, then stopped halfway across the living room. "I mean, Martin. What do you want? Why are you here?"

"Hello, Lani," he said in an ominously low tone of voice. He stood squarely in front of the dining room table, but he couldn't hide the remnants of dinner for two.

Lani glanced from the wine glasses to the candle burning low. Her jaw hung open as her stare returned to Martin's face. Then her lower chin jutted out. "I'm not going back. You can't make me."

"I'm not, either," he said. "That's why I'm here."

"Just to tell me that?"

"Um, no, not entirely. Let me explain. Come sit down, Lani."

Lani didn't budge.

"I'll just go get the coffee started," Jewell said, ducking out of the room. "I'll let you two talk alone."

"Dad?" Lani said. "You know about him, don't you? About my real dad?"

"Yes, Lani, although I like to think of myself as your real dad. Maybe not your biological one, but your real one. I'm the one who's given you a home and a name and everything."

"That sucks. I don't blame you for leaving her. That's what you're doing, right? Leaving Mom?"

Martin twisted his collar away from his Adam's apple, which bobbed furiously. "Um, your mother left me long ago, Lani. She puts up a good front, and that's what she's done all these years."

"And now you're standing up to her? It's about time. Why didn't you do it a long time ago if you knew about my real dad?"

"I just... Well..." He tugged on his earlobe. "I'll tell you what. It's that Nolan Penrose. You know? He said something about time running out before we reach for our dreams, and it hit me. That's what I've got to do."

"Huh? Your dream is getting mad at Mom for having another man's child?"

"Well, not exactly. Your mother and I have never really been suited for each other, and it took Nolan to make me realize that."

"So you're not mad at Mom? I am. I have a right to know who's my real father. You know, don't you? Who is it, Dad? It's okay, you can tell me. I don't care about him. I just want to know the truth, that's all. I want everyone to stop pretending and to face up to what's what for once in their lives."

"Lani, life is more complicated than that. I don't know who he is."

"Jewell knows. I'll make her tell me."

"Jewell doesn't know. You can leave her out of this."

"That's not fair, Dad. Jewell makes up her own mind about things. That's why she's so cool. I'm living with her now."

"And so am I, Lani. That's what I'm trying to tell you. Your mother and I... We've never been right for each other. But Jewell... We recognized that long ago and have suppressed our feelings until now. Until Nolan gave me the courage to go after what I really want. No one will let you get what you're after, Lani, unless you make the commitment to go for your dream yourself. You only get one chance at life."

"What? Dad? You...and Jewell? No way! Get out of here! Gross me out! And I thought I could trust her! You...you two make me sick." Lani turned and stormed out the front door, slamming it behind her.

# EFFIE

**Effie Boatman didn't** take kindly to cowards. Cowards was all she saw these days. Cowards came to her store every day, took up space in the conversation pit, talked their faces off about the war and tapping and the new girl. They didn't do nothing but talk and talk. Least they could've done was buy from her, but no.

"Effie, you got anymore hot water I can add to my coffee? Make it stretch a bit further?" One of 'em would say. Ruth Teasdale or Adelle or Daisy Somerset or the Widow Wallis Wiley or Arnie Trimble or Opal Ingersoll or Old Man Dent or Kipp Lehnert. They was all the same.

All of 'em, except for Rolph.

Now, there was a fine specimen of a man. Effie had found out for herself just how fine a specimen he was, up there in the barn at Dead Man's Curve before the Teasdale girl come wandering by.

Rolph was no coward. If only the rest of them could appreciate all the trouble Rolph was going to, looking out for them and their future, keeping them safe. Well, they didn't deserve it now, did they?

She straightened up from the ledger book that wouldn't balance, erased some numbers, swept away the eraser crumbs, and tried again.

"Effie, you work too hard. Come sit a spell."

"Effie, you seen Sugar lately?"

"Effie, you got anymore hot water?"

"Effie, you want me to deal you in this round?"

If they only knew.

# OPAL

**They called the new** girl "Sugar" for want of a name. Opal Ingersoll thought it a silly name, but her opinions never mattered. Opal never mattered. Opal was one of the few women in Dillon Falls whose husband kept her warm at night, which made her an instant target of envy and yes, even hate. The women of Dillon Falls wished that Opal didn't exist, and so they treated her that way.

Being an invisible person made Opal feel a sympathetic connection toward the new girl, who stood out in the village, by virtue of her foreignness and the village's small size. Foreigners didn't come to Dillon Falls often. The Ingersolls were the most recent outsiders to settle here, sixteen years ago, shortly after Paul was born, and they still hadn't been accepted by the locals, not entirely. The pastor was also an outsider, but he had a purpose here. Opal and Rolph had no purpose, other than being on the lam, and that wasn't something you could talk about. What better place than this isolated community to make a new start, where your past couldn't catch up to you?

# EFFIE

**Effie was mighty** tired, and this was only the beginning. The beginning of her war widowhood. Everyone wanted something different of her, and all she wanted was to get by.

"Effie, you must do your duty and allow the League to gather at the store," said the Widow Wallis with a sniff of her aristocratic nose. "You don't want Evil to come knocking on your door, do you?"

"Effie, can you watch Sugar for me this afternoon?" Adelle asked. "Get her out of the house for a while? Maybe she'll talk to you. She won't talk to us, and I worry about her wandering off."

"Effie, you ever seen Kipp Lehnert and Sugar meet at your place?" Arnie's OCD was going to his head these days, and Effie was mighty tired of that, too. She was tired of men thinking they was bigger than what they really was.

"Effie, you got to let me know what you hear folks saying about Sugar," Arnie told her. "I can't always be there, and I'm OCD, y'know. You got to be my eyes and ears."

Even Rolph was all over her, wanting her up at the barn day in

335

day out. She couldn't just leave the store untended at any hour of the day or night at his whim. She wasn't so sure his load of rifles was ever going to get picked up, and she didn't know how much longer she could hide them. It was risky, running the truck back and forth, but what else could she do when there was only one of her? Already, the Teasdale girl was suspicious, and everyone knew what a mouth that girl had on her.

Besides, Arnie was getting closer every day.

And then there was Sugar.

# OPAL

**Opal took a special** interest in Sugar. Their paths crossed around town, at church, in Boatman's, at the post office. Paul brought home stories about the new girl at school. Opal encouraged his interest. Anything, to get him away from that little Teasdale tart.

Opal couldn't help but wonder why a girl who claimed to have amnesia would have so much regular business at the post office. Who did Sugar correspond with if she didn't remember her own past? Opal tried to draw Mr. Lehnert into conversation about the purpose of Sugar's visits, but he wouldn't talk.

Opal thought it possible that Sugar went to the post office to mail Mrs. Somerset's letters to the pastor, since Sugar owed the Somerset women for their hospitality. But if that was the case, then why was Mr. Lehnert being so coy about it? Why not just say so?

Opal smelled a conspiracy. If anyone knew about conspiracies, it was her husband Rolph. That's what had brought them here in the first place.

# IMOGENE

**Grandma Moses brought** the new girl to school, and Imogene couldn't remember ever having so much excitement before in Dillon Fell.

Well, outside of her run-in with Paul's dad in the woods. Now that she was safe from his reach, she thought about that day the storm hit as her big adventure, as surely it was. But now that the adventure was over, she couldn't help but wonder what Paul's dad was up to.

Whatever it was, it had something to do with Mrs. Boatman and her truck and the load in the rear that Mrs. Boatman didn't want her to see under the blue blanket.

Like the blue blanket Mr. Trimble found Sugar under out there in the sugarbush. Word got around in a place like this.

Like the way word got to Troy before Imogene even had a chance to tell him about her and Paul. She'd never seen him so mad. Never, ever. The way he stormed out of study hall like a crazy person. Headed up to the pond. She never thought anybody's face could get so purple. Like he was holding his breath, and he was going to explode, only when it happened, it'd be a bomb, like what was happening everywhere in the world except here in Dillon Fell.

# ADELLE

**Adelle couldn't be sure** what she remembered anymore. She was so certain she'd heard Sugar pronounce those unpronounceable words before lapsing into unconsciousness. German, Mr. Lehnert had said.

Now she couldn't be sure. She didn't know what was real and what was not.

When Sugar awoke, you'd never know she'd had a near brush with death. She awoke the next morning as if she'd awakened every morning of her life in little Gloria's bed.

"Good morning," Sugar had said that morning and every morning since then. English, clear as Adelle had ever heard it spoken. Not German. Was Mr. Lehnert wrong?

Sugar had no memory of the days that came before. It was as if she belonged here. As if she'd always belonged here. As if none of them were strangers. As if she'd come home.

# ARNIE

**After Arnie thought** on it some more, it all began to add up. The summer man coming early to these parts. The way he stood up for Sugar. The way they met in the post office.

"Oh, Lordy," he told Adelle. "It's not Kipp. I was wrong. It's Lyman. I thought Lyman was running away from something, but I was wrong. He was running to a place. *Here*."

"I heard him tell you that," Adelle said. "He said you were wrong."

"He wants to eliminate me. Get me out of the way. Seeing as how I'm OCD, Lyman's assignment has got to be to eliminate me, and possibly to receive contraband, awaiting the arrival of Nazi infiltrators."

# EFFIE

**"Get away from** there, girl. What you think you're doing? You ain't got no business poking around my truck."

"Why are you hiding rifles back here, Mrs. Boatman?"

"Go on, girl. You haven't seen nothing, y'hear? Get away from there."

"What's this, Mrs. Boatman?" Before Effie could count to three, the Teasdale girl scampered back to the rear of the truck, lifted the blue blanket, and yanked out the first rifle she could lay her hands on.

"Put it down, girl, real slow." Effie made her voice go low, so as to emphasize the importance of her words. It didn't matter, though, she told herself, not really. None of them was loaded. "They're just hunting rifles," she said. That was the story. Inventory. "Put it down. NOW." She shouldn't have to tell a kid to mind her own business, but she didn't want to be tested.

And then before she knew it, the rifle went off in the girl's hands, knocking her backwards, throwing her to the ground. At the same time, someone's yowl sounded, and Effie turned to see

Kipp Lehnert on the ground. Blood trickled from his leg. That's what he got for sneaking up on them like that.

# OPAL

**Then one day Opal** found out. All of her waiting and watching and crossed paths round town finally paid off one day when Opal happened in on them at the post office. Sugar didn't have any letters to mail, but Lyman did. Letters to that university where he used to work. Sugar was sweet on him.

# EFFIE

**Effie couldn't take** it any more. The ledger books wouldn't balance. The rifles out of her control. Her own life out of her control. The mistakes she'd made. Harold. Rolph. There wasn't much left of the store these days.

So she drove her truck up to Dead Man's Curve and forgot to steer round the bend. The nose of the truck aimed straight for the cliff. Those ticking seconds were the longest seconds of her life before the truck cracked through the ice of the pond. Cold, icy water seeped into the cab as she plunged to the bottom of the pond, and her last thought before passing out was wondering what part of her too-short life had mattered most. Exactly *what* about life was real? The living part? Or the footprints you left on the world, once your living was done?

# TWENTY-TWO

I drown in the white.

The white is both cold and hot. The white hurts, but I do not know what hurts, other than white, the color of hurt.

They look at me, hurting. I do not know who they are, but I think I once knew them. They are from the rooms of my mind. They are me. And they are not. They are who I would've been, if not for the white, and they are prisoners of my mind, not me.

Not me!

# OHIO: MARCH, 1943

**Rosamonde didn't mind** saying goodbye. Because this wasn't the end, no no, this was the beginning. The glorious beginning of the next phase of her life, the part that would finally count as real! She couldn't wait to put Corning behind her and follow her new husband to...

Well, she didn't know where, not exactly. He wasn't allowed to say. They were on the train, rumbling and jiggling toward Chicago, and after a brief honeymoon there, they would board another, a special one, Hank promised, a private car his boss would arrange just for them, and then after that it was a mystery. She thought of this adventure as following the tracks. She'd follow her heart. It was for the war effort, and that was good enough for her.

With her fingers, she traced a heart in the fog of her breath on the window. Through the heart, she watched the rolling hills slip by outside, flattening out into dishpan land that drained the central plains. Yes, it was good to leave this place behind, for it was a place of death. The air back there had filled her sister's lungs with tuberculosis until she couldn't breathe anymore, and then her heart had given out.

Hank put his arm around Rosamonde, and she leaned her head against his shoulder. He sensed her pain. They didn't need any words between them. She sighed and nestled against him to absorb his love. She could soak his love into her soul, and it worked like a salve to heal her heart.

He didn't know.

That was okay.

He didn't need to know about her sister who died in this dying place.

Let him think that it was home she would miss.

Not so, but who knows? Maybe she would. After all, home was where the heart was, they said, and this home of hers (former home, she corrected herself) might be capable of yanking her back by the heart strings one day. She hoped not, and with Hank at her side, she didn't think that was possible.

Because she'd had enough of that place to last her a lifetime. The endless hills closed their damp shadows of valleys around her and smothered her with gray skies. She'd seen enough soot in the air to fill her lungs, just from smelling the filth that billowed from farmhouse coke stoves.

Besides, home wasn't a place. Home was people. She would always hold Mama and Papa (and her sister who died) in her heart, and she would build a new life with Hank, and she would never look back. Hank, being from Chillicothe, not too terribly far away, would be all the reminder of this general area that she would ever need.

Now, they were bound together for the wide open spaces of the west. Some folks claimed that the air out there could heal tuberculosis patients, and if that was true, then it would be good air. Air that was bound to keep her heart from missing Mama and Papa and her sister's grave. It was too late for her sister. She might've been saved if only Rosamonde had met Hank sooner. If only Rosamonde weren't really Rosamonde. She would've taken her sister out west with her, had there been time.

Spring, that time of renewal, was her favorite time of year, and there was no place on earth (not that she really knew) more beautiful than springtime in hill country with the dogwoods and redbud in bloom.

Yes, she'd miss spring here, but she suspected Hank could more than adequately fill any empty spaces in her heart. When Hank walked into her life almost three weeks ago, she thought her heart would burst. Theirs was a storybook romance, only Rosamonde was smart enough to recognize at the outset that Hank was her Rhett. They wouldn't have to waste the best part of their lives fighting the force of their love. They were smart enough to give in to their passion, to the raw chemistry that bound them together. It was useless to fight. And now they'd spend all of eternity together. They were made for each other, two peas in a pod. Everything that went before the moment Rosamonde met Hank meant nothing anymore. She only looked ahead, never back.

She had expected Mama to whine, but Mama gave them her blessing with a kiss, a welcome to the secret club of true love kiss. Papa shook Hank's hand and slapped him on the shoulder in some kind of male secret club.

Too bad Hank's family down in Chillicothe had snubbed them. Even that, Rosamonde kind of understood. After all, Hank was older. Not that he was *old*, but rather that Rosamonde was young. And more importantly, inexperienced, as compared to Hank's experience.

He'd been married before. Naturally, his family tasted doubt in their mouths about Rosamonde. They blamed Rosamonde for the scandal Hank had brought onto them. Yes, she could understand that they were old-fashioned and believed in loyalty, not divorce. That they were still attached to that first one, the mistake, Hank called her. Rosamonde might not like it, but she couldn't fault his family for not accepting his divorce.

What stuck in Rosamonde's craw was the way Hank's family blamed all the ills of the world on women who didn't know their place. Times were changing, didn't they know? Furthermore, they had no right to call Rosamonde a teenager — and horrible other names even worse than that — which couldn't be farther from the truth. She was all of twenty years old. For two entire months she hadn't been a teenager, technically.

Her aunts had always said "My, but don't she grow just like a weed? Can't hardly recognize her no more." And that was true. She'd been an early bloomer. Why, she'd even had her first period when she was eleven and a half, which was sooner than any of her friends. Sooner, too, than her older sister who died.

So, she didn't need any of them. She had Hank now, and that was all that mattered.

It wasn't fair that her sister who died had died. She'd been so beautiful, so exotic, like a living, breathing porcelain doll. Too beautiful, perhaps, too fragile and fine, for she never breathed well. At night, in the dark in the room they shared, she listened to her sister's shallow breaths, gasping, gurgling panting breaths as if she ran with lungs full of water instead of slept. Dolls were never meant to live, not really, and so the charm that her sister lived under, the charm that allowed her to taste life, wore off all too soon in a place like this. This wasn't storybook land. No. Vermins thrived in the soot clouds and dripped into the valleys and wrapped a shroud around her sister, smothering her at night when she thrashed and fought for breath.

It wasn't fair. Everyone loved her sister, not just her. Her sister had held every popularity title the school district could dream up, starting with Miss Sixth Grade and ending with Prom Queen her senior year of high school.

Her fiancé and two former boyfriends delivered eulogies at commencement that year.

It wasn't fair. Her sister had loved *her* best, and her sister was the only real person she'd ever known who was as exotic as the characters in all her library books. Books were her only friends — her *real* friends, her true friends. Books, and their exotic, mysterious, romantic-sounding names and places. (Heathcliff came to mind, now *there* was a name!) And so she promised back then, when her sister died (although she was only twelve years old at the time, she had already tasted the world through her books), that she would always keep her sister Rosamonde alive.

# ZANESVILLE: FEBRUARY, 1943

**"What's your** name?" he asked.

A simple question, a fair question, but when she opened her mouth to answer, no sound came out at first. She thought of her name and the ugliness, the ordinariness of its sound as compared to the resonance of names that streamed through her head, names such as Ishmael, Karenina, Bovary, and Allworthy. "Rosamonde," she said. Then she ducked her head and flushed.

"Rosamonde?" The lilt of his voice was like a kiss that tilted her chin up and forced her eyes to meet his. She'd never before seen such intensity in a pair of eyes before, blue eyes, as fiery as ice. Ice-fire. "That's a beautiful name," he said, and she flushed again. She felt as if she was on fire. It was all she could do just to breathe.

"You're not from around here, are you?" She held her breath, waiting for his nod of confirmation. Her lie depended on that. And once her lie was done, it was done. There was no going back now. She leaned into him and smiled. "You can come 'round with me, then, if you like. C'mon! I can tell you lots of stories about this place, and you can tell me all about where you come from."

He came from the forest, he said. He tapped maple trees for their sap, he said. He made maple syrup for its sweetness and for sweet things like her, he said.

They spent a magical day together, that first day they spent together, telling each other stories about who they were and who they wished they were. They served as each other's light in an otherwise dark time. The day's rallying event was actually a scrap-metal drive, but with Hank at her side it felt more like a winter fair.

Or magic. His train had stopped here, on its way to Chillicothe — home of his family — and something (the magic!) had whispered in his head that he must, he must get off here. He hadn't planned to. But he'd been vague to his family about when they might expect him for the weekend. And through the window of his coach, he'd spied a junk store next to the train station. You never knew what you'd find in a place like that, and Hank was a collector, had always been a collector.

That's where he found Rosamonde. She'd come to Carl's Curios to collect what scrap metal Carl would contribute to the cause.

Hank didn't believe in magic, but he did believe there were forces he didn't understand, and right now the forces fielded around Rosamonde like a halo. He stumbled into Carl's place after the girl and broke his focus from her only long enough to notice a tiny movement inside a display case up front by the cash register.

It was a cameo. There it went again, jumping like a Mexican jumping bean. While Rosamonde talked to Carl, Hank blinked to clear his vision, and then the piece of onyx jumped again, and it spun round and round before his eyes — he swore to God! It was a miniature whirlpool of onyx roulette, and when it stopped spinning, the woman's face in the onyx smiled and winked at him, melting his heart, and he recognized her face as Rosamonde's.

The world stopped around them that weekend of collecting. They scoured snow-covered hills, and they danced together and talked together under an unusual winter sun. White light reflected off snow and blinded them and ignited their love.

# HONOLULU: TODAY

**Hank felt himself** slipping. The time was drawing near that his connection to this world was fading.

One last task, and then he could let go of his hold on this world. He sank into Melody's space and gave her the image of a graveyard high on a hill overlooking a pastoral valley in Ohio...

It was time to turn this mess over to others. Let someone else be responsible for a change. This was like retirement, and he and his Rosie would have a blaze of glory to look forward to.

"Gran? Gran? Are you all right? Mom, what's happening to her? She's...smiling, and...she's different... Her face...it's like the old stuff is draining out of her face, and...she looks...happy. She looks *young*..."

#

**I was wrong.** I am always not right. It is not hurt that touches me, but its opposite, which is the all-good. They do not know that. I know that they think I must hurt, buried in snow, swallowed by beach glare. I know that the white hurt is their hurt, not mine. I feel their hurt.

I cannot hide in the white. Still, you hide from me. There are no shadows in the white, and I shall find you. I am coming.

I reach out to them, and I touch them, and I feel their white hurt, and they feel my all-good, and they do not hurt any longer.

Hank! Old Spice and engine grease surround me, fill my head. I know you are here. White light mushrooms into a ball of light, and snow rains down on me, and... I drown in white.

#

**The storm passes,** and the sun shines down in a blaze of Trinity white. Sugar and Lyman stand there together in the snow, and the snow glares around them as if solidified. Hank and Rosamonde stare blindly at each other, lost in each other, lost in time. The world stops around them. In each other, they've found sanity amidst the madness of the world.

# TWENTY-THREE

*I*t's okay. I've found my Rosie. We're together again, at long last.

They fluttered over a graveyard not far from Zanesville, like kites tethered to Rosie's coffin. Hank didn't mind fading, losing directional control, but he would've enjoyed visiting some of the other residents here for a brief flare before he and Rosie would head out together, into the sunset, so to speak. After all, he hadn't been here — in corporeal form, that is — since they buried Rosie's mother. She'd died of a broken heart, not two years after Rosie's father died of crud in his lungs. The legacy for most of the folks around here who'd made their living and given their lives to coal mining. Rosie's family was no different.

Melody was busy directing the gravediggers. "Yes, I want her right next to her own mother. Daughters need their mothers, you know. And likewise. Mothers need their daughters. I want Mom to always have her mother nearby. Dad? We'll move him next to her. You assured me there's a plot available, and I've already started the inquiries of moving him out here from Baltimore."

"Hey, Mom, come look at this." Lani called from the other side of the cemetery, a knoll overlooking the valley and protected by a gnarled oak tree. "Here's a person with Gran's exact, same name."

"There must've been a lot of Ayres around here."

"This person was Rosamonde Ayers, too, but she died on May 5, 1935. She was only eighteen years old. Huh. How about that."

Rosie's secret didn't matter anymore. What's in a name? By taking her sister's name, she'd only enriched herself, as far as Hank was concerned.

Together, they fluttered above the new grave, and they drifted in the currents of each other. The voices of the corporeals hummed, recovering the order of their world. It wasn't Rosie's and Hank's world anymore. They had each other. They were two elements that came together and made one. Never to be asundered apart again.

With the last shovel of earth tamped onto the new grave, Lani and Melody walked away, leaning on each other, bonded by grief. The kites released, and they drifted away together, melding with puffy clouds, clouds that were shaped like a heart traced with piano fingers in the breath fog of a train window.

Lani looked up. "Do you s'pose that's where Gran is now? Up there?"

"I don't know, honey. You may be right." Melody sighed and frowned. The toothpaste smile wiped away for now.

"It's like a message of some sort. Gran was meant to come

here. Weird, that you figured out to bury her here."

"I don't know, it just felt right somehow. I guess I need to trust my feelings a bit more. One thing I know for sure: I feel really grateful that you and I have each other. Nothing else matters as much as family."

The hum faded to a murmur as Hank and Rosie's tethers released them from earth, and they spiraled away together, soaring toward the welcoming light. One person's reality was another person's madness.

# ABOUT THE AUTHOR

Cameron Kennedy writes women's fiction with a touch of magical realism. When not focusing on her family, she enjoys designing and sewing garments, raising orchids, and painting landscapes. She can be contacted at cameronkennedyauthor@gmail.com.

# To Witch a Woman

by

Cameron Kennedy

The full story is available in the collection

*The Next World is Always Better*

Originally published in *E-scape*

"*Señora!*"

The woman's whisper sliced through the suffocating noise of the airport like a machete through papaya. We were approaching the exit tax window, which remained mysteriously uncrowded in this crunch of tourists, and I paused to catch my breath.

Quentin strode to the window, glanced at the sign that read "we don't take traveler's checks" and thumbed through a wad of *colones*. Carefully, he selected his grubbier bills to unload for the tax. Only when he was certain of his count did he glance back at me. "Feel okay, honey?"

"Mmmm," I murmured, leaning against the cool cement of the wall, resting a hand on my belly's five-month swell. I scanned the flocks of tourists, who clutched their papers and elbowed from one mob to another. Where was she? The woman with the penetrating whisper?

Quentin organized his change by denomination, clipped it all together and tucked it into his fanny pack. "Okay, we're out of here." He shouldered his carry-on and headed for the throng at *migración*.

"*Señora!*" It came again, this time more urgent, carried on a whiff of garlic. I pulled away from the wall and searched to my left, opposite of the direction Quentin was heading.

I saw the nurse's cap first. It was one of those pointed things perched firm by some miracle on the crown of her head. White, trimmed in pink, its style came straight out of the early nineteen fifties. Grandmother had worn one like that. I'd seen her picture taken at the San José orphanage where she'd worked after the rebellion of 1948 left behind too many orphans in her care.

Odd, I thought. Here we were in San José, some sixty years later, combining pleasure with a hunt for my heritage that not even Quentin's money had been able to find. And this woman of the voice would have come from Grandmother's time, judging from the amount of gray hair springing out from under the cap and the wrinkles that withered her away next to nothing. However, the white apron over the pink frock was fresh, as if it had been store-bought yesterday, slapped through a wringer washer and crisply ironed by a hand who still knew her art, leaving no wrinkles. A pity she couldn't do the same for her skin.

My own hand shot up to the sunburn that ringed my neck. Yes, the skin was still firm, but what would happen to it as my baby grew, my own Sara, pushing onward through time? How much was the price of carelessness like that blissful nap yesterday at the pool?

"Come *on*, honey," Quentin said over his shoulder.

His voice stirred me to movement, but as I prepared to lean that way, I couldn't push against the weight of the air. It was too hot and sultry, even here on the *meseta central*. I glanced back at the nurse. Even though her eyelids sagged under a burden of life, the faded brown look that she fixed on me, stuck on me, tangled me up. The spider's web, I thought.

In fact, there *was* a web. I could see it now as the morning light glinted off a single silvery strand looping gently between

372

the nurse and me. Strange, what with all the traffic through here. Strange that it could persist, but then I remembered one of the guides telling Quentin and me about the futile attempts of the U.S. military to duplicate whatever tough essence that a certain forest spider could spin. Now I wished I'd paid more attention as I watched the rhythmic reverberations of that single strand, looking deceptively fragile and tenuous, sagging like the nurse's eyes.

A stream of garlic-laced words gushed from her lips, a thin slash which barely moved, barely disturbed the life furrows of her leathery, lizard-like skin. But all I heard was "*Señora*, for the love of the children..." A wave of nausea passed over me, and I had to steady myself against the wall.

"Honey, are you coming?" Quentin's voice boomed over tourists' heads, his meaning clear that he would not relinquish the spot he'd won in the throng. He held up his wrist and tapped the face of his watch.

But I was fixed there to that spot on the wall. Pregnancy had leeched my strength, made me limp in these tropical climes. The nurse edged closer, so that her garlic breath mingled with my Certs. I tried at least to turn my head away, but my neck muscles were not cooperating (was it the burn?), and so I faced her as she advanced head-on, her faded brown eyes coming to life with a curious sparkle, the fissured skin hinting at stories of a laborer's unprotected life under the sun's damaging rays. Yet, the uniform indicated an indoor life. My head started to spin. Caught in a stream of garlic, I watched as the slit of her mouth opened wider, and I glimpsed not pink but pearly gray. Were there two tips to her tongue? I blinked, and it was gone. I had to steady myself against the wall.

She reached out her hand, and I shrank back against my shelter. "The children need you," she whispered, lightly stroking my abdomen. A flash of ice shot through me at her lizard's touch. "The children are the forest. Do not run away from them, *señora*, as your mothers did before you."

Coolness. I could breathe again. My balance returned to its center; strength flowed through me.

Her hands dropped from my belly, and she picked up my hands in hers, turned them over to examine both sides, stroked the design of my life's story etched across my palms, then stared deeply into my eyes. "You have the healer's touch within you."

Who was this woman?

"I am your *compañera*. I am here to guide you to the *Refugio*."

"The...what?"

"The *Refugio*," she said, smiling at the questions that must be written clearly across my face. "It is a place of protection and healing for plants, animals, children."

"But I can't go anywhere with you." I had a plane to catch, a life awaiting me. We were going home—well, not home, but to our Vail condo for the next month, and then home to Houston.

www.ingramcontent.com/pod-product-compliance
Lightning Source LLC
Chambersburg PA
CBHW050910250626
47155CB00001B/169